For Griffin and Ramona

Saturday was usually a day that Samantha looked forward to; though there wasn't any school (which she secretly loved), there *was* a lot of free time, and on most Saturdays she would go to the park or the museum, or ride her scooter around the neighborhood. Sometimes she'd run into her friend Marvin who would take her back to his house and show her cool things that he could do with his computer. Sometimes, she'd take her dog, Polly, for a walk.

This Saturday, however, was a bit of a disaster. It was pouring rain, a chilly October rain, and Samantha was trapped in her house with her mother, Cindy and her brother Todd. Samantha's mother was young, as mothers go, and single, and was always getting ready to go on some date or another with some boring guy. Todd, who was fifteen, mostly sat around as he was now, playing some stupid video game or another. Samantha watched dully as her mom applied an appalling color of lipstick to her thirty-five-year-old lips.

"Where are you going, Mom?" she asked without much real interest.

"I'm going out," her mother replied. "On a date."

"Who's the victim this time?" Samantha inquired sarcastically.

"His *name*," her mom carefully enunciated, "is Brian. And far from being a 'victim,' he is about to have the time of his life."

"I'll bet," interjected Todd with a chuckle, not missing a step in his virtual commando world.

"Have a little respect for your mother, Todd!," Mom yelled from the bathroom, "And I don't want your loser friends over here while you're watching Samantha, understand?"

"Aww, come on Mom, I was just kidding..." Todd began to protest. An argument of course ensued, as even though Samantha was almost twelve years old her mother still considered her to be in need of a babysitter, which usually meant Todd. Samantha hated being around Todd and especially his friends, who probably would wind up coming over even if their mom said they couldn't. The argument faded into a dull hum as Samantha closed her eyes and focused on the pattering sound of rain on their living room windows, wishing she were somewhere else. Polly was laying on the big, low window sill staring out into the gloom of Brooklyn and looking as much a prisoner as Samantha felt.

The argument was settled, and Todd was given twenty dollars which was supposed to buy Chinese food for both of them, though it would more likely be spent on pizza that he and his friends would inhale, leaving her hungry. At least then she could threaten to tell on him and maybe get to go out for a little bit – but of course, it was pouring rain. Where would she go? The park would be a mess. Mud and small oceans of water – a landscape Polly might enjoy, though the aftermath of wet, muddy paw-prints on her mother's rugs and furniture would surely be nightmarish. Scooter-riding did not sound appealing in this weather either. The museum was her last hope – she could get there mostly by train and could smuggle Polly, (who was a small, obedient Boston terrier) in her backpack as she often did.

Corey and Kevin arrived only twenty minutes after their mother had left, in clear violation of her expressed wishes. On cue they dialed the number to Smiley's, the local pizza place, and ordered a large pizza with pepperoni and mushrooms for delivery. Samantha knew that between the three of them, her brother and his two buddies would blow through it in a matter of minutes. She stared at them as they sat entranced by their video game, which was called *Cyber Wars,* and secretly hoped they would burn their mouths trying to eat too fast.

By the time the pizza actually arrived, Samantha was dressed in her rubber boots and windbreaker and was coaxing Polly into her backpack. Todd paid the delivery man and, as expected, the boys finished the pie within five minutes, all of them painfully scorching the roofs of their mouths. This gave Samantha some small satisfaction, though she grudgingly admitted to herself that she was still hungry, while they were already relaxing into the early stages of digestion. It didn't matter – she hated mushrooms. So did Polly.

It was about one o'clock in the afternoon, and Samantha figured they could make it to the museum in less than an hour. She slipped out the door amidst brief protests from Todd and had had to promise that she would call home in two hours, and in any event definitely be back before five, when their socialite mother was expected to return. Closing the heavy iron front door of the brownstone behind her, she turned right and walked the block and a half on Twelfth Street down to Seventh Avenue, then turned right again and quickly covered the three blocks to the subway station. She zipped down the stairs and swiped her Metro-Card, pushing through the turnstile and descending to the platform. There was a man with a guitar who was singing something about 'Isis,' whom Samantha knew to be an Egyptian goddess of some sort, though the Isis in the song seemed to be a different person altogether.

Technically, Samantha was not supposed to go into Manhattan by herself at all. Her mother constantly reminded her of how dangerous a place it was, though she had mostly only met very nice people on the numerous times she had explored its bustling squares and sky-scrapered thoroughfares. She went to school just off of Fourteenth Street, and her mother typically took this train, the F train, with her every weekday morning. Samantha would get off at Fourteenth Street while her mother would switch to an uptown train to go to work at the Museum of Natural History.

It was her mother's workplace that was currently Samantha's destination. She thought about the museum as the wall tiles that spelled "Carroll Street" flew by the subway windows. She had started spending time there several years ago, mostly after school waiting for her mom to get done with work. In that time she had befriended Professor Smythe ("of the Knightsbridge Smythes," he liked to say), who was from London and held many degrees in 'forensic science'. What this meant was that he got paid to solve fascinating mysteries, using hi-tech tools and deductive reasoning worthy of Sherlock Holmes (who was one of Samantha's heroes). He had a laboratory in one of the museum's basements and was usually preoccupied with carbon-dating prehistoric arrowheads or doing a 'spectral analysis' on a thread from a three thousand-year-old mummy's bandages to find out what sort of things they were soaked in before being wrapped around the body of the deceased. Samantha found all of this to be positively captivating, and had decided early on that when she grew up she wanted to be a forensic scientist.

At this point, though, she was still in training. Just last year she finally came to understand that a spectral analysis was basically a test wherein every little molecule of something was analyzed and labeled as one thing or another, so that when it was done you would know exactly what it was made of. She had tried to do one herself, using Polly as a subject, but did not have the equipment to narrow things down too specifically beyond "dog molecules," or at best "dog hair molecules."

They switched trains at Fourteenth Street, getting on a C train for the rest of their journey. This ride went pretty quick as always, and before long they were rolling into the small Seventy-second Street station and walking up the wet stairs to the street. Unfortunately, the closer Eighty-first Street station had been closed for a few weeks due to some sort of construction or another, but Samantha didn't mind the walk and neither did Polly. Though it was still raining pretty hard, Samantha sensed that Polly was, in fact, getting a little antsy and perhaps needed to do a little 'dog business,' so she crossed the street into Central Park and let her out of the backpack to sniff around.

This was a (usually) lovely part of the park which was called Strawberry Fields, though no strawberries grew in it anywhere that Samantha could see. She thought about this a little and then remembered that her mother (who was occasionally good for some sort of wisdom) had told her the place was named after a man who had written a song by the same name, and who had played in a very popular rock band. Try as she might, she couldn't remember the man's name, or the band's name, but was pretty sure that the man had lived close to here at some time. In any case, it was a pleasant place, even in the rain.

Polly finished her bathroom stop and Samantha got her back into the backpack. They trekked the remaining four blocks and up the many steps to the museum's front doors, then on into the thankfully warm, dry lobby. Immediately they were spotted by Luann, Samantha's mom's co-worker at the ticket sales booth.

"Samantha! What are you doing here? Your mother isn't working today – "

"I know," Samantha cut her off. "I'm visiting Professor Smythe – Mom, uh... asked me to give him something. She's, um, shopping at Zabar's down on Columbus."

"Oh!" Luann processed the information with the speed of a fifty-year-old computer and then smiled a pretty, corn-fed midwestern smile and replied, "Well, that's great! He's, uh, he's down in his office or somewhere near it as usual. Let me know if you can't find him."

"Thanks Luann," said Samantha, already heading for the stairs. Luann was a very pretty woman, Samantha thought, but was rather easy to fool, especially on what looked to be a fairly busy Saturday at the museum. She felt guilty for lying for a moment, then decided it was all for the greater good. Besides, Professor Smythe would be glad to see her. She smiled and thought about him as she wove through the museum's stairwells and hallways. He was a rather small man, about fifty-eight or sixty years old, with what some might call a stereotypical absent-minded personality. In fact, however, Samantha found him to be one of the more focused people she had ever met; people only found him to be scattered because very few of them ever really knew what he was talking about. Samantha thought he was cute – not cute like Jordan Anderson from Heatwavvve (her favorite boy-band) – but just a gentle, funny old man whose British accent made him even more charming.

She rounded the last corner before his office door and ran smack into the man she was looking for.

"Unnnhh!" they both grunted as they collided.

"Oooh – I'm sorry, Professor!," the younger victim offered.

"Samantha!" The Professor looked even more startled than she did. "Tortuous teenagers!"

"What... ?" Samantha answered, not clear on what he meant.

"Oh, that's right, you're – er – not quite a teenager, are you? Oh, but you will be, in time, in time..." The Professor looked somewhat exasperated.

"Professor," Samantha said slowly, "what are you talking about?" Perhaps the man had gone totally loony.

"Samantha," he said, calming and looking straight at her, "what I am talking about is *time.*"

"Time?" she replied hesitantly.

"Yes," he said, looking quickly behind him and trying to shuffle her into his office. "We've got some real problems, Samantha, real problems here. They're all my fault, of course, all my fault. Nattering Nincompoops!"

"Problems?" she asked, letting herself be herded.

"Yes, child," The Professor whispered as they went through the door. She felt frightened for a moment as he hustled her into his office, like something illegal was going on or that someone was watching them. Then they were in the office and the door was closed.

"You see, Samantha – oh! Hello Polly!" Polly had ventured from the backpack and trotted over to the bowl of food The Professor always kept in a corner of his office for her. Professor Smythe then sat in his desk chair and made a conscious effort to relax.

"Have a seat, Samantha," (she sat down), "You see, I seem to have made a bit of a – a mess. With... time. Yes, time. You see? I – I didn't mean to, of course, and I'm still trying to figure out what I did wrong – hmmm. Yes, time. A terrible mess. All my fault."

"You made a mess with... time," Samantha reality-checked. The Professor was mumbling on, barely understandable.

"Yes. Yes! Rather absurd, isn't it? Quirky thing, time – change one little detail and watch out – the whole shebang starts coming unraveled! Forget to turn off a light, turn left at an intersection instead of right, order a *cheeseburger* instead of a *hamburger*. One bloody slice of cheese," he stared, wild-eyed at Samantha. "That's all it takes, Samantha!"

The Professor was manic; Samantha could see his mind's eye shuffling possibilities faster than a Chinese game of ping-pong. It looked like he was going to lose it. Quickly, she decided that someone had to take firm control of the situation, and since Professor Smythe was obviously teetering on the brink of blowing a brain fuse and Polly was quite happily distracted by an unexpected snack, it was she who had to step up to the task.

"Professor," she said firmly, grabbing his flailing arms and making him look right at her, "You've got to calm down."

For a moment the old fellow looked shocked, then shook his head violently as if to clear out a nest of bees or to settle some loose screws back into their proper places.

"You're right, Samantha, of course. This won't do us any good. And after all, I think I can fix it. I think I will, or I do fix it at some point, but I'm not sure, because I'm fairly sure I haven't fixed it already. Yet, that is. Oh, my. I hope I can fix it."

"What exactly is it that you've done, Professor? I'd be glad to help if I can, but I'm afraid I'm going to need a bit more information."

"Yes, yes," The Professor looked as if he was becoming fidgety again, then sat down and looked straight at Samantha. "All right. I'll give you the whole story, then. I suppose you must know if you're to help, and you are already helping, though you don't know it yet... well, anyway, Samantha – I fear that this information is dangerous and I must require that you tell no one what I'm about to tell you. Do you understand? Not your mother, not your friends – *no one.* At least not until I know more about what has happened."

"Well... of course, Professor," Samantha replied, summoning up as much responsibility as an almost-twelve-year-old could, "you can trust me. And – I want to help."

"All right then. Hmmm..." he gazed hard at her for a second then added under his breath. "I suppose I may not even have to worry about you telling anyone..."

At this he got up, took Samantha's hand and led her out of his office; Polly looked up expectantly as they departed but Professor Smythe closed the door, shutting her in. They walked down many back hallways of the museum's sub-basement, The Professor moving very nervously, always looking around as if he were afraid someone was watching them. They picked their way through corridors cluttered with hand-carved totem poles, boxes of unassembled dinosaur bones and some sort of giant ant farm exhibits that had been abandoned down here in favor of newer, more interactive displays. At last they came to a door which had two colossal stuffed polar bears on either side of it, as if they were guarding something in the room behind it. Professor Smythe looked around, then punched in a number on the door's telephone-button-like combination lock and opened it into the darkness beyond.

"In here, Samantha," he whispered, motioning for her to come in.

Once inside, The Professor closed the door and turned on a light switch, illuminating an utterly amazing sight. Inside the very large room was a scene straight out of Pre-Columbian Central America – an entire diorama of ornately carved stone set up in a half-circle, each component block at least ten feet tall. It reminded Samantha of pictures she'd seen of Stonehenge, which she knew was in England, but instead of simple, rough blocks, these were covered in carved pictographs and lots of things that kind of looked like letters. Within the outer ring, in the center of the floor was a huge stone platform with what looked like some sort of gate or doorway set atop it. There were two inwardly-curved, sharp-edged stone pillars coming up from the platform's base that almost met at the top, some nine feet higher. Two steps were cut into the base which led up to the 'gate,' and most notably, in contrast to the surrounding stonework there was a marvelous keystone which sat perfectly in-between the top edges of the two curved pillars, which bore only one symbol. This piece was made of a brilliant, shiny black material that looked almost like glass.

"Obsidian," The Professor noted, sensing what she had wanted to ask. "It's incredibly rare to find a piece so large and so flawless. Just that one piece would be priceless, as a gem. But it is far more than a mere thing of beauty."

Samantha swallowed hard. She had seen many things like this before in the museum, but there was an undeniable uniqueness to this thing, something almost... eerie.

"Where did this come from?" she asked.

"The Yucatan Peninsula," replied The Professor.

"Is it – Mayan?" Samantha remembered that a tribe of Indians called the Mayas had built an impressive civilization on the Yucatan Peninsula, which she knew from her geography lessons to be in southern Mexico.

"One of the strangest things," The Professor mused, "Its markings and pictographs are quite like very early Mayan finds, but I can't translate it very well from the museum's Mayan database. It's sort of an archaic variety, which explains the fact that I've dated the material to almost 5,000 B.C. Samantha, that is long before the earliest relics of any Mayan – or practically any other civilization. This thing is older than Egypt's pyramids! Many scientists would claim there were no people in the region at all at that time. It is a thing out of time."

Samantha stared at the monstrous thing, taking in Professor Smythe's words. She walked closer to the 'gate' platform – it did look very old. But that – that obsidian keystone looked like it was made yesterday.

"We discovered it in a remote, mountainous region, buried under nearly two hundred feet of earth and rock. It's a miracle anyone ever found it at all."

"Well... what's it got to do with time, Professor?"

The Professor sighed heavily and began to look nervous again. He wrung his hands and his lower lip began to tremble slightly as he spoke.

"This – this gate, this ring, these symbols," he said, gesturing, "They're – they're sort of a time machine, Samantha. I don't know how – I'm still trying to decipher many of the symbols – "

"A *time machine?*" Samantha interrupted, rolling her eyes. "Yeah, right. You've been reading too many science fiction stories, Professor. I hope you'll forgive my saying so, but maybe you need a...

a vacation or something..."

"I know it sounds incredible, Samantha, but listen to me – I can prove it to you. Yesterday, I got it to... work. I'm sure I can do it again, but I need more time to study it – I want to be more accurate the next time I try, and more... careful. Samantha," The Professor grabbed her arm gently and led her urgently back to his office, locking the room behind them. Once inside, he pulled out the bottom drawer of his desk and produced a newspaper. A satisfied Polly jumped up on Samantha's lap, happy she had returned.

"Samantha, I bought this newspaper yesterday, in midtown. Look at it."

Samantha looked, and Polly sniffed. The paper was new, and she could almost smell fresh ink on it, suggesting it had indeed been printed very recently. The trouble was, the cover story was about the construction of the Empire State Building, as if it were the latest news. Her eyes wandered to the top of the page, where she read the date: *August 14, 1931.* It looked very authentic.

"It must be a reprint," she said at last.

"No," The Professor replied in a hushed but excited tone. "No, Samantha. I walked around yesterday in the New York City of seventy years ago. It is vividly etched in my memory. The cars, the people's clothing – it was absolutely amazing. An incredible experience."

"I can't believe it," Samantha repeated her skepticism.

"Neither could I," said The Professor. "Even though I lived it. So – I ran some tests, on the newspaper. Trying to date it."

"And?"

"Well, it was strange, Samantha. The ink, though it looks and smells absolutely fresh, is composed of chemicals which were banned from use in printing in favor of more environmentally friendly recipes – in 1957. The paper – and this test allowed me to use very exciting new technology – we can say with near certainty that the DNA in the wood pulp used to make this paper came from an alder tree, an alder tree that grew within twenty square miles of a specific site in western Pennsylvania. Samantha, look at this – " The Professor pulled something else from his desk drawer, a picture.

"This is a satellite photo of those twenty square miles."

The picture showed a large body of water.

"I don't get it, Professor... a lake?" Polly, too, seemed puzzled, but probably more because she was wondering if the picture was edible.

"A lake. Exactly. Man-made. This valley was flooded in 1962. And that's not all. I did some additional research – before it was purchased by the county, the land was owned by the Western Pennsylvania Lumber Company. Their records show that wood collected from this region was sold to paper mills in West Virginia from 1929 until 1936. It's proof positive, Samantha."

It seemed to be. Samantha stared at the picture, then at the paper. *Could The Professor really have found a working time machine?* She pondered all this, entertaining fantasies of winning lotteries and preventing disasters, then recalled the really unnerving part of all that Professor Smythe had said since she had encountered him some twenty minutes earlier.

"Professor, you said that you had... done something wrong. Made a... a mess..."

"Yes, Samantha," he sighed. "I don't know how to explain this, but... since I took the trip, well – some things have... changed."

"Changed?"

"Yes," The Professor continued. "I – I'm not even sure to what extent, but – Samantha, I fear I've done something terribly wrong."

Samantha herself began to fidget now. She felt suddenly uncomfortable, like she was in a strange place that she had never been before. What had The Professor done? Could it even be set right? Would their world be changed forever? And how much had been changed? These were questions that urgently needed to be answered, though she feared in her heart that even the wise, knowledgeable Professor Smythe had no idea how to begin to answer them.

Samantha sat and tried to absorb all the information The Professor was telling her. She had asked for it, she supposed, but it was all very confusing.

"It seems," The Professor continued carefully, "That this building is a bit of a nexus. Or, at least, part of this building... you see, Samantha, you walked in here from the world's natural time sequence – the time sequence that the world is supposed to be progressing in. I fear, however, that if you walk out again, you will experience what I have: A quite... different world, a divergent time sequence, in other words, the evolution of whatever small thing I somehow changed when I went back in time."

"You mean I might not live in the same house anymore?" Samantha asked with a hint of panic.

"Samantha." Professor Smythe sighed. "I mean that what you think is your house is probably not even there now. Or it might be there, but probably underwater." He scratched his head.

"*Underwater!!?*" Samantha practically screamed. "What do you mean!? I have to be home by five! Oh, man, Professor, I think I should go. You're really freaking me out."

"Samantha! Wait – " The Professor tried to stop her, but she was off, running through the museum's hallways, Polly stuffed hastily into her backpack. She felt sort of scared now, and had decided that being at home would make her feel better, even if it was with Todd and his stupid friends. Underwater, indeed! It couldn't possibly have rained that much in the past hour.

She ran up two flights of stairs and through a door into the museum's lobby, noting the lack of people that had been there earlier. She glanced quickly at the ticket counter, but the people at it were strange – Luann wasn't there. Had she gone home? Was her shift over already? Samantha had never seen these ticket sellers at all, and she felt even more nervous. Running through the front doors out onto the steps, she froze.

It was terribly wrong. There was no Central Park West. There was no *Central Park*. It was all water. *All water*. Samantha stared in disbelief. Where the park had been there was now a huge, open space like a great rectangular lake, with clusters of what looked like houseboats floating here and there. She could see an island where Belvedere Castle stood, surrounded by boats, but no other land was in sight. Strangely, there were no trees or even treetops visible. Samantha wondered if trees simply drowned in the event of such a terrible flood as had presumably happened here.

The museum looked pretty much the same on the outside, though its entire ground floor and then some must now be underwater. The surrounding city was in a similar situation, and the blocks that stretched to the north and south reminded Samantha of postcards she'd seen of Venice, Italy, where most of the streets were more like canals and people got around in long boats called gondolas. Indeed, it seemed like New York had definitely gone the same way, as she could see many boats buzzing around in the distance; some were slow, drifting rowboats, some canoes and kayaks, many motorized boats with cabs on top – in fact, they looked very much like taxi-cabs – or at least what she imagined taxi-cabs would look like if New York City were a world of water.

Polly had jumped out of Samantha's backpack and trotted down the few stairs left above the water line, and now stood at the water's edge sniffing, looking around and occasionally gazing back at Samantha with a look of utter confusion. Samantha walked down to her and stooped to pet her. "It's okay, Polly," she tried to reassure her canine friend, "I know this is pretty weird. But it's kind of cool, too, isn't it?" She smiled and looked at her little terrier, who did not seem to agree at all. Polly was not an exceptional swimmer and appeared to be in fact quite distressed that most of the world around her had suddenly been filled with water. She had always hated baths and did not even really like to get wet, unless it involved some nice warm mud. She tried her hardest to express these feelings through whimpers, pitiful looks and a general lack of tail-wagging, and it seemed as if Samantha understood.

"Okay," Samantha said to Polly, "I guess all we can do is go back downstairs and try to help Professor Smythe figure out what went wrong – and how we might be able to fix it. Come on, Polly..."

Polly jumped back into Samantha's backpack and they slipped back into the museum, heading for the familiar door to the basement stairs. Samantha kept going over possibilities in her head as to what could have happened to flood all of Manhattan, her mind trying to picture some huge dam bursting or a rainstorm of biblical proportions. Her mind was so completely preoccupied with these thoughts that she almost walked right into a security guard who was now standing in front of the basement door. She stopped suddenly and gazed up at six and a half feet of uniformed muscle. A quizzical, African-American face looked back at her from atop the mountain of person.

"Can I help you?" the security guard asked, blocking the door.

"Oh," Samantha peeped, "I – I – uh, my mom works here."

"Really?" the guard replied. "And you are... looking for your mother?"

"Well, not – uh – not exactly. I'm looking for Professor Smythe – I know where his office is, if I could just – " Samantha tried to slip by him to the door.

"Hold on a minute," said the guard. He clicked on the radio attached to his belt and spoke into it. "Cal – hey, it's Art up front. I've got a young girl who's trying to get downstairs – says she wants to see Professor Smythe."

"Smythe?" the radio crackled. "What for? Who is she?"

"Well, she says her mother works here – what did you say your name was again, Miss?"

"Samantha. Samantha Smart," Samantha replied nervously. "My

mom's name is Cindy – Cindy Smart. She works at the – the ticket counter."

"Did you copy that Cal?" Apparently 'Art' had been holding on to the 'talk' button on his radio.

"Copy that, Art. No one here seems to know a Cindy Smart at tickets – does she sound familiar to you?"

"Negative," Art replied, staring down at Samantha. "What do you want me to do?" The radio was silent for a moment, then chirped on again.

"Why don't you bring her up here, Art. We can watch her while you go ask The Professor."

"Affirmative, Cal," Art replied, "sounds good." Art gestured in front of him for Samantha to make her way to the ticket counter. Samantha sighed and reluctantly obeyed, praying to herself that Polly would not be noticed. They walked over to the counter and Art left her there, going back towards the door to the basement. His radio crackled again.

"Hey, Art, we're just gonna try to ring him on the phone in his office. He might pick up."

"Roger that," Art responded, resuming his standing position at the door and awaiting further instructions.

Samantha was in luck. The Professor had obviously picked up the phone and the security guard at the ticket counter was talking to him, nodding. Presently, he hung up and motioned her over to his post.

"Professor Smythe says to wait here," he said when she was close to him, "he's coming to meet you."

"Okay," Samantha shrugged. She walked over and sat down in a nearby lobby chair that she remembered having played on as a little girl. *Of course,* she thought to herself, *in this reality I probably never played on this chair – it doesn't even seem as if my mom works here.* Samantha frowned a worried frown. Would she even ever see her mother again? Sure, Cindy Smart was a shallow, materialistic, man-devouring dating machine, but Samantha had to admit she loved her anyway. Who knows, maybe in this reality her mom was a famous poet, a very deep, sensitive thinker who spent exhausting hours upon hours championing noble causes and creating priceless contributions to the cultural commonwealth. But then, perhaps in this reality, this 'alternate course of history,' Samantha had never been born. The world had been spinning off in a different direction since 1931. That was a long time. Thinking like this started to make Samantha's head feel dizzy, and she was glad when she looked up and saw The Professor walking toward her, a sort of bookbag over his shoulder.

"Samantha!" he shouted, waving as he approached. "Come on, then, we're going out. Got some research to do, I'm afraid, that is, if we want to get things back to normal."

Samantha nodded vigorously at this idea and got up, following The Professor toward the main doors. They walked out and down the stairs to where the waterline was, then looked at each other. Polly stuck her head out of Samantha's backpack and sniffed the outside air again.

"We'll have to hail a taxi-boat," The Professor said. "I've been out a few times already, Samantha – in this reality. One doesn't have to be quite as careful about changing things – at least, assuming our goal is to change the past back to normal and eliminate this 'incorrect present' altogether."

"I see," Samantha responded. They stood in silence for a minute, waving for a taxi-boat, which it seemed was no easier to flag down than its wheeled counterpart, the familiar New York taxi cab.

"Some things haven't changed," The Professor smiled, shrugging.

"Professor," Samantha thought out loud as they continued waving, "Is it still October?"

"That," he replied, "is a good question, Samantha. I've always assumed that my calendar was still correct, but I can't say for sure. We shall have to ask someone."

"If it is still October, don't you think it's, well, quite warm?"

"Hmmmph. Indeed. It feels more like May than October, doesn't it? Strange..."

The Professor seemed to drift off into a haze of thought, but his reverie was quickly interrupted by a taxi-boat which had finally buzzed over to them.

"Where to, Mac?" the driver asked, edging the open-roofed boat close enough for them to climb in.

"The nearest newsstand, I think," The Professor offered.

The taxi-boat sped off along what used to be Central Park West, cut right down the former Seventy-fifth Street and then left onto the old Columbus Avenue. There were, in fact, new street signs that had been attached to corner buildings, apparently to replace the street-level ones which were all now entirely submerged. Samantha marveled at the eerily familiar yet vastly changed blocks of upper Manhattan. All the storefronts had been moved to the second floors of the buildings, and all of them had these plastic or Styrofoam docks floating at their doors. There were long stretches where one could even walk along on sidewalks made from the same strange material. Samantha thought they were all terribly ugly, and that they would've looked much better had they been done in wood.

The roofs of the buildings all seemed to have sprouted thousands of antennae as well, large steel things with disc-shaped tops packed eight or ten to a rooftop. Samantha wondered if everyone broadcast their own radio station in this alternate reality, but the receiver dial in the taxi-boat seemed to have no more numbers on it than familiar radios.

"How's this?" the cabbie shouted over his rather noisy outboard motor. They had pulled up at a plastic dock next to Manny's Newsroom, on the corner of Seventy-first and Columbus.

"Superb," said The Professor in his royal-sounding British accent.

They disembarked onto the plastic sidewalk and Professor Smythe paid the driver, noting thankfully that money hadn't changed too drastically either. The taxi-boat sped off downtown and Samantha decided to let Polly out of the backpack. Shaking off a bit of a nap, she walked around a little, unsure of the stability of the floating sidewalk, though it did seem to be anchored quite well into the sides of the buildings. She was, however, unhappy about having to sit outside the newsstand's door as the humans went in to look for clues to why the world had changed so much.

They entered Manny's Newsroom, finding it to look quite like a normal, familiar newsstand, and went to one of the racks that held newspapers. There were a variety of headlines, it (presumably) still being Saturday, though few of them made much sense to them. Still, Samantha read them all and filed them away in her mind for future reference.

"WAVES TAKE FIFTH STRAIGHT TITLE"

"PARK FIRE KILLS TWENTY, LEAVES EIGHTY HOMELESS"

"JAPAN MOVES THOUSANDS OF MORE REFUGEES TO CHINESE COAST"

"CALVIN VETOES BOATER LEGISLATION"

and finally,

"TRICK-OR-TREATERS WAX UP THEIR BOARDS"

"This ain't the public library, ya know," a grating, raspy voice called from behind the store's counter. "Ya think the rent's cheap on this little chunk of commercial real estate? You wanna read a paper, you buy a paper, capiche?"

Samantha knew from an Italian friend of hers that "capiche" meant, "understand," though she thought it always sounded more intimidating in Italian.

"Oh! I'm sorry," The Professor blathered, grabbing a pile of different newspapers and putting them on the counter. The proprietor rang up the purchase, which came to six dollars and seventy-five cents. Professor Smythe paid the rather unfriendly man and they quickly exited back out to the sidewalk, where Polly was waiting nervously.

The three walked down the plastic sidewalk, still marveling at the visual difference between what New York City was and what it had been. They found a dock with a little bench on it and sat down, deciding to see what they could learn from their pile of newspapers.

"Apparently," The Professor summarized, "Gary Calvin is now President of the United States, and has vetoed a bill by congress that would have required tougher restrictions on boat emissions. Poor sots – the last thing this world needs is more greenhouse gases – " The Professor cut himself off, as if something had clicked in his head. "October..." he mused, looking at the date on the newspaper, "It *is* October, Samantha. And ridiculously warm. And, considering the fact that in my two other brief outings into this reality I haven't found any evidence of dams breaking or torrential rains in the last seventy years, I'd say what we're looking at here is the result of global warming."

"Global warming?" Samantha asked, looking up from her paper. " Yeah, I've heard about that in science class. The earth gets too hot and the ice caps melt at the north and south poles, right?"

"Correct," The Professor replied, looking as if he were proud of her for having paid such good attention in school. "Global warming results from an excess of 'greenhouse gases,' principally carbon dioxide, building up in the atmosphere and trapping heat inside. When the heat builds to a certain level, the earth exhibits a 'greenhouse effect' and begins to melt the polar ice caps."

"Right," said Samantha. "That's why they say we shouldn't pollute the air so much, or cut down all the rainforests."

"Precisely!" The Professor beamed. Samantha was, after all, his favorite informal student.

"So, somehow something you did in your trip to 1931 melted the polar ice caps?"

"Well, perhaps not directly – but yes, I think that's the theory we should proceed with."

Samantha shrugged and filed away more potentially useful information. She and The Professor returned to browsing their various newspapers for any other clues they might find, sharing ideas with each other. The "Waves" were apparently some sort of water polo team that rode around on jet-skis and played in a sort of stadium that was somewhere in the huge rectangle lake that used to be Central

Park. This didn't seem like useful information, but the game looked cool in the pictures and so did the stadium. The park fire had been a terrible tragedy in a houseboat community that had sprung up downtown in Washington Square Park. There were pictures of the boats burning and people fleeing in canoes and the like, but the strangest sight to Samantha's eyes was how short and stubby the big arch in the square looked with its first ten or fifteen feet underwater.

The trick-or-treating headline confirmed even further that it was definitely October, with Halloween nearing, and the water-world response to this was thousands of surfboard-type things with little electric motors on them. Again, pretty cool but not much help in solving their mystery. The really good information came from the last front-page article, which talked about the Japanese refugees relocating. This went into great detail about the melting ice caps, confirming The Professor's theory and dating the beginning of the extreme water level rise to sometime in the mid nineteen-eighties.

"Egad!" The Professor exclaimed. "That's extremely fast. Twenty-five years and the sea level rises by twelve feet worldwide? Something acutely disastrous must have occurred."

In fact, at that very moment, something acutely disastrous *was* occurring. Polly had wandered a little ways out onto an adjacent dock where a boat was moored with its motor running at an idle. In one of her bolder yet least intelligent moves, she had decided to jump into the boat, landing squarely on its throttle and lurching the boat forward at an alarming speed, so much so that it broke its slender tether like a string of spaghetti and roared off into the busy river-traffic of Columbus Avenue. Samantha's jaw dropped and she and The Professor stared helplessly for a moment before springing into action.

They ran as fast as they could, dropping all but one of their newspapers, straight to a taxi-boat that was parked nearby.

"Please," Samantha cried, pointing ahead of her, "We have to follow that boat!"

"What?" the startled cabbie looked up from a magazine of questionable taste that he had been reading.

"My Dog! Quickly, my dog jumped into that boat and must've hit the gas! *Please!*" Samantha pleaded in as hurried a voice as she could manage. The Professor nodded vigorously in agreement and they climbed into the boat.

"Right," the driver replied, dropping his magazine and kicking in the motor. "You guys got money, right?"

"Yes," The Professor nodded again, and they sped off in hot pursuit of the boat that Polly had inadvertently stolen.

The cabbie opened up the throttle and they roared into high gear, the Polly-driven boat just on the edge of sight ahead. Amazingly, it appeared to be somehow maintaining a mostly straight course, though was not stopping for any of the traffic signals and had almost caused several accidents already. The cabbie dodged crosstown traffic as he wove through the same intersections, gradually gaining.

"Great galoshes!" The Professor exclaimed, hanging onto his hat as they barely swerved around another crossing taxi-boat, inspiring honking horns and a flurry of non-English curses. They were now only a block behind Polly but had already traversed eight or nine blocks, veered left onto Broadway and were heading straight toward the huge, busy intersection of Columbus Circle.

With an extra burst of speed, the cabbie zoomed within a hundred or so feet of the terrified dog in her runaway boat, and Samantha could see her little head poking up over the side. It looked like she was going to jump.

Despite Polly's general disdain of water and her overall fear of this new water-world and everything in it, jump is exactly what she did. The boat was moving so fast that she actually skipped across the water, was almost hit by another boat and then came to a floating halt, totally dazed. She began to paddle, just trying to stay afloat, and the cabbie downshifted, slowing down to pull alongside of her.

"Polly!" Samantha shouted, waving her arms as they approached her slowly, "Polly, over here!"

The dazed terrier seemed to hear her and changed the direction of her paddle towards their boat. When she was within arm's reach Samantha grabbed her by the collar and began to pull her aboard, The Professor aiding in the process.

"Keep the seats dry!" the cabbie yelled, letting them know that he was less than excited about having a wet dog in his taxi-boat, especially after a harrowing chase. Trying to ignore him, Samantha hugged her soaked canine companion, very happy to have her back in one piece.

"Are you okay?" she asked, almost in tears, inspecting Polly for any wounds or missing parts. Amazingly, she seemed to be intact.

The 'stolen' boat, however, had not been so lucky. It had blazed right into Columbus Circle, was hit by several other boats and was now being bashed around in traffic near the circle's central hub, where a statue of Columbus and perhaps six feet of column base were all that now divided this new, broader roundabout. The Professor and Samantha looked at each other with pale faces. A decision had to be made, fast.

"Here," The Professor shoved all of his money, about two hundred and thirty-four dollars, into the cabbie's hand. "Take us to the steps of the Natural History Museum and forget you ever saw us."

The cabbie looked around, checked his mirrors and quickly ascertained that no police seemed to have arrived yet, and no one seemed to have noticed that their taxi-boat had been the source of all the excitement. He smiled and closed his fist on the money.

"You got it, Mac," he replied, pulling a sharp left onto Sixty-first street and then another onto Central Park West. At first they crept a little slowly, trying to blend in, but quickly picked up the pace. Samantha held Polly low in her lap, trying to hide the wet dog from any passing police. She was very nervous; Samantha wasn't accustomed to breaking the law in any sort of way, and she felt bad for the owner of the 'stolen' boat and the other boats that had been involved in crashes, and she prayed that no one had been hurt by the actions of her usually smarter dog. The Professor, though also quite nervous, seemed to sense Samantha's unease and attempted to be a soothing adult voice to her frightened adolescent ears.

"It'll be all right, Samantha," he said, whispering. "Remember, we're trying to make sure that none of this ever happens. Though I admit this would seem to be a small setback."

"A small setback!!? Professor, we're outlaws here now!"

"Yes, well, we're banking on the hope that no one saw us, or can really pinpoint the source of the runaway boat." He paused, looking at the cabbie, "And so is our friend here."

The cabbie appeared calm, reached Seventy-seventh street, swung a quick U-turn as no oncoming boat traffic was evident and pulled alongside the museum steps, settling into a little cove that the water had created beneath the statue of a mounted Teddy Roosevelt. The fugitive trio hopped out, looked at their driver with very serious expressions and received a slight smile in return, the cabbie holding up the last of The Professor's cash and miming zipping his mouth shut with a zipper. The Professor nodded and the driver eased back into Manhattan boat traffic, waving a last goodbye.

"Leaping Lozenges!" The Professor blurted out after a long moment of silence, wiping his sweaty brow with a sleeve. "Have you got a leash for that monster!?"

Samantha smiled slightly and nodded sheepishly, pulling Polly's leash out of her backpack. Polly sat with hunched shoulders and looked as best she could like a dog who was very sorry, and certainly hadn't meant to be bad.

Polly sat calmly in the corner of Professor Smythe's basement office as Samantha eyed her. It was hard not to be angry at the little Boston terrier for all the chaos she had managed to cause in this strange alternate timeline, but she was after all just a dog. Samantha made a mental note to always keep her on the leash anytime they ventured out again into this bizarre, otherworldly New York. At least it seemed like their chaotic activity had gone unnoticed; it had been a day and a half since the boat had gone charging, driverless, into Columbus Circle traffic. They had made themselves beds in the office out of fourteenth century Peruvian blankets, neither she nor The Professor being confident that their homes were still where they had left them back in the 'correct' timeline. Professor Smythe had assured Samantha that he was allowed to be at the museum at any time and frequently worked entire nights there. Whether or not this was true, or at least familiar to the museum guards of this timeline, security seemed to be leaving them alone in their obscure corner of the building's basement.

In the last thirty-six or so hours, they had read their one surviving newspaper from front to back, and had ventured out once in another taxi-boat to purchase several more. It appeared that Professor Smythe's ATM bank card still worked in this timeline – apparently he had not been bankrupted or indeed snuffed out of existence altogether by the dramatic changes the world had gone through. "A fortuitous thing" The Professor had called it, though it had seemed quite unlikely to Samantha.

The Professor had also expressed continued fascination with the forest of antennae that seemed to dominate the entire skyline, and they had made a plan that today they would investigate this phenomenon. It didn't take long for The Professor to discover something about them just by re-reading the newspaper.

"Suffering Cephalopods!" he exclaimed. "Trees! Trees, Samantha!"

The Professor shoved the newspaper in front of her, pointing to a marginal advertisement for some sort of tree maintenance company.

"Look at the picture," The Professor indicated a tall, slender, antenna-like photo at one side of the ad. It was indisputably one of the things they had observed on almost every city rooftop, though it could be seen in much greater detail in the photograph. Its bottom base, which they could never see from street level, was a roughly trapezoidal shape with what looked like computer controls and a digital readout on it. The advertisement talked about regulation of CO_2 intake and oxygen output, which clearly intrigued The Professor to no end.

"Artificial trees, Samantha," he began in a hurried voice. "Thousands upon thousands of them. Artificially processing carbon dioxide and outputting oxygen. Amazing! I must see one. But – " Samantha could almost see smoke coming out of The Professor's ears as she watched him thinking steps ahead of her, "That would mean – *could* mean – " he looked again at the newspaper, then grabbed it and began marching towards his laboratory.

"Come on, Samantha, I definitely would love to see one of these amazing devices, but first we need to run a quick test on this newspaper. If my hypothesis is correct, we may have the answer to our question of how this global warming sprang so suddenly on this alternate timeline." Samantha shrugged and followed, closing Polly in the office behind her.

The Professor's lab was a pretty impressive place. Samantha had been in it many times before but still only understood what half of the hi-tech machines were for. The machine they were currently at was scanning the newspaper The Professor had placed in it, with lasers, x-rays and other invisible forms of light or energy, according to him.

The results, which appeared in columns on a computer screen, were in abbreviations and percentages that made little sense to Samantha, though she had seen this spectral analysis performed once or twice before by her erstwhile mentor.

"Cotton, hemp. Alfalfa! Atrophied Aztecs! There's not one speck!"

"One speck of what?" Samantha asked, trying to understand the numbers on the screen.

"Look," The Professor pointed to the abbreviations, explaining them, "Cotton, 62.5 percent. Hemp, 27.83 percent, Alfalfa, 9.64 percent – there's no wood, Samantha. Not one iota. This newspaper is made entirely without wood pulp."

Samantha looked and began to understand. Artificial trees, newspapers made purely of cotton and hemp, massive global warming. It was beginning to add up to a somewhat sickening conclusion.

"Professor," she said quietly, "Does this mean what I think it means?"

"It certainly seems so," he replied, shaking his head sadly. "Samantha, I think it is quite possible, in fact likely, that in this alternate timeline *there are no trees.* At least not in this part of the world."

"The floating plastic sidewalks," she thought out loud, "I thought they would've looked much better in wood. Now I understand why they made them the way the did. But Professor – no trees!? How could such a thing happen?"

"I believe," replied Professor Smythe, "that that is the next mystery we must unravel if we are to set things right."

It was quite a mystery. Fortunately, The Professor early on concluded that the answer to it might indeed lie right under their noses. They were, after all, in the basement of the Natural History Museum. While they had reasonably assumed that their little corner of basement seemed relatively immune to the effects of the time disruption, it was also true that the entire staff upstairs seemed to have changed, and it was therefore likely that the other parts of the museum had been affected.

They wove their way upwards through the building, The Professor having decided that they should head for the section that primarily dealt with ecology and climate, if indeed it would even be in the same place that it had been before. They climbed four flights of stairs, avoiding the elevators in order to encounter as few security personnel as possible and exited into a magnificent reconstruction of an Amazon rain forest. A huge canopy of expertly-crafted vines and branches stretched out overhead, while they were flanked on either side by every kind of tropical bush, tree and moss one could imagine. Hidden speakers played the sounds of rain, shifting leaves and hundreds of different birds and animals. Samantha remembered being in a similar exhibit here before, but couldn't remember if it had been in the same exact location or not.

"This way," Professor Smythe indicated. It seemed he was perhaps more familiar with the wing; Samantha always found the massive building hard to navigate. It didn't help that exhibits would frequently change.

After passing through an African desert, a Himalayan mountain scene and an Arctic refuge complete with walruses, killer whales and polar bears (not live ones, of course), the pair came to a sort of nexus where the walls were lined with large, backlit displays full of writing, diagrams and illustrations. It didn't take long for The Professor to locate something relevant; in the next moment he was reading aloud to Samantha from one of the more interesting-looking ones.

"In 1973, a disease was discovered in trees of the lodgepole pine family by Dr. Emmond Hesparius, a researcher for the U.S. Forest Service." The Professor pointed to a diagram of the fungoid-type organism's molecular structure. "The disease was considered contained until the summer of 1975, by which time it had mutated to affect several other species of pine. Emergency research grants were applied for (largely at the behest of the timber industry) but did not arrive until the spring of 1976, at which point the aggressive fungoid had spread to infect all species of pine trees and several other spruce, fir and other coniferous subspecies as well. By 1977, though research funds were now pouring in from around the globe, the disease had spread to four continents and had continually mutated to infect deciduous trees as well, and by 1980 almost every tree on the planet was dead. The fungoid had mutated to also affect some bushes, shrubs, flowers and, most alarmingly, algaes that helped maintain the planet's temperature, but by this time a neutralizing agent had been developed. The remedy proved to be too little too late, however, for without rainforests and many marine organisms, the bulk of the earth's atmospheric processing apparatus was irrevocably crippled.

"Dramatic increases in global temperature were recorded in every subsequent year, having been raised an average of twenty-three degrees worldwide since June 6, 1981."

"Yikes," Samantha piped in, "No wonder it's so warm."

"Ocean levels began to rise shortly after global temperatures," The Professor continued reading. "At an average of sixteen inches per year, the level has risen an estimated 8.8 meters since November of 1981. Despite massive emergency efforts to build walls, dams and breakwaters, most coastal cities were flooded considerably by 1997, including the U.S. Cities of New York, Boston, Philadelphia, Baltimore, Miami, Houston, New Orleans, Los Angeles, San Francisco and Seattle, as well as several other smaller cities."

The Professor paused in his reading here, having noticed a symbol that directed the reader to a huge, interactive map. He pressed the button next to it, and he and Samantha watched an animation of the rising sea level superimposed on a map of the world as it had existed in 1981. Major cities of the world were labeled and indicated with red or green lights, turning red at points as the water level rose to affect that city, usually indicating serious or total flooding.

"Jumping Jackelopes!" The Professor coughed out after some period of having held his breath.

"No kidding," Samantha replied. "Whatever you did, Professor, it sure was a doozy."

"Say again?" The Professor snapped out of his spellbound trance. "A *doozy?* Hmmm... yes, very *American* sort of expression. Hmmph. I suppose jackelopes are fairly American as well." (At this point he was basically mumbling to himself) "A doozy. I assume you mean that whatever I did had a far more profound effect than even *I* could have imagined. And that certainly is the truth... Samantha, all I did was go to a newsstand, buy a paper and a cup of coffee and come back to the museum! Unfortunately, the way time seems to work, I suppose I could have unknowingly kicked a pebble on the street which rolled down a drain, struck a rat right between the eyes which angered it enough to run out of its hole, bite a German shepherd in Central Park, giving it rabies and causing it to become mad enough, weeks later, to run into the street, causing an accident that killed the world's foremost... tree expert. Hmmm... perhaps there's something to that, Samantha..."

"You mean, maybe we should go back and make sure you don't kick any pebbles?"

"Well," The Professor said in a frustrated tone, "Unfortunately, I haven't figured out how to be that accurate with the time device yet. I'm afraid we'll have to do as much research as possible on this end first. But – the tree expert. That might be something to look for."

The two decided to go back down to the basement after examining a few more relevant exhibits. To their dismay, the museum's computer database had been updated that year, and they had decided that whatever 'tree expert' they were looking for had probably died before 1973 or else had never been born at all in this timeline. The Professor looked up from the terminal they were seated at with a blank look, then broke into a large smile.

"Good thing I never trusted computers," he said, springing up from his chair and opening a door at the rear of his office (which he had to move several piles of things to get to). Polly was awakened from a pleasant nap by his shuffling and trotted over to sniff around the area of excitement.

Behind the door was a sizable room of bookshelves from floor to ceiling, an impressive personal library that they both prayed fell within the unaffected zone of time displacement. Professor Smythe skimmed titles with his finger, circling the room at least twice before settling on *Who's Who In Botany, Forestry and Horticulture, 1997*.

The Professor shot Samantha a wink and pulled the rather large volume from the shelf, lugging it back to his desk before opening it.

"What we want, I think, is an entry for lodgepole pine diseases," he said, paging through the index. "Or at least pine diseases in general – ah, here we are – " The Professor looked a bit dismayed; Samantha could see the index entry over his shoulder and noted at least thirty page references – some for multiple pages.

"Oh dear," The Professor sighed. "We may have a bit of reading to do Samantha." He closed the book and handed it to her. "You read this one – I have another copy – though it's the 1993 version. I think it will probably still have our man in it, though, or – our... woman."

Hours passed in the windowless office, the two immersed in reports on tree diseases. Polly had begun to get antsy and Samantha decided to take her for a walk, tucking her neatly into her backpack to smuggle her out of the museum. She left The Professor to his research after borrowing ten dollars for a taxi-boat to and from Belvedere Castle, the only grassy area left above water for some ways and hence a favorite dog walk. It was a short and relatively cheap boat ride, and Samantha hadn't had any trouble flagging down a boat-cab.

A sort of dock-like area had been built into the high ground the castle sat on, which was known to New Yorkers as Vista Rock, where she and Polly got off to start their walk. There wasn't all that much grass about the place, it being mostly rock, either natural (*Vista Rock*) or man-made (Belvedere Castle). Off in the distance Samantha could see the obelisk known as Cleopatra's Needle, of which a good sixty feet (at least) still protruded from the water that was Manhattan's new 'base level.' Even further out she could see the upper floors of the Metropolitan Museum Of Art, which she had been to several times and hoped had been salvaged as well as the Natural History Museum had been. She thought it would be a terrible loss if much of its priceless collection of art from around the world had been ruined.

Polly was unhappy about being kept on the leash, but Samantha had had enough mischief from the terrier for one week already, and so would not let her loose. She did, however, run around a little bit with her dog, who was after all young and energetic and needed a healthy bit of exercise and play. Samantha enjoyed the running about too, though she quickly became hot and sweaty in this sweltering July-like October they were having. Global warming, she decided, was for the birds.

When they returned, (having rang The Professor's phone again from security), they found the gray-haired Englishman feverishly scribbling down Mayan translations from his computer screen. Polly lay down, panting, in her corner while Samantha attempted a conversation with The Professor. It seemed, however, that "Shhhh!" was the only reply she was going to get for a while, so she went into the bathroom across the hall to wash up a bit, feeling sticky from the hot sun and exercise. She had developed a real yearning for an actual shower, not having had one for days and growing less and less satisfied with her sink-baths. She was fairly sure there weren't any shower-equipped bathrooms in the museum, but she vowed that she would find one somewhere soon as she scrubbed behind her ears with the last bit of pink liquid hand soap.

Professor Smythe practically assaulted her as she strolled back into his office, waving papers at her and babbling too fast for her to understand.

"Slow down, Professor," Samantha said, drying her hair with a Peruvian blanket that was probably worth thousands of dollars.

"Sorry, sorry. Sorry, Samantha, but listen – I found our tree expert, I think. In both editions there are entries for a man named Dr. Elliot Bergen. He supposedly isolated and crafted a cure for an extremely aggressive fungoid tree disease in 1974, a disease found in lodgepole pines. *But* – when I put his name into the museum's computer database, which we have established is continuous with *this* alternate timeline, I get nothing. He doesn't exist. At least, not as any person of renown in history or the sciences."

Samantha scratched her head, digesting the new information. "So what next, then?" she asked.

"Well," The Professor continued, looking at one of his papers, "I have all his information. He was born Elliot Vincent Bergen, in 1936 in Chapel Hill, North Carolina to parents Vincent Bergen of Atlanta,

Georgia and Violet Edelstein of New York, New York. His father was (not surprisingly) a professor of biochemistry at the University of North Carolina and his mother a published writer of poetry and short stories. He would be seventy-five years old this year.

"I've done some further research," The Professor cleared his throat. "In this timeline, there does in fact exist an author of poetry and short stories, in New York City, a Violet Edelstein. According to the museum's database she is still alive. Ninety-six years old, Samantha."

"So, you think we should find her – this Dr. Bergen's mother... what do you think she could tell us?" Samantha wondered.

"Well, for one thing," Professor Smythe went on, "She could tell us whether or not she ever married a man named Vincent Bergen, and if they in fact had a child. That could help us a lot to narrow down the time-area that's been so largely affected by whatever my error was."

"I see," Samantha chimed in, catching on. "So, if they did get married and have Elliot, we know something happened to *him,* but if they were never married or never had him, then we know something must've happened to *them.*"

"Precisely," The Professor beamed. "Now, Samantha – I have an address for you here – it's for Ms. Edelstein's agent. I've made an appointment for you at three o'clock this afternoon to meet with him under the pretext of some school report you're doing..."

"School report?" Samantha interrupted, a bit alarmed.

"Just make something up," The Professor went on. "School report, school paper interview, I don't care – we just need to get to Violet Edelstein and ask her about Vincent Bergen and any children they may or may not have had."

"But those are pretty personal questions, Professor!" Samantha protested.

"Samantha, do you ever want to see your home again?" The Professor asked sternly. "I, for one, would really like to. *And* I would like very much to see your mother again, as I know you would as well. Just come up with some more innocent questions and slip in the bits about marriage and children, all right?" Samantha swallowed and nodded. "Good – now get along then; here's forty dollars and the address," he thrust some money and a bit of paper into her hands. "I've written down some essential questions you may want to ask her. You'll have to leave Polly here for this one, I'm afraid, but don't worry, I'll be here trying to get this befuddling Mayan time machine to work a bit more accurately; I believe we're going to be needing it soon."

Polly looked forlorn as Samantha left, but The Professor was right – she had caused quite enough trouble already in this timeline and would most certainly not be welcome in the offices of some esteemed literary agent. It was almost two o'clock, so Samantha had to rush a bit as the agent's office was downtown in Chelsea. She read the address, at Seventh Avenue and Twenty-sixth streets, to the driver of a taxi-boat she managed to flag down, and she was off like lightning to explore more of the freakishly changed cityscape.

The sun felt good on her back now, and Samantha took in the sights around her as they sped down to Columbus Circle and onto Broadway, which cut diagonally over to Seventh Avenue. It seemed to her that overall there were far fewer boats in the city than there had been cars, and as a result of this it appeared that all 'one-way' rules had been abolished, so that any boat could go either way on any given 'street.'

Most of midtown Manhattan's skyscrapers seemed perfectly intact if thirteen feet shorter – they all still looked monstrous to Samantha. Seventh Avenue had a more open feel as they turned onto it, though going past Thirty-fourth Street she still felt tiny in the shadow of the Empire State Building on their right, while she wondered if trains even still ran through Penn Station to their left. There were huge plastic sidewalks floating all around the perimeter of Madison Square Garden, and homeless people were, sadly, evident in numbers huddled up there under wood-free newspapers and old blankets. *At least,* she thought to herself, *New York's become quite a bit warmer.* It was the only thought she'd had since the world got all strange that made this timeline seem better – for some – than the one she and The Professor were trying hard to restore.

The taxi-boat pulled up on the corner of Twenty-sixth Street and let her out onto a plastic sidewalk. Samantha paid the driver and thanked him, then walked to a store on the corner. It was still only half past two by her watch and she was hungry, not having eaten that day. She purchased a huge turkey sandwich at the deli which she figured she'd eat half of and save half for The Professor. She also bought a pint of orange juice and a bag of dog food for Polly, which she stuffed neatly into her backpack.

Walking back outside, Samantha found a little bench and sat down to eat her half-sandwich and drink some orange juice. She found it quite strange that the juice carton read "Georgia Orange Juice" instead of "Florida Orange Juice," but then remembered the interactive map at the museum which had showed large portions of Florida to now be underwater. *Georgia,* she mused as she licked mayonnaise from her lips, *must be the new place to grow oranges.* She hoped that this hadn't affected the traditional Georgia peach crop too heavily, as she had always been a big fan of peaches.

Just as Samantha was packing up the half-sandwich she was saving for The Professor, a young man walked around the corner and asked if he could share the bench with her. She almost choked on her last bite of turkey when she looked up at him – it was Jordan Anderson from Heatwavvve, her favorite boy-band in the whole world.

"S-Sure! I mean, absolutely – by all means!" she fumbled with her words, totally awestruck. "Would you, um, like some... sandwich? Or some orange juice?" she offered. She knew she was totally blushing. This was unbelievable – entirely at random, Jordan Anderson had come and sat down next to her on a bench. She wished she had a picture of the moment to show to her friend Brianna – Samantha knew she would totally flip out.

"Thanks, but I don't eat meat," Jordan replied, smiling his million-dollar smile. "I feel like it slows me down, and I have a very active life."

I know, Samantha thought. She struggled to think of something to say that would keep the conversation going.

"So – aren't you in that group Heatwavvve? I mean, I'm sorry but you – you look almost exactly like – "

"Jordan Anderson?" Jordan interrupted. "Yeah, that's me. Do you know the band?"

"I – I actually have every one of your songs. I – " Samantha broke into a nervous giggle, "I'm actually kind of amazed to be meeting you. I have... a huge poster of you... on my wall, or, I, um, used to."

"Used to?" Jordan sounded slightly surprised. "Have you outgrown Heatwavvve already?"

"No... no! I still love Heatwavvve. I just – well, I kind of had to... move recently, and I don't really have any of my stuff."

"Oh, well – that's a shame. Hey, tell you what," the gorgeous dreamboat said, flashing that smile and patting her on the back, "my manager's office is two blocks from here. If you want you can walk over there with me and I'll give you a brand new poster, signed by the whole group."

"Wow, that'd be awesome," said Samantha, still in dreamland.

"Come on, then," Jordan began, getting up and lightly taking her arm to lead her. She let him pull her to her feet and began floating along like a scarf tied to the singer's arm, his touch sending waves of pleasure-electricity through her body. They made it about a block before she even thought to look at her watch, though when she did it alarmed her.

"Oh, wait – " she began, trying to stop. Her watch read 2:55. "Jordan, I – I'm sorry, I can't actually go right now."

"Aw, come on," he continued pulling her, "it'll just take a minute! It's right up here..."

"I – no," Samantha pulled backward, halting their progress. "I can't Jordan, I have to be somewhere, like *now*."

Jordan's grip tightened on her arm and he continued to protest, saying again that it would 'only take a minute.' At last Samantha pulled her arm free of his hand, almost yelling at him.

"*I have to go.*"

"All right!" he replied, putting up his hands and looking around somewhat shiftily to see if people were watching them. Then he calmed down a bit and apologized. "I'm sorry. I'm sorry, Samantha," he began, trying to look cool and collected again.

"How," Samantha asked looking straight into his eyes, "did you know my name?"

"Samantha," he continued, looking strange and nervous again. "You told me. Just now."

"Whatever," Samantha replied, feeling that something weird had just happened but needing to get moving. "I have to go, Jordan, but if you want, I, um, I walk my dog every day around noon at Belvedere Castle in the park, uptown."

"Okay," Jordan smiled his winning smile again. "Well, maybe I'll see you there sometime. I'll try to bring you a poster."

"That'd be great. Bye, Jordan, it was, ah, nice meeting you."

"Yeah, you too. Take care."

Odd, Samantha thought to herself as she turned around and headed back towards Twenty-sixth Street. Had she told Jordan her name? She couldn't remember; she felt, in fact, like the whole conversation had been a strange dream. It was like he had been, well, *was* the only person other than The Professor who had existed in both the normal timeline and the new, altered one that she was walking through now.

She shook her head to clear it of confusion and dreaminess. It didn't matter right now – she was at the door to the building whose address matched the one on the piece of paper given to her by The Professor. She scanned the board at the entrance with her eyes and found the name she was looking for – Alan Horrowitz And Associates – and noted the call number next to it, 060. Her fingers dialed the number on the phone-like keypad and a voice answered.

"Alan Horrowitz and Associates," it said in a bored, nasally voice. "Who's calling, please?"

Samantha cleared her throat and thought quickly, spewing out the best thing she could think of.

"Hi, this is Samantha Smart – I'm here to interview Ms. Edelstein for my, uh, school newspaper, the... *Roslyn High Examiner...*"

"One moment please," the voice replied. This was followed by a long silence. After what seemed like an eternity of staring at the little metal speaker, the buzzer buzzed to let her in. She almost didn't snap out of her daze in time but caught the door and opened it just before the sound stopped.

Samantha made her way to the elevator in the lobby's far right-hand corner, located the agent's office on the directory board and walked through the doors when they opened, pressing the button on the inside for the fifth floor. The doors closed and she began to move slowly upward, watching the numbers light up as she passed floors two, three and four. As 'five' lit up, the elevator stopped, opening its doors and ringing a little bell that sounded like it belonged in a Japanese economy car.

Apparently the whole floor was occupied by Alan Horrowitz And Associates, as there was a sort of lobby here, too, with a receptionist's desk straight in front of her. She walked up to it, noticing that the receptionist was on the phone, and stood waiting patiently.

"No, Mr. Horrowitz doesn't represent *children's* authors," she was saying to someone. "I – know that adolescents aren't *exactly* children, but as I said – " more silence as the persistent author continued in a minuscule voice Samantha could almost make out. "Yes, well, again, I'm very sorry, but I'm afraid your book just isn't our kind of material. Thank you!" The receptionist hung up, looking peeved at the caller, then noticed Samantha and instantly painted a somewhat patronizing smile back onto her face.

"You must be Ms. Smart," she said in a voice that dripped with feigned honey. "We've been expecting you." Samantha smiled and nodded.

"Come on, then," she said, getting up from the desk and motioning for Samantha to follow her down a long hallway. "Ms. Edelstein doesn't usually give interviews, but I think she was a bit charmed by the notion of a young girl from a high school paper. Right this way..." She opened a door to a large, sunny office with Alan Horrowitz's name on it. Samantha was led in and seated in a comfortable chair in front of an impressively large desk, and the receptionist pressed a button on the desk intercom and spoke into it.

"Mr. Horrowitz, Samantha Smart is here from the school paper."

"Right! We'll be in in a minute," a man's voice replied from the plastic box. The receptionist smiled at her and started towards the door.

"They'll just be a moment. Can I get you anything while you're waiting?"

"No, thank you," Samantha replied politely as the spokesmodel-esque woman exited.

Think fast, she said to herself. She pulled out a little notepad on which she had scribbled some 'cover' questions on the taxi-boat ride down, in addition to Professor Smythe's 'essential' questions. She had to play this like she was actually interested in Violet Edelstein's poetry and short stories, though she had read none of them. She realized, in fact, that she had never really interviewed anyone before, except maybe her brother Todd, for some dumb school assignment. She hoped she could pull off the charade.

After five minutes or so, a side door into the office opened and a well-dressed man in his forties appeared, helping a very old woman walk to the chair opposite Samantha's. She gave Samantha a smile as he helped her sit down, then the man walked over and shook her hand.

"Hello, Ms. Smart. This is the elusive Violet Edelstein." He indicated the old woman.

"Hello," Samantha replied, looking at both of them.

"I'm Alan Horrowitz, Ms. Edelstein's agent. Ah, if you don't mind, I've got some business to attend to, so I'll leave you two alone." He smiled and exited back through the door they had come in through.

"So," Violet Edelstein said after a brief but somewhat uncomfortable silence. "You write for your school paper?"

"Yes," Samantha blurted out. "But I'd like to write other things someday... like you."

"I wrote for my high school newspaper," the aged author began dreamily, "*The Pelham High Gazette.* My, that was a long time ago."

"Um – did you like writing for the paper?" Samantha asked,

pretending to take notes.

"Well... I suppose as much as you seem to," she replied, staring at her with knowing eyes. "I always wanted to write fiction, though. And of course poetry, though," she chuckled, "I certainly never expected to make money off of that. Fiction and poetry, they're much more... imaginative. More fun to envision, you know?"

"Absolutely," replied Samantha. "What would you say is the key to any successful story?"

The old woman thought for a moment, then lifted her finger and pointed at Samantha.

"Research. A story, a person, a place – all of these things are always more believable, more tangible if they are thoroughly and earnestly researched. Wouldn't you agree?"

"Yes," Samantha chewed her pen. "I would indeed. Do you, ah, do you remember when your first story was published?"

"Why, of course," Violet responded. "Like it was yesterday. I was very young and naive then, but – " she smiled devilishly, "I also had the fires of love in me.

"My first story to be published was about a man who wanted to cure cancer, a man who wanted nothing more than to, well, to help his fellow man. It was called *The Mad Scientist.* He wasn't really mad, of course, just very passionate about pursuing something that, well, that thousands of young scientists are still pursuing today. Curing cancer has proved to be quite a difficult task." She chuckled.

"To be sure." Samantha smiled back. "And was this man completely made up, or was he based on someone that you knew?"

The old woman eyed her thoughtfully. "There was a man I knew," she began, hesitating. "He was very charming – not in the way that most girls might find a man to be charming, but very... admirable. Dedicated."

"Dedicated," Samantha repeated, scribbling. "And how did you come to know him?"

"We – well, we... dated for some time. A long time ago, before all this flooding business. We... we thought about getting married, actually – but that was back when every boy a girl dated was thought of as a potential husband, you know." She chuckled again, looking up at the ceiling as if she were remembering something distantly pleasant. "He used to write me the sweetest letters..."

"Well," Samantha pressed on after a bit of silence. "What, ah, what became of this charming, dedicated fellow?"

"We... we lost touch, I suppose. He had talked about moving, to North Carolina, I think. He said he had a big opportunity there, that he was going there to 'check into it' and that he would write me again when he settled into a place – he had lived in Brooklyn up until then – but I never got his letter, if he wrote one. Then there was a – a terrible fire at my house and I had to move as well. It was all rather dramatic, really. I suppose we were just – never meant to be. But that's all ancient history."

Samantha's mind was racing. A letter that wasn't delivered, or was delivered to a pile of ashes. A wedding that never happened. A child who was never born? It was clutch time, and she decided to blurt out a blatant question.

"Ms. Edelstein," she said a little shakily. "That man – was his name Vincent Bergen?"

Violet Edelstein looked shocked and seemed to become most pale, as if she had seen a ghost, and Samantha was briefly afraid she might have a heart attack or something.

"Why, yes – yes, it was. But how... how could you know that?" she asked in awe.

"Perhaps you were meant to be together," Samantha replied, getting up and taking the dumbstruck author's hand. "Thank you, Ms. Edelstein," she said firmly but gently. "You have been a tremendous help. I think I have enough here for the story I wanted to write." She moved toward the door, confident that this was all the information she needed.

"W – Wait," the old woman squeaked out. "How do you know about... Vincent?"

"Research," Samantha winked, exiting the office.

Samantha smiled as she walked in the late afternoon sun up Seventh Avenue. She had totally pulled off what she considered to be a very professional impersonation. Not only had she got the information she was sent to get, she had extracted it smoothly and cleverly, saving the blunt question for last, when she had been pretty much sure of the answer already. As much as she loved forensic science, this sort of work was very exciting, too. Perhaps she could be some sort of detective or private investigator – it was much the same as forensics, the basic gist being to gather the facts and try to make a logical conclusion. The exciting thing about this sort of work, though, was that you got to be out "in the field," interacting with people in the real world and developing skills like impersonating school reporters. It was definitely less dull than sitting in a lab analyzing newspapers under a microscope, though her smart and logical side (of which she was very fond) told her that the latter job probably paid more, and The Professor's bank account seemed to confirm this. She shrugged to herself; maybe she could do both. She was a young, energetic girl.

She felt so energetic at the moment that she decided to walk at least part of the way back to the museum. Taking taxi-boats was fast, certainly, but Samantha hadn't done enough real walking lately, and seeing as she was in no particular rush, she availed herself of the opportunity to fit in some healthy exercise. Seventh Avenue (and apparently all the avenues) had floating plastic sidewalks lining them all the way up, and where they crossed the water-filled streets they bridged them with iron over-walks that were bolted into the buildings on either side. It was a lot of up and down walking, but it at least allowed one to walk around the city. It was also like a natural Stairmaster for the thighs, and though Samantha was not in any way fat or even flabby, she reminded herself that "cellulite is the enemy," as she had been thoroughly informed by every major teen magazine. The workout was nice, and Samantha worked up a sweat after only three or four blocks, she walking at a brisk pace and the day being still quite warm and sunny. When she reached Madison Square Garden and had descended from the Thirty-first Street over-walk, she was again confronted with the huddling masses of homeless people, looking hungry, half-drunk and very much beyond their years. She felt very bad for them, and wound up giving an old woman with a sort of floating shopping cart ten of her remaining twenty-or-so dollars. It was silly, she knew. In the real timeline, the woman may never have been born, or, who knew, she could be a powerful investment banker. It was probably stupid to put her resources into something she was working to eliminate (anything in this alternate timeline), but Samantha was a compassionate person and had felt the need to do something, even if it was just to make one woman more comfortable for a short period of time that might not even exist if she and The Professor accomplished their mission to right things, time-wise.

She continued walking uptown, staying on Seventh Avenue, though when she reached Forty-second Street, where Broadway cut its diagonal path across midtown, the over-walks became very jumbled, and at one point she found herself plopped down in Times Square on a large, plaza-like floating plastic triangle with benches and artificial trees on it. It was bizarre, like and yet unlike how she remembered it. There was still a large digital billboard of sorts, though it seemed to be advertising strange, unfamiliar products, among them artificial trees and motorized surfboards. Samantha wondered if they still celebrated New Year's here, if they still dropped a ball at midnight. *Well,* she thought, *if it's October now, I suppose we'll find out if we don't get this mess straightened out in a few months.*

She spied a music store to one side of the plaza and, looking at her watch, decided she could duck in for a few minutes. Music was very important to her and she realized she hadn't heard a good Heatwavvve song in a while. Even with all her new responsibilities as investigator, forensic scientist and possibly time-traveler-in-training, she maintained that it was only fair to let herself be a young girl at times.

The store was bustling with lots of people, many around Samantha's age. It seemed compact discs had still managed to get invented, though they looked somewhat bigger and were packaged a bit differently. None of the musical artists on the wall's posters looked even vaguely familiar, and this gave her a feeling of discomfort – it was one thing to not be "hip" because you hadn't exposed yourself to new music; it was another thing entirely to be a girl who just *really* didn't belong in a certain time and place. She was sort of staring at a poster of some axe-wielding heavy metal singer when a store clerk came up and jolted her out of her queasy reverie.

"Can I help you find anything, Miss?" A good-looking young man in a red vest and nametag asked her.

"Oh – uh, yeah, maybe," she sputtered, feeling even more uncool. "Do you, um, do you have Heatwavvve, the, uh, singing group?"

"Heatwavvve?" the clerk started walking through the aisles, beckoning Samantha to follow. "Um - I'm not sure if this is what you want, but..." they reached a stack that the clerk thumbed through and pulled out a disc. "Is this what you're looking for?"

Samantha took the CD from him and looked at it. The cover was all red and looked like some kind of nuclear explosion, though it did say "Heatwavvve" on it. She flipped it over and read some of the song titles, "Baby Butcher," "Chained and Hopeless," "March of the Frost Giants" – this was definitely not the same Heatwavvve. She confirmed this assumption by reading the names of the band in the liner notes, which were all wrong.

"Um – no," she replied. "This isn't them. Don't you have Heatwavvve, you know, the boy-band with Jordan Anderson?"

"Boy-band? Jordan Anderson? I'm afraid I don't know who you're talking about. The only Heatwavvve I know of is these guys," he said, taking the disc back from her and replacing it in the stack. "And they play like thrash-metal."

"Heatwavvve," Samantha emphasized, frustrated. "They're huge! Everyone knows who they are, they've sold millions of CDs and are in those ads on TV for soda and barbecued ribs and stuff. They're everywhere! How could you not know them?"

The clerk scratched his head. "Are they British?" he asked, "or Australian?"

"No! They're totally American – I just – and this was incredible – I just met one of their singers, Jordan Anderson, downtown. He was going to get me a signed poster..." she drifted off into the memory of her moments with Jordan. The tingly feeling she'd gotten when he touched her had been amazing, and she wished she could feel it again.

"I'm sorry," the clerk shrugged, smiling slightly at her obvious adolescent crush and causing her to blush. "Maybe you could get a CD from him, too; we don't have one."

Samantha thanked the clerk for his help, and after a brief and futile self-performed search of the "A" stack, hoping to find something under "Jordan Anderson," she left the store. Her watch read 4:48, and though it surely didn't feel like it, it was October and hence the sun was rapidly going down. She decided to hail a taxi-boat from the huge floating triangle-plaza, figuring she didn't want to be walking around in the dark unless absolutely necessary. She had ten dollars left and figured that would cover her ride back to the upper west side, and it didn't take her long to find a cab.

The ride uptown was uneventful, and Samantha mostly spent it trying to figure out why Jordan Anderson existed in this timeline and yet no one at a big chain music store had ever heard of Heatwavvve. Perhaps they weren't quite as famous in this reality, and Jordan had just been playing himself up as a superstar simply because she had heard of his group. *That wouldn't be so bad,* she thought to herself. *If he wasn't so famous, maybe he'd even consider... well, dating someone like me.* She quickly dismissed this as silly girlish thinking, he was years older than her, though perhaps a definite spark of hope remained in her mind.

The taxi-boat pulled up and dropped her off at the museum steps and she gave the driver her ten dollars, tipping him two dollars and twenty-five cents as the fare had been $7.75. She did the usual rigamarole with the security desk, though by now the "new" people sort of recognized her and would generally let her find her own way down to Professor Smythe's office once they got the telephone o.k. from him. She was almost knocked over by a Boston Terrier blow to the chest when she entered the office; Polly had obviously missed her. She gave her dog a good bit of affection and then looked over to where The Professor was tinkering with something on his desk.

"Hi, Professor!" she said in a peppy voice.

"Oh, Samantha!" he replied, looking up from his work. "I've just finished making a prototype for a wristband-communicator," he said enthusiastically. "It runs on a closed-circuit microwave band that, if my theory is correct, should be unaffected by temporal displacement."

"Say what?" Samantha tried to adjust back to The Professor's speed of thinking.

"Time travel, Samantha. The wrist communicator is joined by a sort of a closed-circuit microwave band to this desk unit here." He indicated a larger sort of radio thing. "They should function no matter what sort of 'timeline' one might be in, and of course throughout the course of any of these timelines, at any point along the way."

"Cool," Samantha said earnestly, walking over to the desk and looking at his work. "Where did you get the parts to make this, Professor?"

"Radio Shack." The old Brit smiled a toothy smile. "Well," he said, turning back to the desk, "we shall have to test this, then. And that means using the time machine, Samantha."

"Professor," she interjected, "don't you want to hear about my interview with Violet Edelstein?"

"Bellowing bugbears!" he exclaimed. "I'd totally forgotten. Sometimes I just get so involved in a new project that I sort of forget what the last one was for," he said apologetically.

"It's okay, Professor," Samantha said, patting him on the top of his head. "But listen!" Her voice became as excited as his. "I got to 'interview' Violet Edelstein – a very neat woman, by the way - you would've been so proud of me, I did such a good job as field agent, impersonating a school reporter – " The Professor was nodding in anticipation. "Anyway, there's no Elliot Bergen in this timeline, he was never born. Ms. Edelstein said that she *had* been dating a Vincent Bergen, but that he had moved, probably to North Carolina, to pursue some opportunity, and that he was supposed to have written her, that they had been considering marriage, but then her house burned down and she had to move as well and they lost touch."

"Oh dear." The Professor frowned. "Do you think I did something in the past that caused her house to burn down?"

"Well," Samantha replied, then paused for thought. "I hadn't thought of that. I was thinking that perhaps he had written a letter and that for some reason it hadn't been delivered."

The Professor assumed a look of deep thought, scratching his chin and appearing to be searching his memory.

"You know, I vaguely recall walking by a postman that time in 1931. But – I didn't touch him or even interact with him in any way. Still, perhaps something could've happened..."

"Well, okay," Samantha said. "What do we do with this information?"

The Professor looked at her in a focused way, then looked back at his desk.

"Well," he said, "no matter what, we're going to have to use the time machine. We need to try and get back to that short period of time I spent in 1931 and correct whatever went wrong. We now know that something I did either caused a house to burn down or a letter to not be delivered. Did Ms. Edelstein say when exactly her house burned down?"

"No, I, um, didn't ask her," Samantha pouted, a little deflated.

"It doesn't really matter. In fact, I think the letter theory is a bit more plausible. And I seem to remember something about that postman – he... yelled or something, it made me turn around and look, but I was halfway down the block from him at that point. I hardly noticed it, but... now for some reason it sticks in my memory.

"In any case, someone has got to go back and fix it, and as much as I would rather do it myself, I don't think that would be a very good idea."

"I'll go!" Samantha volunteered, biting her lip in excitement and eyeing the nifty wrist-communicator.

"Hold on a moment," The Professor put his hand up. "I'm not so sure if that's such a good idea either, sending a young girl alone back in time – you could get hurt or lost – I'd feel simply horrible if anything happened to you."

"I'll take Polly with me!" She beamed, nodding as if this were the obvious solution. Polly wagged her little stub of a tail and looked back and forth between Samantha and The Professor.

"That dog has caused enough trouble already, don't you think?" The Professor looked at Polly and spoke in a scolding tone so that she cowered slightly from him.

"Oh, she didn't mean it, Professor. And I'll keep her on the shortest leash, the whole time!"

"Well," The Professor grumbled, "unfortunately, I fear that I absolutely mustn't go myself. I'm afraid having two Professor Smythes in the same time and place might produce some disastrous result, though I'm not sure what exactly would happen." He looked at Samantha long and hard. "I suppose it has to be you. I can't rightly draw anyone from this timeline into our little mess. I thought about asking one of the museum security guards to do it, but then my mind got to wondering – what if they weren't meant to exist in that timeline, *our* normal timeline. Would they be able to exist there as we are able to exist here, or might they simply blink out of existence upon reaching *our* 1931? Though presumably, our timeline and this one were one and the same up until that specific point when I goofed something up." The Professor shook his head. "There are too many ifs, Samantha."

"Well then that settles it," Samantha said firmly. "If there are too many ifs, Professor, one logically has to follow the course with the most certainty, even if it isn't one hundred percent. If you're not sure what will happen if you go yourself or send some security guard, you have to send me. You know that I won't cause any 'double-occurrence' like you would, and it's less likely that I'll blink out of existence than someone from this new timeline, and I'm the only one in this timeline besides you who even knows half of what's going on here. Do you think some security guard is going to be easily talked into walking into some crazy Mayan time machine because you've just explained to him that he and his whole world weren't meant to exist, and that we need to fix that?"

Professor Smythe frowned.

"You certainly put forth a very compelling argument, Samantha." He sat brooding for a few moments, seemingly going over their very limited options. "All right. But I want you to take Polly – *on a short leash.* And before I let you anywhere near that time machine we're going to give this communicator a real test."

"Okay! Fine – I mean, it's a deal. I need to take Polly out anyway – how far do you want me to go with it?"

"As far as you can," The Professor said, strapping the small, watch-like device onto her wrist. "I'd actually like you to take a cab down to Battery Park, at the bottom tip of the island."

"I've been there." Samantha assumed her worldly tone and looked down at her little Boston Terrier. "Polly, do you want to come for a *walk* ?"

"Walk" being a word that even most dogs of far less intelligence understand and celebrate as a key to some promised land, Polly became very excited and started sproinging around (a word Samantha had made up), panting and yipping in her little bark-voice. Samantha smiled and scratched her between the ears, then looked up at The Professor.

"Don't worry, Professor. We can take care of each other, really. We've been doing it for years. Polly's smarter than she acts sometimes, you know."

"Hmmmph," The Professor snorted, turning away. "I'll believe it when I see it." He started digging in his pocket then turned back to her. "Do you have any money left?" Samantha shook her head. "All right then, here's twenty dollars. I want you to take a taxi-boat straight to Battery Park, we'll test the communicator while you walk the dog, then I want you to come straight back. Here – " he handed the money to Samantha. "Shall I show you how it works?"

"Absolutely." Samantha grinned.

The Professor flicked some switches on the desk unit then reached for Samantha's wrist.

"This button," he indicated controls as he spoke, "is to turn it on. *This* button is to toggle on and off whether you are in the same time as the desk unit or not – I can't really explain how – I hope – that works, (if it even does), but it sort of modifies the bandwidth and pulse of the signal. And this big dial is your fine-tuner. Use it to tune in if your signal gets weak or starts to break up." Samantha nodded as she received each instruction, even though Polly was still sproinging a bit and distracting her slightly. "If you *are* in the same time as me, as you will be in Battery Park in half an hour or so, keep the right button *out*. If you are in another time, keep it pushed *in*. Got it, have you?"

"Yup," Samantha said, already getting her backpack ready to stuff her little dog into.

"Testing..." The Professor spoke into the communicator master unit. Samantha pressed the left or 'on' button on the wrist unit and made sure the right, or "time setting" button was left "out." She could hear his voice coming out through the tiny speaker in the wrist-communicator's face. From across the room she replied,

"Professor – is there a 'talk' button?"

"Oh, yes! Stupid of me, really – it's that large bar at the bottom – it's a button too, just shaped more like the space bar of a computer keyboard. You don't need to hold it in the whole time you're talking, but you need to press it at the beginning and at the end of each time you speak. Its normal state is a 'listening' one." Samantha followed the directions and was able to get a message through successfully.

"Testing – testing – Professor Smythe, of the Knightsbridge Smythes, eats worms..." she giggled into the unit.

"Thunderous thumb-suckers!" he yelled gleefully at his new invention. "It works!" He turned to Samantha, who was packing up

Polly. "All right – off with you. Call me from the park, just as I showed you, then come *right back,* okay?"

"Yeah." Samantha rolled her eyes a little. "Okay. Really, I'll be fine, Professor. I just want to let Polly run a little bit."

"Just remember, Samantha, we're a team now. Without each other, neither of us has much hope of setting things right again. Please be careful." The Professor was most affectionate and protective, and Samantha almost blushed. Instead she nodded and headed up the stairs to the surface.

*

Battery Park was certainly a bit different, even perhaps more so than the average spot in flooded New York. Being at the foot of Manhattan Island, it had essentially become part of the bay, or the Hudson River, technically. You could still see the very tips of some of its stone walls and smaller monuments, but mostly it had become largely saltwater. In a sense, the Hudson and East Rivers had been entirely blended together into one big bay, and the water that had drowned the streets of the city was actually quite salty thanks to the ocean's encroachment. You could still see the Statue of Liberty from the floating plastic sidewalks that lined what used to be the park, but it looked smaller now and farther away. Samantha concluded that this was probably a sort of illusion; a good portion of the statue's base was now underwater, and essentially the global rise of the sea level had made the horizon line a bit higher. This gave the viewer the impression that Lady Liberty's feet were down to or below the horizon line, which made the statue appear to be farther away. It was an eerie effect, and it made Samantha really soak in the apocalyptic feel of this unfortunate alternate reality.

She had, of course, been foolish to assume that there would be any grass remaining here, and Polly whimpered as if she had been robbed of a proper walk. There were a few little strips of sodded floating sidewalk that Samantha found and offered to Polly, who grudgingly did her business. Samantha picked up the dog-doo with a plastic bag and deposited it in a close-by trash can that had obviously been put there for just such a purpose. *Pew!* Samantha thought, *I need to start feeding her something else!*

They found a little beach and Samantha sat down, looking around a little nervously as it was about six-thirty or seven in the evening and pretty much dark already, though there were plenty of lights shining out from the city that apparently still never slept. She rolled up the sleeve of her sweatshirt and turned on the wrist-communicator. Tapping the big talk bar, she spoke into its tiny condenser microphone.

"Professor? Professor, it's me, Samantha. I'm at Battery Park now." She tapped the 'talk' bar again and listened. A crackly, staticky voice came through the little speaker. She couldn't quite make it out, so she turned the fine-tuning dial until she had a much clearer signal.

"... mantha, are you there? This is Smythe, 'comin' back atcha,' I suppose. As one of your Midwestern truckers would say."

"I hear you, Professor," Samantha replied, tapping the talk bar on and off.

"Samantha? Wonderful! How does the park look, Samantha?"

"Like part of the bay. You should see the statue, Professor, it's really sort of creepy. Like an end of the world sort of vibe."

"Yes, I can imagine what it might look like. Low in the water, I should guess."

"Yeah, it looks that way, more even than most other things."

"A trick of perspective," the wrist-speaker squawked. "All right. Come on home, then – I just wanted to give this a real good distance test before we try to use it through time. Hopefully by the time you get back I'll have fetched us some supper. Do you like Chinese food?"

"Sure!" Samantha beamed. She always wanted Chinese food, but her stupid brother was always taking all the mom-money and ordering pizza.

"All right," the speaker continued. "Get back as soon as you can. I'll try to meet you at the front door so you don't have to go through all that phone-security business. And I'll try to make us up some nicer sort of beds. My back's been paining me lately. Smythe out."

Samantha pushed the off button and sighed deeply. It was a nice, summer-like night, even though it was technically October. She took a moment to relax and think about things she had sort of put off thinking about, feelings she had put off feeling. She missed her mom a lot. There was this sort of gut-wrenching feeling she had that somewhere her mother was really worried about her, and she didn't want her mom to worry. If she could only make a phone call to the world she was trying to get back to, to tell her mom she was all right, she would feel much better. But she couldn't.

She missed her friends, too. Hanging out with The Professor and doing exciting investigative things was cool and made her feel very responsible and grown-up, but sometimes she just wanted to let loose a little and have fun. She and her friend Brianna Knowles used to spend hours in Brianna's penthouse apartment trying on clothes and dancing around, listening to Heatwavvve CDs. Sometimes their friend Suki Han would come over too and show them the hottest new fashions of Tokyo, Japan, where she spent half the year with her father. She even missed her friend Marvin Santiago, who was a chubby sort of Hispanic boy who lived not far from her in Brooklyn. He was weird in that he liked computers as much as he liked basketball, and wrote equal amounts of computer programs and mediocre rap songs. Samantha smiled, remembering a day she had been sitting in Marvin's room when he had just hacked into a distribution company's files and switched two orders, so that a wedding catering company would receive fifty stun-guns and a prison upstate would be delivered fifteen boxes of lemon mousse and chocolate-chip cookies. "Move along, move along," they had taught his pet parrot, Flacko to repeat as they rolled on Marvin's floor in laughter, imitating caterers prodding guests away from the conspicuously diminished desert table at some snobby wedding. Perhaps, upon reflection, it had been a trifle cruel to ruin someone's wedding, but Samantha thought that since a lot of prisoners were probably happy for a day, it would make up for it. Most of them were there for not much good reason, as Marvin liked to point out.

"Well," Samantha said to her only remaining friend (other than The Professor), "thank goodness for you, Polly." She picked up her little dog and hugged her tightly and Polly licked her face, returning the affection. "I suppose we should head on back, then."

After another pleasant but uneventful taxi-boat ride, Samantha found herself stuffing her face with Crab Rangoon – an absolute favorite of hers that The Professor had ordered in what Samantha thought was one of his especially brilliant moments. The two sat and talked more about their predicament, the information they had and didn't have, and tried to devise a plan for the controlled use of the mysterious Mayan time-machine. The night drifted on and they settled down to sleep on their respective piles of Peruvian blankets, listening to the slimy sound of Polly licking sweet and sour sauce from an empty food container.

"Professor?" Samantha mumbled sleepily.

"Mmmphh – yes, what? What is it, Samantha?"

"Have you ever heard of Heatwavvve?"

"Say again?" The Professor replied.

"Heatwavvve. An American singing group. Very popular."

"Oh, heavens no." The Professor turned over on his side facing away from her. "Why?"

"How likely would it be, Professor, that an immensely popular group that was topping the charts in our timeline would also exist in this one?"

"Hmmmpph. Extremely unlikely, I should think. Not impossible, but most unlikely indeed."

"Hunh..." Samantha began to ponder his response, but the two were asleep within minutes, and the only thing still making a sound was Polly's tongue.

*

Morning came again without a sunrise, as it always did in The Professor's windowless cave of a basement office. The only way they ever really knew it was morning was by the clock on his cluttered desk. Both he and Samantha agreed that the lack of natural light was getting a bit depressing, and they decided to both take Polly for a walk over at Belvedere Castle before diving into the risky and uncertain activity of time travel. The museum lobby was bustling with school children, and they slipped out largely unnoticed, Polly stuffed neatly into Samantha's backpack. They hailed a taxi-boat and were soon disembarking on the island formerly known as Vista Rock; Samantha let Polly out of her backpack while The Professor paid the driver.

"Sumptuous sunbathers!" The Professor exclaimed. "It's quite nice out. I haven't been getting out enough, what with all my time-machine researching and inventing spatio-temporal wrist communicators! Is it always this sunny, Samantha?"

"Oh, yes," Samantha replied, clipping Polly's leash onto her collar. "It's been like this every day. Very nice, really, though I imagine it's easier than we might think to get a bad sunburn."

"To be sure," The Professor said in a somewhat serious voice as he pulled a little folded-up cap from a pocket of his lab coat and fitted it onto his head.

Polly was quite unhappy to be on her leash, with all the rare grass to run around on, and kept tugging insistently, dragging Samantha this way and that (as much as a Boston Terrier can drag anyone). She had to sniff every square meter of ground, of course, though she found most places to be generally unremarkable. As they walked, Samantha and Professor Smythe discussed their plans for time-traveling.

"So, assuming I wind up in the right place – at the right time – what should I do, Professor?"

"Well," The Professor answered, "I think the best thing to do would be to follow me, the 'me' in the past, perhaps not letting 'me' notice that you're there. I know that sounds strange, but I think that the less obtrusive you can be in another time and place, the better. And I don't imagine that The Professor Smythe of that moment would understand at all what you were doing there – and *then* – and it would take a whole lot of explaining in any event."

"Okay. So, stay out of sight."

"I think that would be best. And for God's sake, don't touch anything! Don't talk to anyone, don't bump into anyone, don't even interact in any way with that world if you can possibly help it, except to correct my mistake."

"How can I correct your mistake if I don't know what it is until it happens?" Samantha asked.

"Hmmmm." The Professor thought out loud, his brow furrowing. "I suppose you'll have to anticipate it, to some degree. Remember, it probably has something to do with a letter, and I *know* there was a postman nearby in that time. Whatever happened – aaah, this is frustrating! I would say to look for a postman, and to pay attention to whatever I'm doing around the time you might see him."

"All right." Samantha's mind processed the information.

They had been walking in a semi-circle around Belvedere Castle, and now ascended some stone steps to a sort of terrace that stretched out like a grand, outside dance floor. They were still walking and talking when Samantha noticed that Polly had frozen in place.

"Polly, come on, girl," Samantha intoned, pulling gently on her leash. She still would not budge, and seemed to be staring into the distance at a person who was leaning on a stone wall about fifty yards away. Her ears were straight up in the air and she seemed to be extremely on edge.

"Polly, what is it, girl?" The Professor prompted her. She turned for a half-second at the sound of her name, then immediately snapped back to looking at the distant figure, who was now walking toward them. It appeared to be a young man in a dark red leather jacket, with an average build and a gait of calm confidence. As he grew closer, Samantha began to recognize him. It was Jordan Anderson. Her heart began to thump as she remembered the feel of his hand on her arm – half a feeling of danger and half one of excitement. She gulped hard as he approached them and The Professor took note of her reaction. Polly began to growl.

"Samantha, right?" Jordan asked, stopping in front of them and flashing his blinding white smile like a mirror in the intense sunlight.

"Hi, Jordan," Samantha gushed. "I – I forgot I told you about this place – Polly, stop it!" She slapped her dog lightly on the head to cease her growling.

"Well, it certainly is a nice place," Jordan replied, his eyes darting from Samantha to The Professor to Polly.

"Oh – I'm sorry," Samantha continued, trying to assume an air of womanliness. "This is my friend Professor Smythe. And this is my dog, Polly. Polly, *stop.*" She grabbed the canine's face to quiet her continued noises.

"Good to meet you," Jordan said, shaking The Professor's hand.

"Likewise," The Professor said somewhat suspiciously.

"I – uh, I met Samantha downtown yesterday. She said she was a fan of my band. Oh – here, I brought that poster in case I ran into you," he said, turning to Samantha and pulling a small poster from an inner pocket of his jacket. "Signed by the whole band."

"Oh, thanks! Thanks for remembering," Samantha peeped, taking the poster and unrolling it. It was truly the same Heatwavvve she remembered, with all the members' signatures signed in what appeared to be fresh black marker underneath each of their faces. She was tickled pink, but then remembered her strange experience at the Times Square music store.

"Jordan, I tried to find your discs at the store the other day and –"

"They didn't know who we were?" Jordan interrupted.

"Well, yeah," Samantha said, blushing a little.

"Yeah, well... we're not that big – yet. I was actually surprised you knew who we were, Samantha. It's nice to have a fan. We've been trying to get our albums in the bigger chain stores, but, well, it's tough, you know?"

"Oh, sure," she responded, once again taking on an air of maturity and nodding as if she knew all the ins and outs of the music business. Inside she breathed a sigh of relief; that explained a lot and dispelled most of the uneasy feelings she had had before.

"Where can one purchase one of your recordings?" The Professor piped in, still eyeing the young man warily.

"Oh - um, well, you can get them at Al's music, down on Fifty-seventh and – oh, I think it's Third or Fourth Ave."

"Third or Fourth?" The Professor raised an eyebrow.

"Yeah. That's – I think that's one of the closer places, though I'm not sure. They're at other stores, too, just not that many, and you kind of have to dig a little. You can download them for iTunes too."

"Cool." Samantha smiled.

"So – how did your appointment go? Yesterday." Jordan asked her.

"My – oh! Oh, it was great; I went to this literary agent's office to..." The Professor subtly pinched her, rather hard, an action obviously meant to tell her she was perhaps talking a bit too much. "To – uh, do an interview. For my school paper."

"Really! Whom did you interview?"

"Oh, uh, it was this... children's book author. A man named Mark Farmer. Have you heard of him?"

"'Fraid not." Jordan shrugged. "What did he write?"

"Ah – *The Frog Prince*," she struggled out, wincing to herself for coming up with such a stupid answer.

"The Frog Prince? I thought that was a really old story."

"Right. I mean, it is. He just, oh, modernized it."

"I see. Good story. One of my favorites," Jordan responded. There was something of a dire gleam in his eye when he said this, and he had the slightest hint of a mischievous smile on his face. Polly began to growl again.

"Well," he said, breaking his stance. " I suppose I should get going. We've got a photo shoot later this afternoon. It was good to see you again, Samantha." He took her hand and kissed it, making her shiver with pre-teen crush feelings. Polly growled loudly and he let her hand go, shaking The Professor's again. "Nice to meet you, Professor," he said. The Professor just nodded and stared as he walked away.

"Thanks for the poster!" Samantha blurted out belatedly, waving to the cutest boy she had ever seen, who had just kissed her hand. He turned around and shot her a gun-shaped finger as if to say "You got it, kid." *What a smooth operator,* she thought.

The Professor turned to her with a look of concern.

"Heatwavvve?" he asked. Samantha nodded. "Seems like a bit of a loose cannon, that bloke. I get a funny feeling about that lad. You watch out for him, Samantha."

"Oh, Professor!" she shot back. "It's just an act. He's *supposed* to come off as the 'bad boy.' I'm sure what we just saw isn't at all the *real* Jordan Anderson. There are probably very few people that really *know* him, you know? I mean, really know him well." She drifted off into fantasy-land, wondering if she could be the one to really get to know Jordan.

"Hmmph," The Professor snorted, looking at her as if she were suddenly just another, average pre-teen girl.

"I think your judgement is a bit... clouded, shall we say. Anyway – it's not that I thought he was, well, your typical, roguish young man, it's just – well, I didn't trust him. He's lying about something."

"What!?" she chirped defensively.

"I don't know," The Professor scratched his chin. "But it's more than just the popularity – or lack thereof – of his band. Mark my words."

The two walked in silence for a little while longer until Polly had had her fill of the great outdoors, then hailed a taxi-boat at the shore and returned to the museum, where they sat down in The Professor's office and went over the last-minute details of their plan, working out various contingencies and worst-case scenarios that could in fact occur in the unpredictable world of time travel. The Professor explained that to get back to the present, she would have to return to the museum and the sub-basement room that contained the massive Mayan time-machine and stand in exactly the same spot that she had arrived in.

"Trace your feet with this," he said, handing her a piece of odd-looking chalk. This, he further explained, was part of the machine, this chalk, and it was not to be lost at all costs. "One must place one's feet *exactly* within the markings to return properly," he stressed. That was how he had gotten back to the present from his journey into the past, though now it was *this* present, a present altered by his actions back in 1931.

"If you get confused," he reassured her, "remember, we'll be in constant communication."

Everything was ready. Samantha had checked her wrist-communicator, had her backpack on which contained ten tuna-fish sandwiches, sixty-four ounces of water and some pepper spray (in case of emergencies), and was wearing a heavy wool coat as they did not expect 1931's October to be as balmy as this one in the altered, globally-warmed timeline. She stood on the stone platform in the middle of the time machine's ring of monolithic outer stones while The Professor fiddled with what looked like primitive black glass beads on the panel directly in front of her. She held Polly in her arms, who looked a bit frightened though she did not squirm. In her left hand she clutched the "magic" chalk.

"All right, Samantha, brace yourself. As I recall, this feels a little strange."

The word "strange" did not even begin to describe what Samantha felt in the next minute. It seemed, suddenly, that she had become transparent, like a ghost. Her body felt like every cell had been connected to an open socket of cool electricity. The room around her began to flicker in and out like a TV screen that kept short-circuiting. In between were brief flashes of a world of darkness enshrouded in billowing blue mist. Sounds warped and echoed; she could hear Polly whining, though the sound of her little dog-voice seemed to come in waves, from all around her. The flickering grew more rapid and The Professor began to appear and disappear, his being becoming something more and more distant, as if it existed only in a far-off dream world outside the immediate bubble of her self. She gritted her teeth and closed her eyes, the electrical buzzing of her every atom intensifying, and she thought at that moment that something had gone very wrong, that the machine must have malfunctioned and that she would surely explode at any second. Weird Mayan symbols danced across the insides of her tightly-clenched eyelids and then – it was over.

Slowly, Samantha opened her eyes. It was very dark. Luckily, she had thought to pack a flashlight in with her tuna-fish sandwiches and water and she slowly put Polly down and extracted it from her backpack, turning it on. Immediately she was startled by a gargantuan sabre-toothed tiger that could only have been three feet from her face. She stifled a scream and almost instinctively jumped straight backwards, but her intuition thankfully kept her feet glued to the floor. If she moved before she traced them with chalk, she might never get back.

The tiger, of course, was not real. She shined the flashlight around to reveal a small jungle of apes, mammoths, cave bears and miniature horses, all posed dramatically to reflect their individual prehistoric natures. It seemed that, yes, she was in fact in the very same room she had been in a minute ago, only in another time where it was occupied by (very convincing) replicas of ancient mammals instead of a huge stone time-machine. She let out a breath she had been holding the whole time, bent down and traced around her shoes with the Mayan chalk. The outline that it made was rather amazing in itself; the lines glowed in a bright neon blue and had a pearlescent quality to them that made them appear to be moving. Samantha found herself momentarily mesmerized by their brilliant patterns and stared at them for a couple of minutes until a small, thin voice snapped her out of it.

"Samantha? Are you there?" The Professor's British accent crackled from her wrist-communicator. She adjusted the fine-tuning until the signal was clearer, then pressed the talk bar to respond.

"I'm here, Professor," she said slowly, still shining the flashlight around. "I'm in a room full of, well, artificial tigers and mammoths and stuff."

"Ah!" the voice said knowingly. "Sounds like the right place. Or time, rather. Did you trace your feet with the chalk yet?"

"Yeah." Samantha yawned. She had not slept well in anticipation of the day's possibilities. "The marks are glowing, moving almost. They're a beautiful blue, Professor."

"Indeed," her wrist replied. "They'll fade, though. As you move away from them, they become invisible. As you move closer to them, they will light up again. It's a remarkable phenomenon, really. I ran a spectral analysis on that 'chalk,' you know. Mostly gypsum, phosphorus and gold, though there are traces of aluminium and some other compound I have yet to identify. I do hope it isn't radioactive, though if it is, its readings are negligible."

Samantha shared that last hope as well and gulped at hearing of the possibility that something in the chalk might be dangerous. She decided to wrap it tightly in a handkerchief she had and stuff it in the outermost pocket of her backpack. She couldn't help but smile a little when The Professor said "aluminum," though, for he pronounced it *al-u-min-i-um,* as the English were known to. It was somehow a more ticklish-sounding word when you said it that way.

She called for Polly, as the little terrier had already snuck off to explore their new surroundings, but came trotting back quickly from in-between some shaggy Yak-like creatures. Samantha quickly clipped the leash onto her collar, not wanting her to drastically change anything here and more than a little worried about losing her dog in a strange and unfamiliar time.

"Okay," Samantha said after tapping her wrist-communicator again. "Now what, Professor?"

"You need to get out of the museum. Put Polly in the backpack and try to be sneaky. No one's expecting a strangely-dressed young girl to pop out of the museum's basement."

Samantha felt momentarily peeved at The Professor's comment that she was strangely dressed, until she remembered that she was, hopefully, in 1931. Of course they would consider her strangely dressed. Luckily, the wool coat covered most of her clothes and looked like it could have been bought seventy-five years ago. She pulled it close around her and tucked Polly into the pack, then set off to sneak up to the museum's lobby, and was doing just fine until she came to a place with a wall where a stairway should have been.

"Um... Professor?" she whispered into the communicator. "You know the first stairway you go up from your office? Well, it's a wall here."

"Oh, dear," the tiny speaker squeaked. "Hang on a moment, Samantha..." She could hear the sounds of papers shuffling and things being moved around. "There," said The Professor, "I've got blueprints from 1928. Hopefully they haven't had the money to change anything since then. You are in the Great Depression, remember."

Samantha just hoped that she was even *in* 1931.

"Okay," The Professor began, "keep going down the hallway, there should be a right turn – " she did as told, following his directions. "Follow the right turn, then take your next left. This passage should terminate at the old front stairway. It's been bricked up for decades, here, I mean now. Do you see it?"

"Yes," Samantha replied, walking up the first few steps of the old stone staircase. "Should I go up this way?"

"Yes, yes." The Professor made more paper-shuffling noises. "When you get to the top, walk quickly to the... right, along the lobby's back wall. Then try to blend with the people coming and going through the left main lobby entrance."

This is getting complicated, Samantha thought, though her feet began to move and she soon arrived in the lobby, in a little space between the large staff/information desk and central back wall, where the general public was not really supposed to be. She crept as silently as she could along that wall, trying not to be spotted, and quickly slipped into a stream of people heading out of the museum.

It seemed to work. Shuffling out onto Central Park West with a throng of museum-goers, Samantha couldn't help but gasp slightly at the vastly different view. There was Central Park and its corresponding avenue, not drowned in water and almost like she remembered it should be, though not quite. The park was much more wooded than she remembered it, and far fewer tall buildings crowded the midtown skyline to the southeast. If she had, briefly, entertained the thought that she was home again, in her proper time, the illusion was boldly shattered by the automobiles that passed by on the road in front of her. They were clearly old and large, each one a classic that would probably be worth a hundred thousand dollars or more to collectors of her time. They were also conspicuously few and far between; it seemed not nearly as many people drove cars at all in 1931. *Of course,* she thought, *there weren't nearly as many people to drive them either.*

Samantha ducked into a little cove around the north side of the museum's steps and pressed the talk button on her communicator.

"Okay, Professor," she said, letting out a deep breath. "It certainly looks to be about the right year. What's our next step?"

"All right," he replied. "I want you to walk down Seventy-seventh Street to Columbus Avenue. Take a left there and walk down three blocks. There should be a newsstand there that sells coffee. Stay out of sight as best you can and contact me again when you get there. Got it?"

"Got it," Samantha acknowledged. She began walking, pulling her coat close around her and trying to stay close to the buildings. It was, indeed, a much colder October here, and she shivered, being unaccustomed to it. It did help to keep her fairly anonymous, though, as most people were sort of bundled up and just looking straight ahead as they walked. The Upper West Side looked mostly the same, though most of the characteristic brownstones looked practically brand new, and perhaps a few more trees were in evidence. She reached Columbus Avenue without incident and swung left, walking at a brisk pace.

Three blocks later she saw the newsstand. It was halfway between Seventy-Third and Seventy-Fourth Streets, and the pleasant smell of coffee wafted from its open front.

"I'm here, Professor," she tried to speak inconspicuously into her wrist.

"Good, Samantha," the thin, electronic voice replied. "Now I'm afraid there's a bit of waiting involved. See if you can find an out-of-the-way stoop or basement stairway, one you can see the newsstand from."

"Roger," Samantha responded. She had already spied out a set of basement steps that perfectly fit the need, and quickly made her way over to them, hunkering down on the third step from the top and keeping an eye on the newsstand through two rungs of a little iron fence that surrounded the stairway. "Okay," she spoke into her wrist again, "What am I waiting for?"

"Well," The Professor chuckled, "you're waiting for *me,* Samantha. I tried my hardest to insert you an hour before I was at that newsstand, but I could have been as much as three days off."

"*Three Days!!?*" she exclaimed. "I'm supposed to sit on these steps for three days!?"

"You do have plenty of sandwiches," the now giggling Professor reminded her. Samantha got the feeling he was enjoying this.

"It's cold out here, Professor! You're crazy if you think I can stay here, awake, for three days! What about Polly?" Polly stuck her head out of Samantha's bag upon hearing her name.

"All right! All right! Relax, Samantha. In all probability, it won't be nearly that long. Just sit tight, and if you see me coming, by all means watch everything I do and stay out of sight."

"Right," she sighed, signing off. Evidently, being a secret agent time-traveler had its boring moments as well as its romantic, action-packed ones. She patted Polly on the head and pulled out a tuna fish sandwich. Luckily, they were sealed tightly in zip-lock baggies and had therefore evaded the probing nose of her little Boston terrier. She unwrapped one, broke off a piece for Polly and then started munching on the rest, keeping a watchful eye on the newsstand from her mostly-concealed perch.

*

Several hours had passed, and it was now mid-afternoon. Samantha had watched several people buy newspapers and coffee, and was beginning to wonder if she was even staking out the right newsstand. The Professor had assured her that this was the right place, though he had conceded that his memory told him it had been about three o'clock in the afternoon when he had stopped there. She blinked and rubbed her eyes, trying to wake herself up more as that hour was probably approaching, though it was cold and she felt sleepy. Polly had had to pee at the bottom of the stairs, and the resulting smell had been less than pleasant for the last hour or so. Just as she was about to doze off, her eye caught a glimpse of something odd.

Samantha shook her head and stared at the newsstand. There was a man standing next to it now, a young man, and quite handsome at that. She squinted at him as he stood there, just sort of hanging around as if he, too, were waiting for something to happen. As she studied him further he began to seem eerily familiar, the way he stood, the way he moved his body – Samantha almost yelled when it dawned on her. She was looking at Jordan Anderson.

She was sure of it now. Though he had a more conservative haircut and was dressed in clothing that fit the time period, it was clearly him. Samantha's mind raced. What in the world was Jordan Anderson doing *here,* or rather, *now*? It seemed that The Professor had been absolutely right about him – there was definitely something suspicious going on.

Snapping out of her momentary daze, she inched back down the stairs and tapped the talk button on her communicator.

"Professor," she whispered loudly.

"Yes, Samantha?"

"Remember that boy I introduced you to in the park?"

"Yes... the – the roguish fellow, ah – Julian. Er – Justin..."

"Jordan," she corrected him. "Jordan Anderson. From Heatwavvve, the boy band."

"Right, right, Jordan. Why do you ask?"

"He's standing right by the newsstand."

"That's impossible!" the wrist communicator crackled.

"I swear it's him. He's dressed all like – like someone from this time, his haircut's all funny but – I know it's him, Professor. What is he doing here!?"

The communicator was silent for a moment.

"I don't know, Samantha. At this point, you've seen this chap in every timeline you've been in. I knew there was something fishy about him. Is he still there?"

Samantha peeked her head up above sidewalk level and then quickly popped back down.

"Yeah, he's still there. It's like he's... waiting for something, or someone..."

"Oh, dear," The Professor replied. "We can only conclude from this that we are not the only people capable of time travel. I fear, Samantha, that your man Jordan is there waiting for *me,* just as you are, and that in the grand scheme of things, there are forces working against us. Are you absolutely sure it's him?"

Samantha poked her head up again and stared intently at the loitering man. She tried to visualize every Heatwavvve poster in her now distant bedroom, remembering every line of the face she had been crushed-out on for years. There was no mistaking it. Somehow, this cute pop singer boy was far more than met the eye.

"I'm positive, Professor," she said as she slid back down the stairs. "What do I do?"

"Stay put," The Professor responded. Samantha could tell that his famous brain was calculating every possibility in this bizarre situation. "Keep waiting for me to show up. If Jordan begins to follow me, follow us both from a safe distance – but close enough to see if anything happens. I fear we may have to keep this mission strictly one of observation, and plan another one once we know where – and when – something critical occurs."

"Roger that," Samantha whispered. Her mind was spinning and she no longer felt the least bit sleepy. Polly was sniffing at her feet, her canine senses acutely aware of some change in her human's state of being; a scent of fear or excitement must have begun to seep from her glands. She patted her little dog and waited, watching Jordan pace back and forth in front of the newsstand.

She didn't have to wait long. A minute or two later, Professor Smythe came ambling up Columbus Avenue and walked up to the newsstand. Samantha quickly stuffed Polly back into her pack and tried to keep an eye on the scene. Jordan had definitely noticed him as well, and was trying to look nonchalant, glancing at his watch, perhaps waiting for someone else or else trying to make it appear as if he were waiting for someone else. The Professor said hello to the newsstand clerk, bought a newspaper and a cup of coffee, then tipped his hat and began walking on north up Columbus Ave. Jordan began walking almost right behind him, and Samantha felt adrenalin rush through her body. It was time to move.

She sprang up and grabbed her dog-, chalk- and tuna fish sandwich-filled pack, trying to stay more towards the buildings and pulling her coat closer around her so as not to stand out. She stayed about twenty feet behind Jordan, who was only walking five or so feet behind the apparently oblivious Professor. Luckily old Smythe was setting a fairly leisurely pace, and Samantha could see him gazing around in wonder at the "historical" surroundings. They crossed Seventy-fourth Street and continued uptown, back along the route she had come hours earlier. As they strolled up the block, Samantha kept a sharp eye on everything around her, noting every person that walked by in the opposite direction or came near The Professor. They crossed Seventy-fifth Street and were halfway up the block when something caught her attention. Coming the opposite way was a man in a blueish-gray uniform, possibly Air Force but more likely a U.S. postal worker. That set off a trigger in Samantha's memory and she tapped her talk button as discreetly as she could.

"Professor, there's a postman coming towards... you." It was a strange thing to say knowing that she was talking to The Professor Smythe of another time and place.

"Watch him, Samantha," he replied in an urgent tone.

She watched. She even sped up her pace a little so she could see more closely. Then, almost instantaneously, a number of things happened.

Professor Smythe stepped to the right, presumably to get out of the path of the oncoming postal worker. At the same time, Jordan sped up, passing The Professor on his right, and threw his left arm into The Professor's right hand, in which he was carrying his cup of coffee. As there was not, Samantha reminded herself, any such thing as plastic in 1931, the cup had no convenient lid, and the coffee flew all over the postman's overstuffed bag, where it soaked several letters that were sticking out, unbeknownst to the postal worker, who seemed to be in a hurry anyway and continued walking at a very quick pace. The Professor made a startled sound and looked around to find out what had happened (he had been staring at a horse-drawn carriage across and up Columbus Avenue), but by this time Jordan was five paces away and had blended successfully into a crowd of identically-clad gentlemen who were turning up Seventy-sixth Street. The Professor eyed them as if trying to figure out who was responsible for the mishap, let out an indignant "Hmmmphh!" and continued walking slowly, sipping the drop or two of coffee that remained in his cup.

Samantha stood at the intersection, trying to decide what to do. She tapped her talk button and spoke quickly into the communicator.

"Professor, Jordan just whacked your cup of coffee all over the postman's letter bag and disappeared into a crowd before you could notice him. He's going... east on Seventy-sixth, the postman is going south on Columbus and you're going north back toward the museum. What should I do!!?" Her heart was racing.

"Listen to me, Samantha. I think we know what we need to know. You need to run back to the museum as quick as you can without causing a stir. Walk quickly past me, not up Seventy-Sixth. As soon as you get to Seventy-Seventh, run when you turn the corner. You need to get back before me, put your feet in those tracings and I'll do the rest. Are we clear?"

"Clear," she responded, taking a deep breath and speed-walking around the still-ambling Professor. She pulled her coat close around her as she hurried past him, praying he wouldn't recognize her. When she reached Seventy-Seventh Street she tore off in a sprint, dodging a street sweeper, an old woman with a cane and a child playing Jacks on the sidewalk. She turned up Central Park West and "turned on the turbo" to cover the remaining distance to and up the building's main steps. She slowed down here briefly, cutting through a medium-length line and through the main lobby, heading for the stairway she had come up earlier. People began yelling as she elbowed by them, and she noticed a security guard had eyed her and started moving quickly toward her.

"Hey you – stop!" he yelled, starting to jog after her now. She broke into a run again, bursting through the door to the stairs and down, at least one guard hot on her heels. At the bottom of the stairs she turned and made a beeline for the time machine room. By this time, Polly had become quite agitated and was poking her head out of the backpack. Samantha plunged through the familiar door and into the dark room filled with motionless mastodons and still saber-tooths. She felt her way through the forest of artificial animals, trying to get a sense of where its center was and cursing her eyes for not adjusting faster to the darkness.

"In here!" She heard the guard's voice yell somewhere toward the doorway. She could also hear the sounds of more running footsteps coming into the room.

"Where's he at?" asked a new voice.

"He went in here," replied the first one.

"There ain't no other way outta here," a third interjected. "I'll watch the door, you two spread out."

Suddenly a flashlight beam cut through the dark.

"Where's the light switch in here?" the first guard grumbled.

"It's here," said the voice of the second. "It's burned out."

"Damn! All right, fella," said the first voice. "We know you're down here."

Samantha searched desperately for the chalk outlines, crawling on her hands and knees so as to avoid the beams of the flashlights and more easily navigate the herd of stationary beasts. Polly began to growl.

"Sssshhhh! Polly!" she whispered, her heart pounding like a hammer inside her chest.

"There!" the first guard's voice shouted. "By the tiger!" His light-beam had fallen right on her. The men began shoving their way through the animals toward her and she scrambled to escape the light. Then she saw it.

Ahead of her and a little off to her left, she could see a faint blue glow on the floor. She scrambled towards it, having to use one arm now to hold her panicked terrier's collar to keep her from jumping all the way out of the backpack. She scurried closer and the glow became stronger; it was her set of footprints, sure enough.

"Samantha?" her wrist crackled. She hit the talk button with her teeth just as she was standing up in the footprints, holding Polly firm and staring at a security guard that was no more than six feet away and closing fast.

"NOW, PROFESSOR! NOW!!!"

Mayan symbols exploded in her head once again, the world turning blue and flickering in and out. The security guard had stopped dead and was staring at her in disbelief, but he too began to flicker along with the darkness and prehistoric beasts, and images of the great stone time machine with The Professor at its controls began to replace those of the room in 1931. In a moment, it was all gone and Samantha found herself in the more familiar room, staring down at her feet on the thick slab of granite that made up the time machine's platform. She thought she saw a light puff of smoke as she stumbled off of it, letting go of Polly and collapsing onto the floor.

*

She awoke moments later to her dog's licking tongue and The Professor's worried voice.

"Samantha!? Samantha, are you all right?"

"I – uuuhhh – yeah, I think so." She sat up, looking around. "I must've... fainted," she thought out loud.

"Come on now, girl, just relax. Take some deep breaths."

Samantha did as she was told; she couldn't, she felt, have done much else, actually. The running and the adrenalin surge had left her soaked in sweat, and she took off the heavy wool coat and shook her head. She felt very tired.

"Professor," she said weakly, "I think I need to sleep for a little bit."

"That's fine, Samantha. Not a problem." He was listening to her heartbeat with a stethoscope. "Come on over here and lay down." He took her, standing her up slowly, over to the pile of Peruvian rugs she had come to know as her bed, and helped her lay down, stroking her forehead.

"Just for a little," she mumbled, and then she was out.

*

When she awoke again, The Professor was sitting over her, a steaming cup of tea in his hands.

"Posthumous Postmen!" he blubbered. "Had me scared there, Agent Smart! How are you feeling?" He handed her the cup of tea.

"How long was I asleep?" she asked groggily, taking the hot beverage and sipping it.

"Hours," The Professor replied. "But I've got some good news for you. After I determined you were all right, I took Polly for a walk to get some tea – I, I locked you in – I hope you don't mind – just for about an hour. I rented us a bit of a hotel room down the road – had to pay extra for the bloody dog," he eyed Polly disapprovingly. "We can all stay there tonight, though. It's got proper beds and a wonderful shower in the loo. Come on, if you're up to it we can walk there. It's only about half-eight – er – eight-thirty to you yanks. Are you hungry?"

"Starving," Samantha gurgled through her tea. "And I would die for a shower."

The Professor helped her up and she put down the empty tea cup, which she had quickly drained.

"Right, then, we'll get you fed and showered up. Then we can talk about what needs to happen next." Samantha nodded, yawning.

They walked upstairs and out of the museum, pausing momentarily to look up at the main lobby's barosauraus, a gigantic assembly of dinosaur bones that Samantha always seemed to take for granted, having walked by it so many times. For some reason she stared at it now; it seemed somehow more alive now that she had traveled through time.

"Professor," she asked, "could we travel as far back as this dinosaur lived?"

"Absolutely," he replied as they exited. "Though I'd say we'd better have a bloody good reason to. I wouldn't imagine that it would be a terribly hospitable time to fragile little creatures like you and I." This was indeed more food for thought, and Samantha's tired mind daydreamed of great trees and beasts as they walked out into the warm night air of the altered timeline's balmy October.

They walked up to Eighty-first Street and then towards Columbus. The Professor explained that the hotel was up on Eighty-fourth, but that there was a falafel place on Eighty-second and Columbus he had found that was "absolutely delicious." They traveled by over-pass as they walked, traversing the flooded Manhattan streets like nothing was amiss. They both had grown somewhat accustomed to the strange reality after having been stuck in it for nearly a week.

The falafel place was more of a to-go window than an actual restaurant, but Samantha happily inhaled one of their creations and smiled at the amused-looking Professor with tahini dribbling down her chin.

"If anyone asks at the hotel, you are my daughter, Samantha Smythe."

"Samantha Smythe," she cooed, affecting a British accent. "Yes! And I'm – I'm studying ballet with a prominent, world class instructor!"

"Yes, well, no need to play it up too much, now," The Professor chuckled. Samantha wiped off her chin with a napkin and smiled again, and they began walking toward the hotel.

Polly was out of the backpack now, on her leash, as the two arrived at The Wildman Arms. The Professor had paid for her, after all; having found a hotel that took dogs at all was a small miracle in uptown Manhattan, but it seemed as if many of the city's hoity-toity rules had been relaxed since the whole place had flooded. The man at the desk checked them in with an air of pure boredom about him, though oddly enough he seemed engrossed in a book called *The Time Machine* by H.G. Wells. Samantha exchanged a strange look with her 'father,' as he had obviously noticed the coincidence as well. Smythe smiled slightly and shrugged.

Their room was on the fifth floor (which was now actually more like the fourth floor, though the elevator signs had not been modified to reflect this), and Samantha ran through the door and jumped on one of the big double beds, Polly right behind her.

"A bed, Polly!" she shrieked in excitement. "We get to sleep in a bed tonight!"

"Shhh..." The Professor tried to quiet her down. "Are you going to shower? I had one myself when I checked us in; it was most refreshing."

"Definitely," Samantha said in a serious tone, springing from the bed into the plush, fancy bathroom.

*

At least an hour later, Samantha emerged, sparkling, from her first shower in nearly a week. She had used every one of the little 'ketchup packets' full of shampoo and conditioner, and felt cleaner and more relaxed than she had in days. She toweled her hair dry and watched The Professor, who was sitting at a table by the window, tinkering with her wrist communicator.

"Feel better, then?" he asked without looking up.

"A hundred times better," Samantha gushed.

"We should talk about what happened."

"Okay," she said, sighing heavily and sitting down on the closest bed.

"Fill in the missing minutes for me, Samantha," The Professor requested. "Last I heard you were about to sprint past me and up Seventy-seventh Street, and then you were just screaming 'NOW!'"

"Yeah," Samantha giggled. "Well, I did what you told me. I ran up Seventy-Seventh and had to barge my way into the museum through a line of very unhappy people. At some point a guard spotted me and started chasing me. I ran down the stairs, Polly was trying to jump out of the pack, I got to the room – "

"The time machine room?" The Professor interjected.

"Yeah. Only there – I mean then, it's jam-packed with fake prehistoric animals."

"Right."

"So now there are three guards after me, and they have flashlights – luckily the room light was broken – but they're still coming after me, and I'm trying to find the footprints and I'm crawling on the floor to try to dodge their light-beams, holding Polly's collar with one hand – "

"You were very nearly caught..."

"Uh – hello! You don't even know, Professor. I had to hit the talk button on the wrist communicator with my teeth, and when I yelled 'NOW!' I had just stood up in the footprints and had a guard six feet from my face!"

"Hmmmm. That's not good. Did he see your face?"

"I don't know, but I think he thought I was a guy. He kept saying things like 'we know you're in here, fella,' and 'he went in here.' Anyway, he definitely saw the light show when you hit the switch, or whatever it is that you did to bring me back."

The Professor pondered her last statement and hoped that the security guard wouldn't be traumatized for life due to the experience, fail to join the army and fulfill some pivotal role in the war, causing the Nazi war machine to roll unimpeded over the allied forces. Time travel was such a sticky thing. *Well,* he thought to himself, *hopefully he'll just have written it off as an electrical event, a product of faulty wiring, and assumed the intruder had somehow slipped out in the excitement.*

"By the way, Professor," Samantha mused, "how did you get back when you had no one to operate the controls for you?"

"Ah." The Professor snapped back to the present. "Actually, Samantha, that's a very good question. You see, the time machine can be set to work automatically. I figured out the Mayan constructors' measurement of time, as it relates to our concept of it, and synchronized my watch to the machine's controls. When I returned to the museum, I stood in my footprints and simply waited for the correct moment to arrive. It's quite intriguing – did you notice another set of footprints near to yours in the room of 1931?"

"Well," Samantha said, scratching her chin, "I didn't think about it at the time – you understand I was in a bit of a rush – but you know, there may have been another set, larger, encompassing mine. Maybe we were standing in exactly the same place."

"Mmmmm." The Professor nodded. "It would appear so."

The two were silent for several moments, each processing their thoughts and trying to make sense of them. Finally, The Professor spoke again.

"You can't go back, Samantha," he said grimly.

"What? But – don't we have to prevent this from happening?"

"Yes, we do. Somehow. But, for the same reason I couldn't go back this time, you cannot go back next time. To have two of the same person in the same time, especially if they were near enough to meet, I fear would be particularly disastrous."

"Well... what, then?" Samantha asked hopefully.

"We need someone else," her mentor replied. "And, honestly, I don't know who. Or where we're going to find them. This is going to take some serious thought, Samantha."

They both sat staring into space, brains aflutter, trying to think of a way to overcome this latest obstacle in their quest to restore the reality that they knew. Neither of them came up with an answer.

"Let's get some rest," The Professor said at last. "Perhaps the morning will bring some fresh inspiration."

"Okay," Samantha agreed, getting under the covers of her bed. At the moment, she did not have a clue as to what could possibly solve this latest problem, and as she closed her eyes she felt farther than ever from the world that she knew as home.

Samantha and Professor Smythe sat in the basement office, she drawing circles on a piece of paper and he staring into the middle distance, chin on folded hands. They had had a wonderful night's sleep and had each had another shower in the morning at the Wildman Arms. They'd walked Polly out to the park and fetched themselves a delicious breakfast at an uptown crepery on Broadway, and had leisurely made their way back to the museum. None of these activities, unfortunately, had jarred loose any ideas about how to solve their current predicament. They knew where they had to go and what they had to do, but the problem remained that neither of them could go and do it. They hadn't really made any trusted friends in the altered timeline and in fact the only other person they'd hung around more than once was Jordan Anderson, who now seemed to be, if anything, some sort of enemy. They had thought about asking Violet Edelstein, who'd seemed like a wonderful and tough old woman, but had decided she was both too old and too directly entwined in the time-knot they were trying to untie.

One entertaining distraction, at least, was the growing number of costumed people on the streets. Today was October 31, and young folks everywhere were gearing up for an evening of trick-or-treating. Even the *New York Times* had an especially eerie-looking front page, adorned with pumpkins, witches and black cats in its margins and with the huge headline *HALLOWEEN* written in bold, gothic-looking type. Even though she fancied herself a bit old for that sort of thing, Samantha thought it might be fun to go out in the watery city seeking whatever kind of candy it might offer, or at least get a hold of one of those mini-surfboard scooters that looked so cool.

At the moment, though, they were twiddling pencils and the like, hoping some idea might hit them. Suddenly, The Professor lifted his head and opened his mouth, raising one finger in the air as if he were about to have a revelation. Samantha's pen stopped moving in circles and she looked at him in hopeful anticipation, but then he closed his mouth into a frown and put his hands and head back down. She resumed wearing a circular hole in her piece of paper as she drew mindlessly with the pen. Finally, she plopped it down on the paper.

"Look, I'm going to take Polly to the park. Can I have a few dollars for a taxi-boat?"

"Mmmmpph," The Professor acknowledged her, absently fumbling in his lab-coat pocket and handing her a crumpled up wad of bills.

"Thanks." She sighed, coaxing Polly into her backpack and turning to leave.

"Oh, Samantha – " The Professor came out of his thoughts for a moment. "Try to steer clear of that Jordan fellow."

"I will," she replied, departing. She was almost certain that Jordan had not spotted her in 1931, but still was, herself, quite nervous about running into him again. *Though,* she thought, *I could perhaps try to learn more about whatever it is he's doing, and why.* Her thoughts and feelings about Jordan tumbled around in her head and heart as the rest of her body trudged up the stairway to the main lobby, and she pushed open the door at the top of the stairs. She walked briskly by the massive barosaurus skeleton and was headed toward the main entrance when she heard a voice that made her stop dead in her tracks.

"Samantha!" a boy's voice yelled. "Samantha Smart!"

She was briefly terrified. There was only one boy in this alternate timeline who knew her by name, and that was Jordan Anderson. But the voice didn't sound like Jordan's; it was a little deeper and sounded almost... Spanish. Slowly, she turned around, trying to pinpoint where the voice had come from, though the most likely source seemed to be a trio of costumed kids about thirty feet away.

Two of them seemed too small for the voice; they were dressed as an Arabian princess and a cute kitten of some sort, while the likely shouter stood in between them wearing some bizarre, grayish animal outfit that could have been a pig or a turtle or –

"Samantha?" The princess spoke now.

"Brianna!?" Samantha replied hopefully, walking towards them now. "Brianna, is that you?"

"Of course, silly," the princess quipped back in a snooty tone, taking off her mask. The others lifted their masks as well, revealing her other two best friends Suki and – Marvin! *Of course,* she thought, *the Spanish voice...*

"Marvin!? Suki!?" Samantha was overjoyed. "I can't believe you guys are here! I've missed you all so much!" She hugged them all in turn, almost tearing up as she embraced little Suki. "How did you guys get here!?"

"Um, Brianna's chauffeur," Suki replied. "Where's your costume? I thought we were all meeting here to go to the Heatwavvve show. You knew we were supposed to dress up, right?"

Samantha looked at all of them and her smile faded. They had no idea what was going on, where they were.

"Yo, your mom's been looking for you, Samantha. She's really freaked out, I think. Maybe you should call her." Marvin let out.

I wish I could, Samantha thought.

"Yeah, she called my house, too," Brianna said. Where've you been, Samantha?"

"You guys don't know about the flooding. You must have – Marvin, come with me for a second. Can you guys wait here for just a minute or two?"

"Sure... I guess." Brianna crinkled up her brow in a puzzled expression. "What do you mean, flooding?"

"All right – everybody just – follow me for a sec, okay?" She pulled Marvin's hand and the rest of the kids followed, out the main entrance and onto the steps, where they could see the flooded streets of Manhattan and the island of Vista Rock.

"Damn," Marvin said in disbelief. "When did that happen?"

"We – we just walked in here a moment ago," Brianna said, starting to panic.

"This isn't possible," Suki contributed.

"You all had better come with me," Samantha said, leading them down to a taxi-boat and motioning for everyone to get in. "Belvedere Island," she said to the driver, who sped off toward the castle.

Her friends sat dumbfounded as they approached the shore, and everyone got out of the boat while Samantha paid the driver. She let Polly out of her backpack, and she immediately began jumping all over Marvin, who had frequently walked her with Samantha back in Brooklyn.

"Hey, Polly! Hey, girl!" Marvin stooped to pet her affectionately. "Still sneakin' in the museum, huh?" Polly licked his hands and made little whining noises.

"Samantha, what is going on here!!?" Brianna demanded at last.

"Come on," Samantha said. "I'll try to explain this as best I can." She found a bench under a shady tree and sat her costumed friends down. She then proceeded to explain the whole predicament of the alternate timeline, the tree diseases, the global warming, the postman, Vincent Bergen and Violet Edelstein, the coffee, the letter and at last, the sinister true self of Jordan Anderson.

"So that's what's up here," she finished. "Somehow, you guys must have wandered into this timeline just as I did, at the museum." There was a long silence.

"Right," said Suki.

"Like, I'm sure," Brianna offered.

"Check, please!" Marvin shouted, getting up.

"You don't believe me," Samantha sighed. "I don't blame you. This is all extremely hard to believe. All I can say is, you will come to believe it. Look at Central Park," she said. "Those are your own eyes you're using; I'm not projecting a movie on the insides of your eyelids."

"Though that would be phat," Marvin chuckled. He was always funny and good-natured, no matter what the situation.

"So, you're saying you've been sleeping in Professor Smythe's office, in the basement of the museum, and that yesterday you traveled back in time, using an ancient Mayan time machine made out of... out of – big rocks, to try and change some event in the past that caused this – this reality here to happen?" Brianna summarized, still in disbelief.

"Pretty much," Samantha nodded, grinning hopefully.

"Cool," Suki smiled.

"Well, I guess the Heatwavvve show's off, then." Marvin shrugged. "Fine with me. I always thought they wuz chumps. I was just goin' 'cause I knew da ladeez wanted to check it out."

"Marvin," Samantha said, chuckling, "what exactly are you supposed to be in that costume?"

"Yo." He got up and began to go into one of his mediocre rhymes, "I'm an Aardvark, chillin' hours before dark, makin' my mark on the bleak remains of Central Park, yo, it's all so sudden, time machines and global floodin', Heatwavvve's hunk is proven a villain, but Dr. Marvy's still willin', chillin'..."

"Ugh. Please make him stop," Brianna said disgustedly. She was not taking this as well as the others. "What about my family? All our families? What about Mrs. Newberry?"

Mrs. Newberry was Brianna's family cat, a pure white, long-haired monstrosity that wore a collar of what looked like diamonds around her neck. The Knowles family was pretty well-off.

"Believe me, Brianna, I miss my family too, even Todd. I haven't seen them for days... but you have to understand - chances are, any of our parents were never even born into this alternate reality. I know it – it takes a bit of getting used to, but the only way I've figured out to even try to get back home is by doing what Professor Smythe says. I'm... I'm sorry."

Brianna pouted, and the others all looked more thoughtful now, too.

"Listen," Samantha sighed. "Don't take my word for it." She tapped the talk button on her wrist communicator.

"What's that!?" Marvin marveled.

"Shhh!" Samantha shushed him. "Professor? Are you there?" She tapped the button off and a crackly voice came back at her.

"Yes, Samantha?" Her friends looked awed.

"Professor, I need you to meet me as soon as you can. I'm on Belvedere Island."

"What is it?" the voice inquired.

"There's been a – a new development," she said, looking around at her friends.

"On my way." The Professor signed off. Samantha turned off the device to prolong the life of its battery, as she almost always did when not using it.

"That was Professor Smythe?" Suki asked. Samantha nodded.

"Where did you get that cool radio-thingy?" Marvin blurted out.

"Professor Smythe built it," Samantha responded. "It works through time, even, believe it or not. It's really quite handy."

"I'll bet." Marvin gaped, shaking his head.

"I want one!" Suki implored, her eyes lighting up like a small child's on Christmas day.

"Well," Samantha chuckled, "you may get your wish. We're sort of... in need of some new people just now."

Brianna was still sitting quietly, looking at the ground. Polly was sniffing at her leg and she reached down to scratch the dog's neck.

"Oh, Polly," Brianna sighed. "If I'd known I was going to be stranded in an alternate future, I would've worn something much more fashionable than this silly princess costume."

*

Professor Smythe arrived on the scene in something like twenty minutes. After Samantha's round of introductions, he sat down on the bench and tried to assess this latest change in their situation.

"Well," he said thoughtfully, "we now have a larger pool of 'agents' to choose from, I suppose." Marvin and Suki looked excited at the word "agents," though Brianna remained obviously unenthusiastic.

"Yeah," Samantha piped in. "I mean, it's kind of a lucky break, isn't it, Professor? These guys showing up just when we needed someone else?"

"Perhaps..." The Professor mused, furrowing his brow. "But it also concerns me. More people from the 'correct' timeline accidentally being ensnared in this 'incorrect' one. Could there be others? What if random people, whom none of us even know, are blundering into this timeline just as you have? What if they, like us, cannot get out?"

"No," Samantha shook her head. "We'd know, Professor. We'd see people standing on the museum steps staring in disbelief at this flooded New York, don't you think?"

"Mmmmm. I suppose that's true. Then I am forced to wonder if your friends' arrival here is really so random at all. You kids say you were going to a Heatwavvve show for Halloween?"

"Yes," said Suki. "It was a big show... a dance party, kind of. I was kind of psyched for it, but I have to say this has turned out to be a lot more... interesting."

"Word," Marvin echoed her sentiments, still staring around him like he was on some giant movie set. The Professor stared quizzically for a moment, translating the boy's American slang in his head as best he could, then shook his head.

"Well," he concluded, "I suppose we may as well proceed according to our plan. We've got the extra personnel now and I can't think of anything new to do to fix our situation."

The group got up and walked down to the Belvedere docks, hailed a taxi-boat and ferried back to the museum. They got some funny looks as they filed down the stairs with The Professor, costumes and all, but no one said anything to them or tried to stop them. When they reached the office, The Professor unlocked the door and let them all in.

"Wow." Marvin drooled. "That's a nice computer. Can I check it out?"

"Em – er – I'd, uh, I'd rather you didn't actually."

"I won't hurt nothin', I promise," Marvin continued.

"He's really good with computers, Professor," Samantha vouched for her longtime friend. "He may even find something useful that we haven't."

"Oh, um, well... very well, it's all right, I suppose," The Professor agreed reluctantly. "But don't mess up the desk!"

Marvin eyed the piles of papers and coffee cups that occupied The Professor's desk and wondered if it could, indeed, become any messier.

"No problem," he said, sitting down at the console. As he began clicking away, Samantha addressed the others.

"So, we need to send someone else back," she said firmly. "I'd go myself and so would Professor Smythe, but as I've told you, we're already there, and so can't go back again. Or shouldn't, anyway."

"I'll go!" Suki volunteered. She was very excited at the idea of time travel, and also relished any opportunity to use a cool electronic gadget like the wrist-communicator as she was very fond of such things.

"I appreciate your bravery and your enthusiasm," The Professor responded. Suki smiled. "However, I am afraid that we must first ask Marvin."

Marvin perked up his ears. "Yo, wassup?" Suki frowned.

"Marvin, I hate to sound, well, sexist, but I fear that this particular mission may in fact involve physical violence. I hate to send any of you young people into such a situation, but as it is utterly necessary, it is my duty, then, as planner and organizer of the mission to make sure I send the most capable person for the job, and the least likely to be hurt. You being, well, frankly, male, and as such almost twice the size of Suki, well, I think you might be best able to handle this."

"Yeah – ain't no hood from Detroit nor Chicago can kick it as good as M.J. Santiago..." Marvin rapped, still clicking on the computer.

"I'm sorry, Suki – but believe me, we may have a mission for you yet before this thing is all over."

Suki nodded quietly.

"What's the 'J' stand for?" Brianna asked Marvin.

"Jelly Jive Jazzmaster Jackson," he replied in his rapper's

egotistical tones. Brianna rolled her eyes.

"It's Jerome," Samantha let out.

"Hey, girl! Why you crampin' my style?"

"'Cause your 'style' is startin' to cramp me," Samantha did her best Brooklyn home-girl impression, waving her finger at 'M.C. Dr. Marvy.' He seemed to quiet down.

The girls spent an hour or so catching up on gossip while Marvin clicked away on the computer and Professor Smythe began fabricating a duplicate of Samantha's wrist-communicator. They talked about music, boys, clothes, school and other normal things that girls their age would talk about if they weren't stuck in an alternate future. At some point The Professor began talking quietly with Marvin, presumably going over the details of the mission with him. It was probably seven in the evening before it was decided they should get on with it.

"This way, then," The Professor led them down the hall towards the two polar bears that flanked the door to the time machine room. He punched in his code and let the wide-eyed adolescents into the huge, high-ceilinged chamber that was just large enough to contain the massive stone time machine. Jaws dropped and they stared; even M.C. Marvin was rendered temporarily speechless.

"This... this is incredible," Brianna gasped.

"It's so big and old," Suki observed.

"Word," was all Marvin could get out.

The Professor moved to the machine's controls and began dispensing instructions to the team of youngsters that had, by chance, assembled itself around him.

"Samantha, I want you to give your communicator to Marvin for now. I've just about finished making another one but it hasn't been tested, and we know this one has." Samantha complied, unfastening the device and putting it on Marvin's much thicker wrist.

"Marvin, are you feeling good about this?" The Professor inquired.

"Yeah, whatever." Marvin shrugged. "Three hours ago I was dressed as an aardvark and going to see a Heatwavvve show, and now I've gotta travel back in time to make sure Heatwavvve's lead singer doesn't spill your coffee on a mailman, and try not to get beat up by him in the process. No sweat, man."

"You're all taking this quite well." The Professor chuckled slightly. "Marvin, if at any time you feel you're in over your head, just look for the footprints and talk to me."

"You know I will," Marvin responded into the communicator, testing it.

"We're going to be trying something new as well," The Professor went on. "I believe I've mastered this thing's controls a little more, so I think I can insert you into a smaller time window – you shouldn't have to wait as long as Samantha did. In addition, however, I'm going to try to transport you spatially this time. This way, you should, if my calculations are correct, appear closer to the spot we need you to be at."

"Whatever you say." Marvin began to shuffle somewhat uncomfortably. They had dressed him in some spare clothes that The Professor kept in a closet in his office; fortunately Marvin was big enough (or The Professor was small enough) that they sort of fit. At the very least they were far less conspicuous than an aardvark suit.

Samantha walked Marvin up to the stone platform and he climbed up and stood in the proper place.

"Fasten your seatbelt." Samantha grinned at her nervous friend.

*

Marvin found himself, suddenly, standing in a stairwell outside a large apartment building. The trip had been dazzling, with blue light and Mayan symbols still echoing visually in his mind. He stood there, somewhat stunned, until a voice snapped him back into awareness.

"Marvin?" It was Samantha's voice, coming from the tiny speaker on his wrist. "Trace your feet with the chalk."

Marvin did as instructed, remembering that The Professor had impressed upon him the importance of this particular step in the time-travel operation. The lines glowed brilliantly as he put the chalk back into the little tubular container The Professor had found to keep it in, a plastic cigar tube, Marvin guessed.

"Marvin – it's Professor Smythe," another voice spoke. "Can you hear me?"

Marvin tapped the communicator's talk button as he had been shown and responded.

"Yup. Where am I?"

"I was going to ask you the same question."

"Um – I'm in a stairwell," Marvin looked around. "Outside."

"Can you walk up the stairs enough to see where you are?"

"Sure," Marvin replied, walking up a few of the stairs and coming eye-to-eye with the street level. "Brownstones," he continued. "It's a side street. I can see the park in one direction, but I'm closer to the other corner. I think it's – yeah, I can see the sign – it's Seventy-fifth Street."

"Perfect!" The Professor cackled. "Now, I need you to go out to the corner of Columbus and just sort of... loiter. Wait until you see us coming. Then try to stop Jordan – I don't care how, but you've got to hold him up for at least, oh, thirty seconds. That should give me enough time to safely get past the postman."

"Okay," Marvin agreed, making his way to the corner.

Almost immediately he saw The Professor, perhaps two blocks down, walking towards him. Not far behind was the sinister Jordan Anderson, and Marvin smiled at having a chance to get in the pretty boy's face, all, of course, for the good of humanity. Further back he could just barely make out the form of Samantha, sticking close to the walls and trying not to be noticed. *Well,* he thought, *she's definitely going to notice me, especially if she's watching intently.*

The Professor passed by and Marvin stepped out immediately afterward, adrenalin pumping, and did the only thing he could think of: he walked straight into Jordan Anderson, their heads colliding.

"Aaaaawwww!!!!!" Jordan moaned, putting his hand to his head and stepping backward. Marvin did the same; it hurt, but he knew he had to hold Jordan up for another twenty seconds or so, so he naturally began yelling at the singer in Spanish.

"¿Por qué no mira usted donde usted va!!? ¿Usted piensa que usted posee la calle, chico bonito!?"

"I'm – I'm sorry," Jordan said, dazed but looking past Marvin and trying to walk after The Professor. Marvin grabbed his arm and held him there, yelling more.

"¿Dónde piensa usted que usted va!? ¡Mire la cabeza!"

"I'm sorry," Jordan repeated, trying to wrestle his arm away. "Look, I don't understand, okay?"

"Look at my head," Marvin said in English, still holding Jordan's arm and indicating a fast-growing lump.

By this time the postman, in his haste, had passed The Professor and was walking by Jordan and Marvin. Suddenly, Jordan turned into the postman, but the postman – at least this is what it looked like – walked *through* him. Both looked startled, the postman turning around and Jordan focusing first on Marvin's hand, which still held him firm, then on his face. He gritted his teeth and his face transformed into something horrid, something evil, and then – he disappeared. Completely.

Marvin and the postman stared at each other for a moment in disbelief, then Marvin spoke.

"Los espíritus del muerto..." He grinned, spooking the postman into turning around and running down the street. Then Marvin heard his name – but not from the wrist-communicator.

"Marvin... ?" It was Samantha, who was walking slowly closer to him. He turned and ran, not wanting to be seen or cause any further knots in time, as quickly as possible back to his set of footprints.

"Marvin, wait! It's Samantha Smart!" He heard behind him as he ran down the stairwell. "Now, Professor!" he shouted into his wrist as he lined his feet up within the glowing chalk lines. Then – he was gone.

*

"It's very strange," Samantha said after Marvin had reappeared on the stone platform. "I remember it differently now."

"Indeed," Professor Smythe agreed. "I do, too. I remember... not spilling my coffee at all."

"And I remember Marvin being there, yelling in Spanish."

They both turned and looked at the latest time-traveler, who was sitting down now on the steps leading up to the platform. He looked a bit dazed but otherwise intact. It was Suki who first walked over and sat next to him.

"Are you okay, Marvin?" she asked in a concerned tone, putting her hand on his shoulder.

"Yeah." Marvin half-laughed, half-sighed. "Yeah, Suki, I'm fine, thanks. Um, my head kind of hurts, though."

"I'll bet it does!" Samantha interjected, walking over to the platform. "I – somehow I knew you would need it so I – I sent Brianna to The Professor's lab – there's a fridge in there with some ice."

"Let Nurse Brianna take care of your boo-boo." Brianna appeared almost on cue, sitting on Marvin's other side and gently holding an ice-filled cloth to his swelling forehead. "Poor, brave time-traveling man..."

Professor Smythe chuckled. Marvin was getting the hero's welcome from the girls and apparently loving every minute of it. Still, The Professor was troubled. There were so many questions.

"Marvin," he called. "You need to tell me everything that happened."

Marvin nodded and got up, taking the ice from Brianna and thanking her, smiling, (she was quite pretty and still dressed, somewhat appropriately, as a princess). They all filed back to The Professor's office, where Marvin filled everyone in on the specifics of his experience.

"And then Jordan... disappeared, right?" Samantha interrupted at precisely the right part.

"Yeah," Marvin said slowly. "But how did you know that?"

"I was... there. I saw it." Samantha spoke slowly, trying, herself, to understand.

"It seems that our memories, in keeping with... reality, have changed accordingly," The Professor explained. "My memory of the event has changed as well. This appears to be another side effect of... manipulating time. There are other questions, though, Marvin. Most importantly, 'who or what is this Jordan Anderson fellow?'"

"I don't know, man, but his face turned into something real scary, like – not human."

"You say you thought you saw the postman walk *through* him?"

"Yeah, Professor, I never seen anything like it! It was crazy!"

"But you had a firm hold on his arm the whole time?"

"Yup."

"Hmmm." The 'agents' all looked at Professor Smythe as his famous brain ticked away, trying to solve this latest mystery. In the end, it was Suki who broke the silence.

"Maybe he can't touch them..." she mused. "Maybe, he can only touch us."

"Go on," The Professor encouraged her.

"Well, I've been thinking about this," she continued. "I mean, if this guy – Jordan – is trying, for some reason, to alter time, then why did he do it like that?"

"Hey, that's right," Samantha chimed in. "Why wouldn't he have just, well, done it himself, when none of us were around? Instead, he has to bump The Professor's hand, spilling his coffee on the postman's letter bag. It seems like an unnecessarily complicated way to achieve the goal..."

"I believe you ladies may have something there," The Professor conceded. "And if you're right, if this strange 'enemy' of ours can only touch through us, then... well, this might be of great advantage to us." He shook his head, mentally switching gears. "In any case, assuming we have succeeded here, time outside the museum should now be, well, normalized."

Samantha was way ahead of him. She was out the door and up the stairs into the lobby. Alas, it was about eight p.m., and the museum had closed. Only a single security guard remained at the main desk. Samantha ran up to him and explained that she and her friends had been learning lessons from Professor Smythe, and asked if she could use the phone to call her mother. The guard obliged, and she dialed the number to her Brooklyn home.

"Hello?" Cindy Smart answered, sounding shaky and tired.

"Mom?"

"Samantha!!? Samantha, Oh my God! Where are you, baby?"

"I'm fine, Mom. I'm at the museum – Professor Smythe was teaching me some forensics things – "

"Oh, Samantha! Where have you been!? It's been almost a week! I was so worried about you!"

"Really, I'm okay, Mom. I just want to come home."

"Stay there, honey! I'm coming to get you – can I talk to the security desk?"

"Sure." Samantha handed the phone to the guard, who had a short conversation with her mother.

"Well," he said after hanging up, "Your mom's quite a bit worried about you. She asked me to keep an eye on you until she gets here."

"Fine." Samantha shrugged. She walked to the museum's front doors and peered out. There it was, in all its glory – her proper timeline, not flooded, not seventy years old, but really... now. She had thought that the sight of it would feel comforting, but for some reason she felt anything but comfortable.

It was Thursday, which ordinarily would have excited Samantha as she would normally have been on her way to school (which, as we have mentioned, she secretly loved), but her mother had been so freaked out picking her up the previous evening that she had asked her to stay home the next day and spend time with her. Todd was allowed to stay home as well, and it appeared it was to be a "family day." Cindy was now dating a guy named Jason, who seemed to have won some brownie points for having hung around to console her during Samantha's disappearance, and now also seemed to be a part of family day as a reward. Cindy had woken up early and (somewhat amazingly) prepared a large brunch for everyone consisting of bagels with cream cheese, scrambled eggs with cheese and vegetables and a delicious blend of cranberry and fresh-squeezed orange juices. Samantha sat uncomfortably at the table, sort of getting the feeling that her mother was being so nice because she thought her daughter had run away. She still didn't believe Samantha's story though The Professor had helped her out on that one; the truth was, after all, pretty far-fetched.

"So;" Jason smiled over his eggs; "your mother tells me you're interested in science."

"Yeah." Samantha nodded politely. "I think... science is pretty cool."

"Samantha does very well in school," her mother said, grinning nervously and serving some eggs to Todd. "English, math, history – she's always had straight A's across the board."

"That's great," Jason voiced his approval with a mouth full of

bagel. "School is important. It's always good to have an education."
Samantha decided that her mom's latest beau was pretty cute, even if
he was obviously no rocket scientist. Sensing her daughter's possible
interest, Cindy took the opportunity to sell him some more.

"Jason sells advertising," she said hopefully, "for the *New York
Post*."

"Oh," Samantha replied. Jason's approval rating silently dropped,
as she preferred the *New York Times*.

"It's actually kind of boring," Jason admitted. "But it does have
its perks." He reached into his jacket pocket and pulled out some
tickets. "Your mom said you were into Heatwavvve, so I got some
comp tickets for you and your friends." Samantha went somewhat
pale.

"Um, thanks," she stammered, taking the tickets from the hopeful
prospective "father figure." She was quiet after that, and asked to be
excused after finishing her eggs. She got up and went to her room,
overhearing whispers at the table as she went.

"I don't know... last week she loved Heatwavvve. "

"Kids are fickle like that. I wouldn't worry about it..."

She retreated to her room and stared at the tickets in her hand. A
week ago, she would've been in seventh heaven, probably on the
phone right now to Brianna, engaged in a lengthy discussion about
which Heatwavvve boy was the cutest or which CD cover looked the
coolest. Now it seemed like all that was part of a dream, a lost
innocence that Samantha could not, try though she might, regain.

Of course, Jason had meant well. He couldn't have known about
Jordan Anderson, even if her mom had tried to relate her truly
unbelievable story to the man. Samantha decided that she would
thank him more properly later on.

She wasn't at all sure what to do with the tickets, though. If she
went to the show, would Jordan just be his unaltered pop-singer self,
oblivious as the next person to the wicked role he had played in the
alternate timeline, or was he some sort of trans-temporal entity,
plotting even now to somehow alter history again? It was, of course,
unknowable, as even if she did go to the show she probably wouldn't

get anywhere near him. Samantha frowned and picked up the phone, dialing Brianna's number.

She wasn't at home. She had, according to her mother, gone to school, which wasn't that odd seeing as she and Samantha's other friends had only been gone for an evening, whereas she had been gone for several days. She sighed and sat on her bed. She felt sad, though she wasn't sure why. Perhaps she was disappointed that her exciting career as a time-traveling investigator had come abruptly to a halt, though she was happy to be at home and in her proper timeline. *Well,* she thought, *I suppose there's still forensic science.*

Her bedroom door edged open and Polly shuffled in, dragging her leash with her. She started wiggling and Samantha scratched her back, causing her to begin sproinging around, obviously desiring a walk.

"Okay, Polly," Samantha giggled. "Let's go for a walk." She picked up the leash and clipped it to Polly's collar, leading her back out into the living room/kitchen area. "Polly needs a walk, Mom," she said.

"Oh, well, of course!" Cindy Smart offered cheerfully. "We'll, uh, we'll come with you, honey. Right guys?"

"Um, sure," Jason intoned pleasantly. Todd groaned.

Samantha endured the moment as the "family" hastily cleaned up their dishes and suited up for a walk in the park. Her mother had been very insistent that she was to no longer walk alone anywhere, and Samantha accepted the new situation grudgingly, hoping that the rules would relax in a couple of weeks. Apparently The Professor had (thankfully) made up some story about her having volunteered for some extended experiment of his, and had reassured Cindy that she had been safe the entire time and apologized profusely for not having contacted her, believing that Samantha had had her full knowledge and permission. Cindy bought this reluctantly, she having even gone looking for Samantha in the museum's basements to no avail. It seemed that Professor Smythe, as well, had been missing during their period of existence in altered time, and was now himself busy making up stories for his colleagues and superiors.

The group bundled up and headed outdoors, Polly in the lead and Todd unenthusiastically bringing up the rear. They locked the brownstone and walked up Twelfth Street and into the park, everyone shivering slightly. It was, of course, November now, a proper November with bleak, gray skies and a real nip to the Brooklyn air. Todd could be heard grumbling away about how he was being "deprived of his education" by missing a day of school, though everyone just sort of snickered at that as they all knew school ranked about as high as root canal on his list of preferred activities.

Polly, in contrast, was quite perky and pulled Samantha along on the leash in erratic jerks and spasms when another dog came into view or a brave squirrel dared to enter the periphery of her scent range. They walked along a path that led down into the basin that was Prospect Park; really, it was quite a beautiful place as parks went. Once you made it down into the athletic fields it was like you weren't in the city at all; the lower ground was surrounded by thick rows of trees that mostly obscured the tall buildings beyond them, though their leaves were mostly gone now and you could see some dark outlines through them as a result. Still, it was as 'in-the-wild' as you could get in New York City, and was also a place that held many fine memories for Samantha.

"Heads up!" Jason yelled; he had brought a football and began an impromptu game of catch with Todd, who despite his generally non-athletic nature seemed up for some activity other than walking. Their mother watched, smiling, then turned to Samantha.

"Jason's pretty okay, don't you think?" she asked honestly.

"Yeah Mom," Samantha smiled genuinely. "He seems pretty cool."

"He, um, he really was good to me when you were... gone, you know. I was a wreck, Samantha – and he stuck it out."

"I'm sorry you were so worried, Mom. I wanted to call you, really, I was just, well, I couldn't stop what I was doing..."

"It's okay, baby," Cindy Smart smiled, hugging her daughter. "You're home now. And I gave that Professor Smythe a piece of my mind," she scowled.

"It wasn't his fault, Mom; he was in it too, he... he sort of gets caught up in his mind and can't get out sometimes."

"Hmmmph," her mother huffed. "Well, he damn near aged me five years with how much I worried about you..."

"Okay, okay!" Samantha giggled, "I'll get a paper route to help pay for your face lift!" It looked for a moment that Cindy Smart was about to smack her upside the head, but instead she burst out laughing and the two of them had a mother-daughter bonding moment. It was kind of sickening in a sweet way, but was just salty enough to feel good and right to her anyway. They walked along some more, following Polly's lead while the males of the clan gradually migrated their game of catch along with them.

"So, what, you don't like Heatwavvve anymore?" Cindy asked with a look of true shock.

"No, I mean, I – well, I think so. I'm just not sure," Samantha replied, fumbling.

"Is there some other group that you like more now?"

"No, no it's not that. And I really did appreciate the tickets. Brianna will be pretty psyched."

"Well, it's at Irving Plaza Saturday night. Jason and I are coming with you – "

"Aaaawww, Mom! Why?"

"Because, young lady, you are still too young to be going to things like that by yourself. But don't worry, we'll give you your space."

Samantha pouted but wasn't really upset. She was, in fact, more nervous about going to the show at all. They walked along the path and her thoughts wandered to Jordan Anderson and his obviously suspect character.

*

Brianna was extremely talkative on the phone that evening. She had sat through school the entire day fidgeting nervously and thinking about their experience in the alternate timeline. She and the others, Brianna related, had kept the entire thing to themselves, sticking with a story that they had, in fact, gone to the Heatwavvve show. When Samantha mentioned the tickets, the line went silent.

"So... Brianna?" Samantha spoke.

"Yeah – yeah, I'm sorry." her friend responded. "I mean – jeez! What, are we gonna go, Samantha?"

"I, um, I don't know, Bree," Samantha said, unsure.

"Maybe we should ask The Professor what to do."

"That's a good idea. I'll call him tomorrow if I can do it without my mom noticing – she's kind of down on him since, well, because I was gone for so long."

"Okay, Samantha. Are you going to school tomorrow?"

"Um... I don't know. I'll call you like, after school's out either way, okay?"

"Okay. I'll talk to you tomorrow."

Samantha hung up the phone and almost instantly, it rang again. It was Suki, and Samantha essentially repeated her conversation that she'd had with Brianna. Marvin, of course, was next to ring her up, and she did her best to make a coherent plan with all her friends.

"Samantha," her mother called. "Who keeps calling?"

"It's just my friends, Mom. Brianna, Suki and Marvin. They, um, just wanted to know where I've been."

"Oh, okay. Do you want to get some ice cream with Jason and I? Come on, I know you love mint chocolate chip."

This sounded suspiciously like another one of her mother's newly contrived 'family' activities, but Samantha had nothing better to do and decided that she would indeed like some mint chocolate chip ice cream, so she agreed to the outing. Todd declined to come, as his alter-ego of 'cyber commando' had reached some as yet unencountered level of the video game world and he was exceptionally absorbed in the virtual reality of lightning-speed combat. Samantha put Polly on the leash and followed her lovestruck mother and her new boyfriend out the door.

They walked down Twelfth Street to Seventh Avenue, where most of the stores were, and up a couple blocks to Tenth Street where the ice cream place was. Samantha stayed outside with Polly while the two adults went in for the goods. *Silly,* she thought to herself, shivering, *who eats ice cream in November?*

"Samantha?" a small, thin voice called her name from out of nowhere. She looked around, saw no one close by, then heard it again.

"Samantha?" Polly was nuzzling her hand and it sounded for a moment as if it was she that had spoken, as though the voice were coming from *her dog.* Then she remembered – her wrist-communicator! She had totally forgotten it was there; her mind had sort of filed it away with the rest of the whole alternate timeline experience as if it were part of an almost entirely faded dream. But there it was.

"Professor?" She whispered into it after tapping the talk button.

"Samantha!" It responded cheerfully. "There you are! I've been trying to contact you!"

"Sorry," Samantha spoke quietly. "I left it turned off – I must've turned it back on by accident somehow – " She eyed Polly's nuzzling nose.

"It doesn't matter," The Professor continued. "I really must speak with you. It's a matter of the utmost importance!"

"Um, all right." Samantha looked nervously over her shoulder into the ice cream shop. The lovebirds were returning. "But not now. I have to go – I promise I'll call you on this thing later, okay? Bye!"

"But – " she shut off the device, just as Jason and her mother returned with ice cream cones. "Here ya go, Samantha," Jason handed her a cone, smiling.

"Thanks," she smiled, taking it and licking it.

"Samantha, were you talking to someone out here?" her mother asked, slightly suspicious.

"Hmmm? Oh, um, no Mom," she waffled. "Just Polly. *Mmmmmm* this is good ice cream!" she quickly changed the subject. "Thanks, Jason!"

"No problem," Jason smiled. "Cheers!" He lifted his cone in a mock toast. "Here's to Cindy Smart, beautiful woman and awesome mom." Samantha lifted her cone, smiling, and her mother blushed, thoroughly forgetting any suspicions she might have had a moment earlier.

"Aaaawwww... shucks," she shrugged, looking coy.

They walked back home, licking as they went, and discussed the virtues of many ice cream flavors such as butter pecan, rocky road, cookie dough, chocolate and cherry and even bubble gum, though Samantha remained deeply committed to the delicious combination of mint and chocolate chips. Polly trotted along, somewhat disappointed in the fact that due to the cold weather, no delicious droppings melted off to fall on the ground within her reach as they usually did in the summer.

Home was pretty much the same as they had left it, though Todd was now completely bug-eyed and sitting tensely on the edge of his seat, thumbs moving frantically on his video game controller.

"Todd, shut that awful thing off!" their mother demanded. "It's driving me crazy and you look like some freakin' zombie!"

"No, Mom, wait, you don't understand," he stammered.

"Oh, yes I do! *Now,* Todd!"

"But Mom, this is *It!* This is the final battle with Mechanor, the leader of the cyborg army!"

"Todd, you have ten seconds to turn that thing off or I'll turn it off for you!"

"Okay!" Todd pressed pause, but continued his arguments.

Samantha slipped off to her room after finishing her ice cream cone and closed the door. She put on her pajamas even though it was still early and crawled into her bed. She pulled the covers up around her and tapped the talk button on her wrist-communicator.

"Professor, are you there?" she spoke quietly into it. "Professor?"

"Ah, there you are, Samantha. I'm sorry about that whole mess with your mother, you know; I had to come up with some kind of story..."

"It's okay," Samantha forgave him. "What's up? Are we in the clear?"

"I'm afraid not," Smythe replied, sounding worried. "I've been doing some research on our friend Jordan, pop icon and time traveler extraordinaire. I've found out some very interesting things I'd like you to read. I've sent the information to an email account I set up in your name at hotmail.com. To access it you'll need to type in your username, which is *timetraveler11@hotmail.com*, And your password."

"What's the password?" Samantha asked excitedly. She had an email account already but was quite happy to have a secret agent one as well.

"*Polly*, of course," The Professor chuckled. "Well, *Polly11* actually. It's good to throw a few numbers in there for extra security. Please read the contents in complete privacy as soon as you get a chance and get back to me tomorrow morning if you're able, all right?"

"Samantha?" Her mother was knocking on the door.

"Okay, Professor! Gotta go – Smart out!" She turned off the device, then answered her mother in a voice that pretended to be sleepy. "Mmmmm... what, Mom?"

"Oh, okay, just checking on you. Can I come in?"

"Yeah, sure," she snuggled up under her blankets. Her mother opened the door, walked over to her bed and plopped Polly down next to Samantha.

"Thought you might want your sleeping buddy," she smiled, sitting down on the edge of the bed. "Tired?"

"Mmmm," Samantha nodded, smiling a contented smile.

"Well, you've had a bit of a crazy week. I think you should probably go to school tomorrow, though – what do you think?"

"Yeah, definitely," she responded, rolling over and opening her eyes. "Yeah, I want to go to school tomorrow."

"Everything's still going well at school, then? There's nothing there that's bothering you?"

"No, Mom. Look – no matter what you think, I didn't run away. I like school; I mostly like home just fine too, I was just – doing something really interesting and really wanted to – to be a part of it. Really."

"I understand, honey," her mother smiled warmly. "I know you're very smart – probably smarter than me even, and my name's Cindy Smart! Just promise me if you ever do anything like that again that you'll let me know about it beforehand, okay?"

"Okay, Mom, I will. I promise."

"Good. I love you, Samantha. I'll wake you up and we'll ride the train together tomorrow, okay?"

"Okay. I love you too, Mom."

Her mother kissed her on the forehead and tucked her in good, smiled and got up to exit.

"Good night, Polly," she said as she closed the door and shut off the light.

*

As soon as she had determined that everyone was asleep, Samantha snuck out to the living room and switched on the family computer. She waited nervously for it to boot up and turned the volume knob down so that it wouldn't make any sounds. When it was ready, she clicked the Internet icon and the browser opened. She navigated to the Hotmail website and typed in the I.D. information The Professor had told her to, smiling as she spelled out the word "Polly."

There it was: An email from A. Edgar Smythe, with the subject heading "Jordan Slane." Samantha wondered momentarily at The Professor's middle name, which she hadn't known, but then shrugged and opened the email. This is what she saw:

To: Samantha Smart
_Re: Jordan Slane, a.k.a. Jordan Anderson.

Jordan Slane was born an only child to Vassily Slane and an unknown mother in June of 1986. No more specific birth date is known. Vassily Slane is known as a powerful, mysterious Wall Street investor of whom not a single photograph exists in the public domain. Doing business largely over the computer or through numerous subordinates, Slane has amassed a considerable fortune primarily in the energy, pharmaceutical and forest products markets, and has also financed his son Jordan's efforts to (quite successfully) popularize his singing group, Heatwavvve. Vassily is of unknown age and unknown origin, but does apparently have a social security number and pays taxes. He wields great political influence and is a large contributor to several conservative candidates' political campaigns, though he also supports medical, geological and biological science research to a very generous degree.

In short, Vassily Slane is a nearly-invisible, non-existent person who nonetheless has done a bang-up job at existing, and is someone we need to know more about. I fear, Samantha, that this is someone capable of great, vast manipulations of the world, and his connection to Jordan makes me almost positive that he is involved in, if not the primary force behind these glitches in time.

Please let me know when we can meet or chat via wrist-communicator to discuss this development further.

Yours,
A.E. Smythe

Samantha stared at the computer screen for a moment and then snapped out of her daze. She hurriedly shut the thing down and crept back to her bedroom where Polly was waiting, her nose sticking out of the door in canine curiosity. Getting back into bed, Samantha pulled the covers up around her neck and lie there, her mind spinning. *Jordan Slane? Wall Street fortunes? An invisible enemy?* All these thoughts made the cogs of her mind turn round and round, and the main gist of her thought process kept coming around to one question: *Why?*

Why Jordan Anderson? Why a powerful, reclusive investor father? *Why alter time?* That was the real question. Why would anyone *want* to alter time, rich, powerful investor, pop music idol or otherwise? What possible benefit could it have for these people? Not fame, Samantha decided. Heatwavvve was far more successful, popular and well-known in this timeline than the altered one, where hardly anyone knew their name. Money? She supposed that a powerful investor could make a fortune in stocks, if they had invested in something like taxi-boats, artificial trees or floating plastic sidewalks, but Vassily Slane seemed to have money in none of these things. "Forest products" was a somewhat suspicious investment, as Samantha imagined that anything made of wood might become rare and sought after, though she failed to see any huge future in anything that basic that would totally cease to exist. No, it had to be something else, something more substantial, perhaps a personal stake in seeing global warming succeed. But what could it possibly be?

Samantha sighed and curled up to go to sleep. She decided she would somehow find some time tomorrow to contact The Professor and discuss this latest information further. Surely his magnificent mind could put the pieces together quicker and more logically than hers. She rested her hand on her little Boston terrier's side and slipped off into a deep, dreamless sleep.

*

School was refreshing the next morning. Samantha forgot how much she missed learning things, even if they weren't things as advanced as those she picked up from hanging around Professor Smythe. The focus of the day was on geography, which Samantha especially liked; they were studying maps of all the countries in Africa, that huge "dark" continent where it was believed humans had originated. Mrs. Wronsky, her sixth grade teacher, was especially keen on talking about Egypt, which was at the far Northeast corner of the African continent and was home to the Great Pyramids. The pyramids, she said, were constructed by ancient kings known as Pharaohs, who ruled the land thousands of years ago and believed that they were immortal, that is, that they were godlike and would never truly die. They ordered the pyramids built to house their bodies when they died, and believed the massive stone tombs would assure that their spirits could live on and roam free amongst the stars of the heavens.

Samantha found all this very exciting, and began to daydream of time-traveling to these ancient places, living amongst their people and seeing the amazing pyramids when they were brand new. Her imagination blossomed while looking at the paintings reproduced in their school books, seeing herself standing next to a Pharaoh as he directed the construction of these incredible monuments. She thought that this would indeed be a grand experience, though she was a bit troubled upon learning that the pyramids had been built mostly by the work of slaves. Slavery was wrong, she knew, and the thought of it sort of soured her daydreaming.

When lunchtime came, she went outside to the school's playground, found a secluded spot and contacted The Professor on her wrist-communicator. He was glad to hear from her; it seemed he had formulated some sort of plan.

"Ah, Samantha! I'm glad you buzzed. Your friend Marvin and I have been devising a plan to get to the bottom of this confounding conspiracy. If you and Marvin can get in touch with Brianna and Suki and have everyone meet here tomorrow afternoon, that would be most advantageous."

"I'll try, Professor, but my mom is keeping a pretty close eye on me these days, I'm afraid."

"Ah – I wouldn't worry about that, Samantha. I had a long talk with your mother this morning up in the lobby. I daresay she's somewhat fond of me again, and has given the O.K. for you and your friends to come down here for a couple hours tomorrow. Oh, and she expects you'll either ride home on the train with her when she gets off of work, or maybe you're going to some show with someone named, er, Jason?"

"Oh. Cool. Yeah, um, Jason," Samantha tried to explain. "He's my mom's new boyfriend. He's kind of okay, actually. I guess he's got some money."

"I see. Perhaps he's the reason your mother seemed so, shall we say, cheery this morning."

"Yeah, probably. She's all *in love* or something. Whatever. Oh – Professor?"

"Yes, Samantha?"

"Jason actually, um, well, he got four tickets to see Heatwavvve tomorrow night at Irving Plaza. I'm really not sure what to do, but he and my mom said they wanted to go with us, me and a friend, I guess. What do you think, should I totally not go?"

The line was silent for a moment. Samantha could almost hear The Professor's brain calculating thoughts at some most alarming speed.

"Let me think about it, Samantha. It sounds very dangerous, but it could be an opportunity for us, too. I'll talk to you tomorrow afternoon. Talk to your friends tonight, and tell Brianna to call me on my office phone if you speak with her. The number is two-one-two, seven-one-nine..."

Samantha fumbled in her backpack for a pen and paper and began writing down the number.

"Okay – got it," she said.

"Good. Tell her to call me tonight if she can, I'll be here. Smythe out." The Professor signed off.

"Right – uh, bye Professor – I mean, Smart out." She turned off her wrist-communicator and shrugged. She knew The Professor was putting together some sort of plan, but resigned herself to the fact that she probably couldn't understand it, at least until he explained it to her in full.

The lunch bell rang and Samantha headed back indoors, happy to come in from the cold playground. The rest of the day's lessons continued on the theme of pyramids, though in the afternoon they learned about Central American pyramids instead of Egyptian ones. This fascinated her even more, for though these pyramids were somewhat smaller and not as old, they were remnants of the Mayan civilization, which was supposedly the civilization responsible for creating the time machine. She listened intently to Mrs. Wronsky's descriptions of how the Mayan people had lived and examined the pictures in her textbook with the eye of someone who had seen many of the symbols presented before. Many of them were similar to the ones engraved into the stone pieces of the time machine, though somehow different as well. She closed her eyes for a moment and could almost see those more ancient symbols as they had flashed through her mind during time travel; still, they meant nothing intelligible to her and she began to develop an even deeper respect for The Professor's ability to research and decipher them.

Jason was waiting for her after school, having made an arrangement with her mother to meet her and ride home with her in a car service car. He worked half the time from home and so, he said, it was really no trouble for him. He did his best to make small talk on the ride.

"So, Samantha," he asked cheerily, "are you psyched for the Heatwavvve show tomorrow night?"

"Um, yeah," she smiled, trying to sound enthusiastic.

"Who are you going to bring?"

"Uh, probably Brianna. Or maybe Suki."

"Cool. Your mom and I won't bother you too much. She's just still a little worried about you, you know?"

"I know. It's fine. I just hope you guys won't be too bored."

"*Bored?*," Jason boomed. "Only boring people are bored, Samantha. I used to sing a little myself, you know."

Samantha rolled her eyes. How many of her mom's boyfriends had said that before. She forced a smile and just nodded, trying to look interested but hoping fiercely that Jason would not begin to sing.

"Yep," he continued, "I played with a band in my twenties. Mostly straight-up rock sort of stuff, but sometimes we mixed it up with some smooth R&B-type tunes, kind of like Heatwavvve but with more of an edge."

"Really?" Samantha squeezed out a response. She was grinning painfully at this point.

"Oh, yeah," Jason went on. "We almost had a little record deal at one point but the bass player decided all of a sudden that he needed to become a Buddhist monk, and then the band broke up." He looked up dreamily at the tall downtown buildings as they passed by. "He's still in Tibet, I think. Man, life would have been a lot different if he hadn't gotten into making those sand paintings..."

Samantha continued her exercise of smiling and nodding as the car rolled over the Manhattan Bridge. *Life would have been a lot different,* she thought, rolling the words over in her mind, *if Elliott Bergen had never been born.*

It was Saturday again. One week had passed since Samantha had walked out of her front door and into a world of mystery and adventure. It seemed like a year. Polly was up early as usual, licking her and whining for a walk, and Samantha groggily got up and staggered into the bathroom to wash her face and brush her teeth. Her mother had already gone to work, it being officially the holiday season, a time which was particularly busy at the museum and hence required overtime hours to be put in by its employees. They had made a plan at dinner last night that they would meet at the ticket counter at four o'clock today, after Samantha and her friends had finished their "study group" (this was Professor Smythe's excuse for them to meet at the museum), down in the basement. Her mother was off work at that time, and they would take the train with Brianna or Suki (whomever Samantha wanted to bring) to a pizza place downtown and have some slices before going to the Heatwavvve concert at seven-thirty. Jason, apparently, would be meeting them somewhere along the way.

Pulling on her most stylish pair of jeans, Samantha looked into her full-length mirror and tried to smile, telling herself that she was attractive as well as bright and that even if Jordan Anderson – or Jordan Slane – was some evil, time-traveling villain, she might still meet some boy at the show who was at least as worthy of her affections. She experimentally applied some of her mom's lipstick, making kissy faces at herself until she finally wiped it off as her mother still didn't allow her to wear make-up outside of the house. Polly sat staring inquisitively, wondering what all the fuss was about and patiently awaiting her walk.

Unfortunately for the little terrier, it was a short one, just up to the park and back, with just enough time to do her business. Samantha still had to shower, eat some brunch and wake up her brother. They had to catch a twelve-ten train into the city, a ride on which Todd had to accompany her according to Cindy Smart's motherly directives. Todd, of course, was equally unenthusiastic about the situation, especially since he frequently slept until one or two in the afternoon on Saturdays. Needless to say, he was not much fun to wake up.

Nonetheless, off they went at about ten minutes to twelve, Polly abandoned once more to the brownstone's big bay window, watching as the brother and sister departed for the F train through a chilly, misty Park Slope. The walk was quick and invigorating to Ninth Street and the train reasonably on time, and Samantha sat down in a corner seat and opened her school textbook to the page on Mayan civilization. Todd sat down next to her with his MP3 player on, blasting some horrid heavy metal noise through his earphones at what must have been an ear-damaging volume.

The book held her attention for most of the ride – there was even a little boxed-off section that was essentially a mini-dictionary of Mayan symbols. Samantha surveyed the ones that stood for *sun, moon, man, woman, day, night* and, most interestingly, a couple which stood for *true* and *false*. She was so into studying the symbols that she walked through the Fourteenth Street station with her eyes glued to the book, instinctively tracing a path to the platform for uptown trains. She was vaguely aware of her brother moseying along beside her, occasionally breaking into an embarrassing display of air guitar when his song came to some climactic moment.

She was still reading when they got off the C train at Seventy-second street, walking up the concrete stairs into the chill air that enveloped Central Park West, and by the time she looked up they were at the stairs to the Natural History Museum. *How odd,* she thought, remembering taking a taxi-boat less than a week ago to this very place. Having spent a while in an altered timeline, she decided, made this proper one somehow less real, no matter how she tried to tell herself that things were as they should be.

They walked up the stairs past Teddy Roosevelt, into the museum lobby and around the ever-present barosauraus, and arrived at the ticket counter where their mother was working, a somewhat long line of visitors stretching out from her ticket window. Cindy Smart saw them and quickly arranged for a short break, coming out to meet them.

"Hi, guys," she said, smiling. "It's really busy right now, I'm sorry. You know, tourists and everything."

"Can I go home now?" Todd asked, momentarily removing his ear buds.

"Todd," Cindy frowned, "thank you for coming here with Samantha. I guess you can go if you want, but call here as soon as you get home, capiche?"

"Yeah, okay," Todd nodded, turning to leave.

"And don't leave the house a mess!" their mother called after him. Todd lifted a lame hand to signal his promise not to.

"Hi, Mom," Samantha smiled.

"Hey, honey," Cindy smiled back. "You look really good. Is that what you're wearing to the Heatwavvve show?"

"Yeah," Samantha replied, shifting somewhat uncomfortably. "Is it okay?"

Cindy eyed her daughter's stylish but fairly conservative outfit, at last nodding an approval.

"Did my friends get here yet?" the younger Smart queried.

"Oh – yes, honey, they're all downstairs with Professor Smythe. You can just go on down if you like, I think they're waiting for you."

"Cool," Samantha grinned. "Um, thanks for letting me have this... study group, Mom. It means a lot to me."

"I know, Samantha." her mother stroked her hair for a minute. "Well, you have a great time. I have to get back to work, but you meet me back here at four, okay?"

"Okay."

"Have you decided who you want to bring yet?"

"Oh – um, no, not yet. I need to talk to everyone first."

"All right. I'll see you at four, then." Cindy Smart blew her daughter a kiss and walked back through the door in the glass-encased kiosk that formed the ticket sales counter. Samantha waved and headed for the stairs.

*

Professor Smythe's office was abuzz with activity. All of Samantha's friends were there; apparently they were becoming a crack team of secret agent time-travelers. Marvin and The Professor were at the computer, involved in testing some new device they had hooked up to it; Brianna was on the office phone to someone who sounded like her father and Suki was engrossed in some volume of the *Encyclopedia Organica,* one in a set of many huge books on all things alive or natural. Their heads all turned when Samantha entered, and Marvin was the first to speak.

"Sammy Smart, Brooklyn's finest work of art! What up, home girl?"

"Hammering Hip-Hoppers!" Smythe shook his head. "Come in, Samantha, we've got a lot going on."

Samantha sat down in the only empty chair in the room, getting a nod from Brianna and a 'hello' from Suki, and The Professor began to explain his latest plan to her.

"We're going to need you to go that Heatwavvve show, Samantha," he said. "We've got a plan cooking to figure out these Slanes, and you and Brianna are going to be our agents of choice for this particular mission."

"Okay," Samantha shrugged, shooting a look at Brianna. "What's up?"

"Well," The Professor began, "we've been able to determine that Jordan Anderson – that is, Jordan Slane – is a bit of an email nut. That is to say, everywhere he goes, whether it be his home, a hotel room or backstage at a show, Jordan always carries a laptop computer. Mostly he seems to just answer fans' emails, but we're hoping that he'll also be in touch with his father, especially if there's something important going on."

"Right," Samantha nodded. "So... are you... tapping into his emails or something?"

"Not exactly," The Professor continued, "but we're hoping to, in a roundabout sort of way. Unfortunately, we can't gather all the information we need from here – all Jordan's transmissions are pretty well encrypted – but Marvin has brought us a wonderful device that I think will suit our needs perfectly, though it requires a bit of stealth and, ah, risk, shall we say."

Samantha shifted her gaze to Marvin, who was grinning like the Cheshire Cat from *Alice In Wonderland.*

"Well," he cleared his throat, trying to sound like a professional adult, "ya see this little baby here?" He indicated a small flash drive with a USB input. "This is serious spy stuff, Samantha. This unit here captures keystroke information from the keyboard, that is, it records everything anyone types on it, up to three thousand characters. I got it from a P.I. guy I know back in the 'hood."

"A... private investigator?" Samantha asked.

"Yeah," Marvin replied proudly, "he owed me a favor for helping him find out some stuff about some people he was checkin' out."

"Cool," Samantha smiled, genuinely impressed.

"We need to hook this device up to Jordan's computer," The Professor broke in. "It plugs right into a USB input, so you should be able to do it fairly quickly. Most laptops have at least a couple of those."

Samantha nodded.

"It's pretty much worked out," Marvin chimed back in. "Professor Smythe even rigged it so it'll transmit the recorded information straight to this computer through the Internet, seconds after it captures what Jordan types."

"Well," Samantha said after a moment of silence. "It seems you two have come up with a pretty nifty plan. But... how do we get to Jordan's computer?"

"Done," Brianna smiled in that horribly precocious 'little princess' sort of way. "Daddy got me a backstage pass to the

Heatwavvve show. It should be waiting for me at the door."

"Perfect!" The Professor cackled. He was starting to enjoy himself again, Samantha could tell. "Brianna, you are our main infiltrator. Samantha, I'm afraid that since – well, since Jordan already knows your face, and Marvin's for that matter, you shouldn't be directly involved."

"Um... okay," Samantha shrugged. "What do you need me to do?"

"All right," Smythe said seriously, "everybody listen to me for a moment. Tonight, Samantha and Brianna will go to the Heatwavvve concert with Samantha's mother. There, Samantha, you will try to stay out of Jordan's sight if at all possible unless Brianna specifically asks for help. I'm giving Marvin's wrist-communicator to Brianna for now so you can both have a link to us and to each other.

"Brianna." He turned to the spoiled little uptown girl, who now looked a bit frightened. "Your task is a more difficult one." Brianna gulped and nodded. "You must use your pass to gain access to the backstage area, locate Jordan's specific personal area and find his laptop, if it's set up. If it's not, we're out of luck, but chances are it will be. You need to plug this," he said, holding up the little box-shaped spy device, "into a USB port, whichever one's easiest or least obvious. Understand?"

Brianna nodded again, smiling nervously.

"Here, try it once or twice with this computer – it's really quite simple." She obliged The Professor and found that it was in fact a simple thing to do, and practiced it a few times to see if she could get the action down to within just a few seconds. The Professor continued detailing the plan:

"If you are successful, Suki, Marvin and I will be receiving signals from the recorder/transponder. If anyone types on that keyboard, we'll be able to read the message only seconds later. We'll also put a trace on any emails Jordan receives while our device is functioning. I have a program that can trace any email communication back to its root server – it's rather handy, I must say. If he receives any messages from his father, we can figure out very nearly where he operates out of.

"Well," Smythe concluded, "if we all know our assigned roles, we can relax until four o'clock. Does anyone have any questions?"

"I got a question, Prof," Marvin spoke up. "Do we 'home base' operatives get any chow tonight? A man's gotta eat, after all, y'all."

"Of course, Marvin," The Professor chuckled. "I'll order something for you and I and Suki. I assume, Samantha, that your mother will be feeding you and Brianna before the show?"

"Ray's Famous," Samantha grinned, referring to the ubiquitous Manhattan chain of pizza shops that was known to almost everyone in New York City and beyond.

"Dog!" Marvin shook his head, looking jealous. Brianna smiled, too; everybody liked pizza.

*

The world seemed particularly crowded as they rode the C train downtown underneath the bustle of Eighth Avenue. Both Samantha and Brianna felt quite nervous, but Cindy Smart just assumed that they were excited about seeing Heatwavvve, and was full of questions for the girls.

"So, you girls must be really psyched, huh?" she asked. Samantha and Brianna nodded and maintained what they hoped didn't look too much like forced grins. "So, okay, who's the really cute one you always talk about, Samantha? Justin? Um – Jared?"

"Jordan," Samantha corrected her. "Jordan Sl – Anderson, I mean."

"Yeah, Jordan," her mom continued, acting herself like a young girl. "Maybe we can try to get an autograph for you guys or something. Wouldn't that be *cool*?"

"Yeah, um, we've got that taken care of, Mom. Brianna has a backstage pass waiting for her at the door," she gave a sideways glance to her friend, who nodded. "She's going to try to get autographs for both of us."

"Wow!" Cindy replied. "That's great! Maybe, well, maybe we can *all* get backstage!"

Samantha and Brianna exchanged uncomfortable glances again.

"Um, actually, that's okay," Samantha fumbled with her words. "I think I'd rather just, ah, watch the show."

"Really!?" Cindy was shocked. "Come on, honey, don't be so shy. I'm sure Jordan's a very nice person."

"I'm sure he is," Samantha lied. If only her mother knew how bad of a boy he really was. "I, uh, I just would rather sit down and watch the show. I'm, um, not feeling that great," she lied again.

"Oh. Well, I'm sorry Samantha. Maybe a little pizza will perk you up."

"Yeah, maybe," Samantha smiled weakly.

They switched to an L train that was heading crosstown to Union Square Station. It seemed like the L was even more packed with people, early Christmas shoppers and regulars alike. At least the ride was shorter, and soon they were emerging on foot from the underground at the small but lively downtown park. After a two block walk, they had arrived at Irving Plaza, though it was still only about quarter to five.

They quickly spotted Jason outside, who greeted them and asked if Samantha had remembered to bring the tickets, which fortunately she had. Since it was early yet, the group decided to implement the dinner part of their plan and they set off down Third Avenue, Jason in the lead. The nearest Ray's was down on Saint Mark's Place, a chilly walk of eight blocks or so. There were closer pizza places, but Jason was dead set on Ray's, and so the company made the trek, Brianna doing her best not to look totally inconvenienced. *Ray's is okay,* Samantha thought to herself, but there were better places, and both she and Brianna knew that any 'Ray's Famous' carried the New York stigma of a tourist trap. She wondered briefly if Jason had grown up in New Jersey, then shrugged and kept on walking; she was enjoying the stroll anyway, it relaxed her nerves.

Ray's was, appropriately, filled with jock-ish guys in baseball hats swilling pitchers of beer and stuffing their faces with ridiculously huge amounts of pizza. Brianna looked positively mortified; her daily meals came from restaurants that sparkled with crystal chandeliers and where one person's dinner would probably cost as much as twenty pizzas from Ray's. Still, she did her best to smile and certainly wasn't particularly averse to pizza by any means.

The wait was only about fifteen minutes, and soon they were seated at a comfortable corner table far enough away from the college-boy ogres that even Brianna felt she could enjoy herself. Jason ordered a pitcher of beer for himself and wine for Samantha's mom, plus two diet sodas for the girls. Together they pored over the menu and decided on two large pizzas, one with pepperoni and the other with onions and green peppers. Their waitress was a pretty girl of about twenty-two, and it was obvious that she was happy to wait on them, probably seeing them as a nice, civilized break from the restaurant's standard Saturday night customers.

After they had ordered, Jason, two beers in already, began to get talkative and, unfortunately, reminiscent of his youth.

"I remember coming here in college!" he chuckled, looking for all the world like he'd rather be yukking it up with one of the tables of college boys. "We used to just *gorge* ourselves on pizza and down *pitchers* of cold beer. Those were the days, I tell ya. *N.Y.U.!*" he yelled, lifting his mug towards the crowd of young louts two tables away. One of them seemed to raise his mug in response, though the girls were embarrassed and even Cindy looked a little perturbed.

"Is he going to be like this all night, Mom?" Samantha whispered in her ear.

"Um... hopefully not," her mother responded in her own whisper-voice, uneasily eyeing Jason's quickly-disappearing pitcher of beer. "We'll try to eat fast."

The pizza was fairly quick in arriving, thankfully, and the gang dug in, devouring the sinfully delicious slices of what was essentially salt and grease. *But mmmm... sooooo gooood.* Even Brianna put aside her usual manners and hungrily scarfed up the dinner, though she notably stuck to the more vegetarian of the two pies – pepperoni pretty much guaranteed some form of indigestion or gas, and she was a person who would probably rather die than release any gas in a public place. Still, she smiled and shrugged, grease dripping down her round but prominent debutante's chin.

Luckily, or by some small grace of the gods of reputations, they didn't have too much time to linger at Ray's Famous, and so try though he might, Jason remained mostly sober and was shot down by Samantha's mother when he tried to order another pitcher of beer.

"Really, we should get going," Cindy smiled, her voice dripping with honey. "The girls are really excited for this show, Jason. I'd hate for them to have to miss a minute of it, you know?" Jason nodded and tried to maturely dab the grease and beer foam from his frowning lips.

"Of course, Honey," he said. "Check, please!" He raised his finger, trying to get the waitress's attention.

The bill was settled and the waitress was left a generous tip, and the group got up and walked back out of the restaurant. They strolled back up Third Avenue, more slowly than they had come down it as everyone was full of pizza and somewhat warmer for having been in a place that was warmed both by high-temperature ovens and the bodies of some hundred or so people. Fourteenth Street was bustling when they reached its wide thoroughfare, and when they turned onto Irving Place they could see a fairly large line forming in front of the club. Many of those in line were girls about Brianna and Samantha's age, giggling nervously and chatting non-stop to each other, probably about Jordan or one of the other cute boys in the group. Samantha watched them with a hint of sadness, of regret – they had an innocence that she could not now regain. She exchanged a kind of knowing glance with Brianna as they slowly shuffled closer to the entrance.

It took a full fifteen or twenty minutes for them to reach the ticket-taking entrance, but they were all pretty happy for the chance to digest their dinner. Upon reaching the ticket-taker, Samantha brought out the tickets and handed them out to everyone. Brianna inquired as to her backstage pass and eventually received it after a good bit of list-checking and I.D. showing. Her pass was neat looking; it was purple and glittery like the sparkles on Dorothy's ruby slippers in *The Wizard Of Oz*. It also indicated something as to her status as a minor, i.e. that no one should give her beer or wine or anything. *Oh well,* Samantha giggled inwardly, *probably a good thing.* Brianna had some very important work to do.

The group walked through the doors and up some stairs. To Cindy's dismay, Jason had quickly spotted a beer vending counter and had agreed to catch up with them at their designated seats. Samantha's heart began to beat fast, strangely, she noted, more because she had never actually seen Heatwavvve live before than for the fact that she knew Jordan was a time-traveling villain who wanted half the known world to be covered with water. She wondered to herself if she could still enjoy the music now that she knew so much about Jordan – she hadn't, she realized, even once put on a Heatwavvve CD since she'd returned from the alternate timeline. She wondered, in fact (and echoing a statement that Jordan himself had made upon first meeting her) if she had outgrown it. The charm and style of a boy-band seemed rather pale and insignificant now that she had traveled through and even helped to alter time; it was like trying to be excited about performing in a local talent show after you'd just signed a major movie deal. Or something like that. (Anticlimactic was the word that popped into her head), and this reflected her general feeling about life even, lately; to have had the most exciting time of her life at eleven and three quarter years of age left her wondering if anything in her teens, twenties or thirties would ever compare to the experiences she was having now. *Ugh,* she thought, feeling her mind wandering. *I'm starting to feel like a washed-up child star whose T.V. show's just been canceled.*

They reached their seats, which were lower level and fairly close to the stage (thank you, Jason) and sat down, taking in the large crowd of people as it moved and flowed like some giant underground anthill. They had checked their coats at a coat room, which gave them more room to stretch out comfortably in their seats. Brianna looked a little twitchy as crowds typically made her a bit nervous, though she was smiling and craning her neck, trying to see down onto the stage, where a few technician people or stage hands were arranging the last-minute details of necessary props or sound system thingies.

It wasn't long before the house lights dimmed, leaving the stage illuminated in rich hues of green and blue. Even these lights then dimmed to nothing, though, and the ambient murmur of crowd noise hushed as every single light in the place went out, leaving them all in total blackness. For a moment, it was absolutely terrifying for Samantha. She imagined Jordan as some grayish vampire creature, swirling in a mist out from the stage and solidifying his vaporous form just long enough to sink his fangs into her neck. She flinched, feeling a chill run down her spine. Then she almost bit through her tongue...

The darkness exploded suddenly. All of the lights turned on at once, blinding the audience. At the same time the music began, booming through the massive sound system – combined with the blinding flash of pure white light, it hit the crowd like a ten megaton bomb. There they were, Heatwavvve, dancing in all silver outfits and singing into their wireless headset microphones – the song was "You Love the Bad Boy," one of their more aggressive and dance-friendly numbers, and the crowd began to move like one huge, rhythmic organism. Samantha smiled in spite of herself and looked at Brianna, who smiled back. How many times had they danced to this song in their underwear, singing passionately into hairbrushes and trying to copy the boys' moves from the video? As much as things had changed, they couldn't erase all those times from their memories.

Somewhere in the middle of the third or fourth song Jason came stumbling down to their seats, carrying an armful of goodies. He handed the girls a soda each, a small drink of some sort to Cindy and kept what looked like a monstrous sixty-four ounce beer for himself. He had also purchased a large bag of chips and some licorice twists, both of which the girls tore into with a voracious appetite, despite their having just chowed a healthy amount of pizza less than an hour earlier. Cindy was a little surprised, but Samantha shrugged and looked at her as if to say 'Hey, I'm young. I have a fast metabolism.' Even though their minds were starting to absorb the feminine propaganda that they should fear sugar, fat and starch, their bodies were still mostly those of children and therefore still contained that extra pocket of stomach which could always hold more sweet things.

In the middle of the sixth number ("Only For You, Babe," a slow, sappy love song), their wrist-communicators went off. Thankfully the adults hadn't noticed, and they excused themselves to go to the bathroom.

"Oh, wait," Cindy began to say, "I'll go with – "

But the girls had anticipated this and were up the aisle and into part of a lobby before Cindy could even completely rise from her seat. They turned a few corners and then found a stairway that appeared to be not much in use at the moment and Samantha answered the transmission.

"Professor?" she spoke hopefully into the little microphone. "We're here – go ahead." She tapped the talk button off.

"Samantha," said a voice that came back through both of their communicators. "Brianna?"

"Right here, Professor," Brianna tried to get the hang of the device, learning to tap on and off.

"Good. Listen, now – you need to get backstage and place our device. Do you know where to go?"

"We can find it," Samantha assured him.

"All right," Professor Smythe continued. "But you need to get back to your seat after you help her find the stage door, Samantha. Are we clear?" His tone was very firm and serious.

"Clear," both girls said in unison. Brianna reached into her purse and pulled out the little spy device, turning it over in her fingers. "All right," she sighed nervously, putting it back. "Let's go find this place."

Locating the backstage area was fairly easy as many staff were willing to help direct them once Brianna flashed her sparkly pass. At the door, the uptown girl turned around and hugged her friend, shaking a little.

"Good luck," Samantha said, hugging her back. "Be careful."

"I will," Brianna replied, somewhat dramatically.

"If there's any trouble," Samantha pleaded, "you know how to contact us." She pointed to the wrist-communicators and Brianna swallowed and nodded. Then she was gone – inside the door.

The man at the door was large and initially tried to keep Brianna out, but then noticed her backstage pass and let her through, though with a conditional approval.

"I catch you drinking and you're outta here, little girl," he said. "And you ain't gettin' back in. Got it?"

"I won't," Brianna promised. She flashed him her patented princess smile and started mingling with the stylists, stage hands and others who were lucky or well-connected enough to have acquired a pass like hers.

The backstage area had an air of general chaos; each member of Heatwavvve had at least three stylists: one for clothes, one for hair and one for make-up. These bustled around like hens, touching up the outfits for the second set, trying out hand lotions on themselves or consulting fashion magazines for the latest tips on hair fixatives or selections of theatrical jewelry or colored contact lenses. There were also sound technicians, stage hands pre-programming fog machines, reporters sipping drinks and hobnobbing with agents and managers, photographers, caterers and a bartender at the far end of the large room who wore a red blazer and was flirting with some girls a few years older than Brianna. She smiled inwardly. *This is going to be easy,* she thought to herself.

It wasn't hard to locate Jordan's section of the backstage world – it was the biggest and most decorated of the dressing stalls, and came with at least one extra stylist. Brianna edged toward the area and started to form a plan in her head.

"Hey!" she said excitedly to one of the stylists, a tall black woman - or perhaps a man made up to look like a woman. "Is this where Jordan Anderson sits?" She tried to play up the part of an infatuated twelve-year-old girl.

"That's right, Honey," the stylist replied, now obviously a cross-dressing man. "And it's Rita's job to make sure he looks his best!"

"Wow." Brianna nodded, smiling and still playing the excited little girl. Her eyes scanned the area until they stopped on a nondescript-looking gray rectangle on one of the counter tops surrounding the large centerpiece mirror. "So, like, does Jordan wear, like, *make-up* and stuff?" she patronized the stylist.

"Oh, Honey, they *all* do. Just because they're boys doesn't mean they don't need a little cover-up, or a slight hint of eyeliner for emphasis!" The drag queen was gesturing as he/she spoke, making Brianna honestly giggle. Another stolen look at the counter top confirmed that the suspicious gray rectangle did indeed have a cord coming out of the back of it - it had to be Jordan's laptop computer.

"Wow," Brianna played along. Her eye followed the cord to a jack in the wall under a counter that was strewn with powders, eyeliner pencils and even lipstick. Suddenly, she decided to act. She lunged for a lipstick even as she was saying "Does Jordan even wear *lipstick?*" She already had the spy device ready in one palm and intentionally knocked the lipstick off the counter so it rolled behind and under it. "Oh! I'm sorry," she squeaked, practically diving under the counter after it.

Her training had paid off. She inserted the device into a port she'd spotted earlier in under three seconds and came back up with the lipstick in her hand. She bumped her head on the underside of the counter as an afterthought, creating some additional chaos and distraction. This caused Rita to become agitated and, along with two other stylists rushing to aid in the process, tried frantically to stop other products from rolling off the counter top.

"Oh, damn!" he/she swore. "Honey, you *have* to be more careful!"

"I'm *really* sorry," Brianna pouted, handing the lipstick back. "I'm just sort of... *klutzy* sometimes."

Rita eyed her darkly, having finally stopped the potentially disastrous motion of the other lipsticks and eye pencils. Slowly, he/she stood up and scowled at Brianna.

"I think you've made enough of a mess, young lady. Why don't you go back out and watch the show?" The sentiment was reflected in the faces of the two other stylists (actual women) who had come to Rita's aid.

"I'm sorry," Brianna repeated, looking down at her feet and starting to shuffle away in mock dejection. Apparently that was all that 'Rita' had to say; Brianna stole one last glance over her shoulder and saw him/her still scowling, trying to straighten the arrangement of make-up items on the counter. She smiled a bit to herself as she walked back into the buzzing central part of the backstage area. Picking her way through the crowd, she kept her little smile as she moved toward the door she had come in. *Mission Accomplished,* she thought proudly. Then her smile disappeared abruptly.

She had walked right into Jordan Anderson. He was just then, it seemed, coming back from the stage for a set break, and he looked down at Brianna with an eerie, quizzical look. He was very handsome, just as much so as in photos she'd seen.

"Do I know you?" he asked.

"Huh? Oh – um – wow!" Brianna snapped back into 'fan' mode. "Jordan Anderson! I can't believe it! Oh, my Gaaawwwwdd! Um, can I get your autograph?" She fumbled in her little purse, trying not to look nervous – at least, not nervous in the wrong way.

"Uh, yeah, sure," Jordan replied, looking like he wanted to get back to his little area (this relieved Brianna). She dug out a pen and a piece of paper and then handed them to him.

"Just – on the paper?" he asked, looking up, pen in hand.

"Oh, yeah – that'd be great," Brianna nodded. Jordan shrugged and began to sign the bit of scrap paper. As he wrote, he spoke, and something frightening and possibly sinister came out:

"That's a pretty cool watch," he said, eyeing Brianna's wrist-communicator and making her almost have a heart attack. "Where'd you get it?"

"Oh, um – The Sharper Image. It does all sorts of things." *Think fast, Brianna.*

"Except tell the time, apparently," Jordan noted.

Brianna was panicking inside now. She felt like she had to do something, so she took a huge gamble.

"Oh, but it does!" she grinned, tapping the talk button. "Wristwatch: what is the time?" she asked, praying silently.

*

In the basement of the museum, the three inactive members of the team looked at each other. Suki shrugged. Marvin said "Que?" The Professor instinctively looked at the clock on his desk, then put his finger to his lips to indicate that the others should be quiet. Slowly, he pressed the talk button on the desk unit and spoke.

"The time is eight-fifty-seven Eastern Standard Time," he said in his smoothest, most proper British accent. Then he released the button and was silent.

*

Brianna breathed a deep but discreet sigh of relief at the sound of The Professor's voice, or, moreover, the words it had spoken. He had understood her need and fulfilled it. He was a very smart, perceptive man.

"Pretty cool, huh?" She resumed her adoring fan persona, switching the communicator off entirely.

"Yeah... definitely," Jordan replied, still seeming suspicious. "I feel like I've seen one before somewhere..."

"Oh! Yeah, all the kids have them," Brianna lied, flashing the princess smile. "Thanks for the autograph, Jordan! My friends won't *believe* this!" She snatched the pen and paper back from him and walked quickly out the stage door.

"Sure..." Jordan said. He still had a disturbing look on his face but was quickly distracted by two reporters who were suddenly at his side, and then some of the other members of the group came in through the stage door, further distancing him from his thoughts of a moment ago.

Brianna walked hurriedly through the lobby hallways, having (in a most unbecoming way, she felt) broken into a bit of a nervous sweat. Her vanity prevailing, she stopped at a bathroom off the side lobby to wash her face and apply a spritz of perfume, and spent a few minutes there to regain her composure. Then she made her way back through the thick intermission crowds and at last down the aisle to where their seats were, but was having a hard time finding them.

There, she thought, scanning what should have been familiar rows, *right next to the man with the navy officer's hat – and the kid with the bright white Heatwavvve shirt that was way too big on him.* But they weren't there.

She dug her ticket stub out of her purse and checked the seat number, the row number. This was the right place. But no Samantha.

"Excuse me," she said to the man in the naval hat. "Did you see my – my people leave, that were sitting here?"

"The ambulance guys took her away," said the little boy in the big shirt. "The lady fainted or something."

"Are you Brianna?" asked the man in the naval hat. Brianna looked at him and then at the boy. A wave of intense paranoia swept over her, and she questioned whether these people were to be trusted.

"Yes," she said carefully after a long pause.

"They said for you to meet them near the front entrance."

Brianna stood, stunned for a moment. She looked back and forth between the man and the boy, who was nodding, trying to detect any hint of a lie in their faces or voices. At last she turned and walked quickly back up the aisle, turning on her wrist-communicator in the process. She tapped the talk button and spoke into it as she stomped.

"Samantha?" she said, now completely on edge. "Samantha? Where are you? Professor? Can anybody hear me? What's going on!?"

"Brianna," Samantha's voice came back over the device. "I'm in an ambulance. My mom is – " she sobbed. "My mom is unconscious – there's a – a thing in her neck..." she trailed off, still crying and unable to explain herself better. "A – like a – a *dart* or something. I think it came from the stage – I, I think it was Jordan! Bree, she's not waking up!"

Brianna felt her friend's pain, continuing toward the main entrance if for no other purpose than to put more distance between herself and Jordan. She wasn't even sure if there would be anyone there to meet her anymore, but if there wasn't, she decided, she would just keep walking out and hail a cab uptown to her home or maybe to the museum. She was just about to ask Samantha what to do when

The Professor's voice chirped from her wrist.

"Brianna," he said firmly. "There is a car waiting for you outside Irving Plaza. You will get into it and meet us all at Bellevue Hospital, on First Avenue and Twenty-sixth Street, in the lobby. That is where they've taken Cindy. Do you understand?"

"Yes, Professor," she came back, still walking briskly toward the venue's main entrance.

"Good. We'll all see each other very shortly. Smythe out." He signed off, sounding like he was getting up to leave the office. "Oh –," he said in an afterthought. "Did your... mission succeed? I just need to know, it's still very important."

"Yes, Professor, though we probably won't get much out of it. I expect our... subject will be packed up and gone in two or three hours, if not sooner because of – well, because of what's happened." They both talked as if there were a possibility of someone listening in on them. Brianna guessed that in the secret agent business, this was always something that could happen, so it was prudent to communicate only as much information as was necessary to understand each other, even if they were on some crazy, time-piercing radio frequency.

"We will maintain radio silence until we see each other, all right?"

"Right," Brianna agreed, spying a driver who was holding up a sign with her name on it and walking quickly toward him.

"Samantha?" The Professor echoed his plea for discretion on the airwaves.

"Yes. All right," Samantha's voice sobbed.

Brianna slid into the back seat of the waiting black car and sped away.

*

The hospital waiting room was a nervous place, as such places were likely to be. Everyone there was nervous about something – either their own health or the health of someone close to them. And all you could do was wait. It was terribly frustrating.

That was what the team of 'adventurers' was doing now, waiting. Brianna sat next to Samantha, who had Jason on her other side. Suki sat across from them with The Professor, mindlessly thumbing through a magazine that would have totally held her attention at any other time. They all watched the hands of the clock on the waiting room wall and thought about time.

SAMANTHA: *If we could go back and prevent this from happening, my mom would be okay.*

PROFESSOR SMYTHE: *I should have realized something like this could happen. I need to figure a way out of this before anyone else gets hurt. And poor Cindy...*

BRIANNA: *I wasn't there. Maybe I could've done something if I had got back just a little sooner. Oh, man, this is so scary.*

JASON: *It all happened so fast! It could've been me. Or Samantha. Why would anyone do such a thing to Cindy? I need another cup of coffee...*

SUKI: *Poor Samantha. I wish there was something I could do...*

Their thoughts were interrupted by the attending doctor, who approached Jason and Samantha. He spoke quietly.

"Ms. Smart is in some sort of coma. The dart in her neck was coated with some sort of toxin. We – well, we don't know what it is. We're running a series of tests on the substance but so far it doesn't conform to anything we know about in standard toxicology. I think it's pretty safe to say that this was no random, childish prank. Someone planned this."

"It just doesn't make any sense," Jason responded in frustration. "Cindy – she sells tickets at the Natural History Museum. She's – she's just a regular person, you know?"

"It's a bit disturbing," the doctor nodded. "We've, ah, we've notified the N.Y.P.D. A detective is on his way."

"Yeah, okay," Jason wiped his brow nervously. He wasn't sure what else to say.

"She's in a stable condition, but until we find out more about what's in her system, I'm afraid all we can do is wait." The doctor formed a tight-lipped expression and lowered the clipboard he was holding, looking around at the gathering of concerned people. "If, ah, if you and... Samantha? If you two would like to stay, that would be great. The rest of you – well, until the detective decides whether or not to speak with you, you may as well go home."

"Of course," The Professor nodded. "I'll leave my number with Jason and Samantha if the police need to reach me." He hastily scribbled his office number onto a couple scraps of paper and handed them to Jason and Samantha, shooting a look to his primary time travel agent. "I'll make sure these two get home," he said, indicating Suki and Brianna.

All the adults nodded, and after Suki and Brianna had also left their phone numbers with Jason, they exited the hospital, having hugged Samantha and told her to stay strong.

Samantha sat, teary-eyed, staring into the middle distance. She was crushed, and somehow had begun to feel as if all of this was her fault. She absent-mindedly unclenched her fist, which was holding the piece of paper Professor Smythe had given her. She unfolded it and looked at it. It was more than just his office phone number. She read it to herself, wiping her nose and trying to focus.

S. - DO NOT mention anything about Jordan or T. Travel to the police. We will figure out how to fix this, I swear. Destroy this note.

For a second she was angry. Wasn't The Professor in over his head here? Her mother was in a coma! Maybe the police *should* be involved... but then she began to realize things. Even if they believed her story, the police would raid The Professor's labs, find the time machine and then... what? The F.B.I. would be called in, the government would seal off the basement of the museum and... no, Professor Smythe was right. They had to try something else. She got up and went to the bathroom, ripped his note into tiny shreds and sobbed as she flushed them down the toilet.

The Professor's office was a busy headquarters once again. He had done his best to indicate an innocent, work-based relationship with Cindy Smart to the police detective, though he was now in constant fear of being under surveillance. He and Marvin had basically scrubbed his computer of any suspicious files and had transferred the massive amounts of time travel information onto flash drives, which The Professor now kept in a locked briefcase that he carried at all times. He was still very nervous, though, when Samantha returned to visit after three days at the hospital, and always locked his office doors now.

Samantha looked as exhausted as the rest of them, if not more so. None of them had slept more than a few hours a night since Cindy had collapsed, but at last Jason had had to go home for a day and had agreed to drop Samantha at the museum under the pretext that she and The Professor were researching natural toxins.

In fact, this was one of the things the group had been doing. The Professor rolled his desk chair back, turning the computer console over to a bleary-eyed Marvin, and began to detail what he could of the situation to Samantha.

"Hello, Samantha. You look tired – have you slept?"

"A little," she replied.

"None of us have, hardly," he went on. "I want to fill you in on what I can, though." Samantha nodded.

"We've got some stuff to show you," Marvin said, bringing up things on the computer screen.

"Of course," The Professor began, "the first thing we tried was the most obvious – you recall I told you in one of our brief communicator talks that we tried to send Marvin back to Irving Plaza, before this happened."

"Yeah," Samantha nodded.

"Well, let us show you why this didn't work. Marvin?" Marvin opened a file on the computer and a three-dimensional image popped up of a building, with bright points highlighted in several spots – floor, walls, ceiling. "Irving Plaza, that is to say, the building itself, has been, well, time-travel-proofed, from a point in time about eighteen hours before you all arrived there. These points you see," he indicated the bright spots, "are some kind of devices that stabilize the space-time continuum to an impenetrable degree, at least to our means of manipulating it. In other words, we can't insert anyone into this area, at that time."

"Can you get anyone in before then?" Samantha asked hopefully.

"We tried that as well," The Professor shook his head. "We sent Suki back, reluctantly, eighteen hours before and tried to have her wait until the show and get in from there, but this failed as well." He looked over at Suki.

"I went, Samantha, I... got in. I saw all of you standing in line, but Professor Smythe told me not to let you notice me. I was on time and everything, but when I walked through the doors of the building, well... the show was over already. Everyone was mostly gone. I can't explain it." She looked back at The Professor.

"Nor can I," the tired-looking man sighed. "It seems our enemies have been getting smarter – figuring out time travel faster than we are. I daresay they have resources that can far outpace ours. They have somehow found a way to completely isolate a segment of space-time, so that anyone or anything that tries to enter it just shoots instantly to its other side, *around* it, but not *through* it. It's terribly frustrating."

"But – what about my *mom*, Professor!? She's still in a coma! They can't figure out what sort of – poison is in her body, and they keep asking Jason and I if she was ever involved in espionage, if we're sure she wasn't a target of some ninja assassin group!" She took a deep breath. "My brother is staying at my Aunt Tina's house in Queens, where I guess I'm going too, if I don't go back to the hospital. Jason's picking me up here in a couple of hours."

"I'm sorry, Samantha. I know this is hard, and we're doing everything we can think of. There is some good news on a couple of fronts."

"What!?" Samantha blurted out in exasperation.

"Well," Marvin cut in, giving The Professor a chance to breathe. "We've isolated the toxin." He brought up another computer display, this time of chemical compounds laid out in 3-D molecular structures.

"We got a sample from the dart," Brianna said. "I had to go back for that one, when your mom was being put into the ambulance on a stretcher. Almost ran into myself, but they got me out in time."

Samantha looked around at her friends. Apparently they had all been taking greater risks with time travel than The Professor had previously allowed.

"It's all right," Smythe came back to the discussion. "I know what you're thinking, but I'm fairly certain we've avoided any major temporal catastrophes.

"The toxin is organic. It comes from a floating, water-lily-type plant that only ever grew on the Yucatan Peninsula – not far from where we dug up the time machine, actually, but I think this is merely coincidence. Unfortunately, its only possible antidote would have to be derived from the same sort of plant, and it's been extinct for close to a thousand years."

Samantha frowned, mentally following the complications.

"Of course, we shall be forced to go back and retrieve some if we hope to revive your mother from her coma."

"So... what are we waiting for?" Samantha almost snapped. She felt instantly childish for doing so, but everyone seemed to forgive her short temper, considering the circumstances.

"Well," The Professor sighed, leaning back in his chair, "consider this: One, we've never tried to travel this far through time *or* space before. Two, we don't know for sure if the communicators will work. Three, I still don't work the time machine like an expert, though I must say I have improved. Four, we definitely need to do a bit more botanical research to make sure we'd send someone to exactly the right area, and with enough knowledge that they could positively identify our desired plant and harvest enough of it so we could extract an antidote successfully. And *five...*"

"Yeah? Five?" Samantha was still impatient.

"Well, five, it smells like a trap, Samantha. Think about it," The Professor folded his hands in his lap and tried to appeal to her rational side. "Our enemies have orchestrated a situation that they know we can only remedy in one way. I assure you, they know exactly what we're trying to do right now, and they *want* us to do it. I don't know why; I'm still trying to put all of our experiences together in a way that might define our enemies' motivations more clearly, but so far it's still fuzzy. Yes, they either want lots of plant life to disappear or the ice caps to melt, or both. But I still haven't the foggiest idea why – Vassily Slane's investments don't explain it, at least not the ones we know of. And Jordan seems more and more to me like just a pawn in the game – I don't know.

"What is obvious at the moment is that they want us in a certain place and time, perhaps to effect something that they can't, directly, as before. I am fairly sure that we have at least one advantage over them: I believe that whatever method of time travel they possess is somehow... incomplete, compared to ours. We can touch and directly physically interact with people and things in other times; they cannot.

"If I had to take a guess, I'd say that they're using a somewhat poorly duplicated copy of our time machine. Perhaps they've built their own from some – some incomplete ancient text that they possess, some half-rotted or insufficiently translated blueprint scroll or clay tablet. One thing is certain, though: whatever their purpose, whatever their motives, plans, means or capabilities, they know full well now that we are out here, working against them. And believe me, not a day goes by that I don't fear them finding out for sure where *our* time machine is, and coming here to take it. Pestering Paradoxes! They might even be able to just send in a spy who could somehow steal whatever secrets they're missing, without even needing to take the thing itself!" The Professor was becoming almost crazed in a paranoid, sleep-deprived way.

"Okay," Samantha said, taking the role of the calm one. "So we have to play along if I want to get my mom out of a coma. What do we do? I'm ready, whatever it is."

"Right," The Professor replied, calming. "Thank you, Samantha – I know this has been harder on you than any of us."

"We're all here for you, Samantha," Suki put in with genuine concern in her eyes. Everyone in the room agreed.

"Thanks, you guys," Samantha almost sobbed, looking around and feeling happy, for a moment, that she was lucky enough to have such good friends. "And thanks so much for taking care of Polly, Bree." Brianna had been feeding and walking her dog for her since she'd been at the hospital.

"Well," The Professor began again, "we need to plan a group mission. I would include myself in this but I fear the police may want to be in steady contact with me and I doubt any of you could properly work the time machine's controls. I'm afraid I must once again resign myself to desk duty. I will, of course, maintain constant communication with you all, and will do my best as well to follow up on our other lead."

"Our other lead?" Samantha raised an eyebrow.

"We're getting close to finding the Slanes," Marvin offered. "Brianna's mission at the show did set us up with some pretty dope info..."

"What our urban poet is trying to say," Smythe translated, "is that we've traced an email that Jordan received on that laptop of his. So far we've followed it back through Los Angeles to the Philippines and then to Guam. We feel it originated out in The Pacific somewhere, most likely from a boat of some sort."

"Oh – wow. So... what does that mean?"

"Well, it means we might be able to figure out where the Slanes are operating from. That would be a decided advantage for us as, despite my paranoia, I do believe that had the Slanes figured out a way to penetrate the sanctity of this building, they would have done so by now."

"They have to know that the time machine is here," Marvin concluded.

"Agreed." The Professor nodded. "They know, at least, that Samantha, Marvin and myself have traveled through time, and have devised their own missions to intercept us or attempt to cause us to change history. I am certain that they are watching this place."

"Then why haven't they tried anything here?" Samantha asked, confused.

"I've been wondering that myself for a long time now," Smythe scratched his whiskered chin. "And I've been studying possible answers to that question. What I've concluded is this: The time machine itself must have something to do with it. As you'll recall, Samantha, the better part of a week that you and I spent in an altered timeline, the area immediately surrounding the time machine, including this office, seemed to remain somehow unaffected. You and I were aware that we were living in an... improper reality, but all of my notes were intact, as I had made them weeks before. My office phone number was the same – "

"The books," Samantha put in.

"Eh? What's that?"

"The books," Samantha repeated. "Remember, we couldn't find Elliott Bergen on the computer network, so we looked him up in your books. We found him noted in a book in your office, and he wasn't ever born, in that timeline."

"Precisely," Professor Smythe replied. "We exist, here, in some sort of bubble, some sort of neutral pocket in time. I haven't been able to establish exactly how far it extends, but I believe that for some reason it is this bubble that our enemies cannot breech. Truly fascinating but, alas, still a mystery to me."

"Don't look a gift horse in the mouth," Suki smiled, pleased with herself to have correctly used a rural western expression.

"And we shan't," The Professor smiled back, looking very tired. "Nonetheless, if we can pinpoint where the Slanes are based out of, we may be able to throw a wrench into the gears of their time-traveling operations."

"And yo, we got homie's password, too," Marvin grinned in his devious hacker's way.

"His password?" Samantha asked, suddenly intensely curious.

"Yup. That little device Brianna planted did its job real good. We can check his email right now if we want."

"Well," The Professor spoke, "I wouldn't count on that."

"No, me either," Brianna agreed. "I'm sure Jordan found that thing when he unplugged his computer. He's probably changed all his information by now."

Samantha frowned. *One step forward, two steps back,* she thought.

"We did get something, though," The Professor acknowledged. "The email we intercepted detailed the plan to target your mother, Samantha. They are clearly trying to draw us into a trap, or at least into performing some other history-altering action on their behalf. Whatever mission we devise to secure the antidote for Cindy's poisoned state, we *must* keep this in mind. I've already begun researching the area and time period we will need to access, i.e. the Yucatan Peninsula sometime before the tenth century A.D. I will continue to keep my mind open to other possible effects of entering this time period and try to plan around not disturbing anything too important.

"We will plan a time when everyone can go. I've mastered the time machine enough so that I am reasonably confident of my ability to get you there and back within an hour, so no one will become too suspicious of your absence. This will be strange, as you may spend many hours or days in the past, during which I will be in constant contact with you. However, I shall 're-insert' you back into the present less than an hour after you've left. Hence, I will probably not remember any conversations we've had beyond that hour, as they won't technically have happened yet. Though I suppose that bringing you back early will change the future, it shouldn't matter as you will already have the required plant."

Marvin sat scratching his head. The others looked equally

perplexed by these complicated conundrums of time, and their confusion was augmented by their general lack of sleep. The Professor sensed their difficulty in understanding and attempted to simplify his explanations.

"All, right, look," he summarized. "I'll send you all back, and you'll be back in the present less than an hour after you left. Just remember that upon your return, I will not remember any of the conversations we've had via communicator, except those that took place within one hour of your being gone. Does that make sense?" Everyone nodded.

"Good. Then when can we meet? I'll need at least two days to do the necessary research. Suki and Marvin, I'd appreciate your help in the lab here as well, if you can spare some time in the next couple of days."

"Okay," Suki nodded. "I'll just tell my mom it's more study group stuff."

"Hey, Dr, Marvy's on call, y'all," Marvin assented. It seemed that, as a boy (and one who did well in school despite his 'rebel rapper' image), his parental rules were a lot more relaxed.

"Samantha, Brianna, see if you two can come here, say, Friday afternoon, after school or – I know you've mostly been at the hospital, Samantha – when you can. Can we say we'll try for Friday at four?"

"All right," Samantha nodded, adding "please, Professor, we need to bring my mom back."

The Professor nodded solemnly, wordlessly promising to do his very best.

*

The next few days were very hard for Samantha. She missed being in school, the learning about other cultures and scientific properties and such, even just the social distraction. She spent most of her time at the hospital, reading magazine articles aloud to her mother, hoping somewhere inside that she could hear them. Jason was there as much as time allowed, and Samantha was beginning to develop a deep respect for him; it was obvious that he really, genuinely cared about her mom. *It must be weird,* she thought, *having to go through something like this with someone you've only been seeing for a week or two.*

Todd was there a lot too, and their mother's sister Tina. Samantha had begun staying with their aunt as well, after an initial few days of falling asleep in the chair in her mother's hospital room. It was all really strange, even for Todd, who seemed agitated and out of sorts, though he attempted to maintain a facade of cool, teenaged detachment. At least it had been nice to be able to be with Polly again – there was no friend in times of trouble like a loyal, canine one, and Polly had gently licked her tears away the past few nights as she cried herself to sleep. In some ways, she had wanted to tell Todd the truth about what was really going on; Cindy was his mom too, and she often thought that he deserved to know. But logic insisted that he probably wouldn't believe her story anyway, that she was lying or just totally crazy, cracking up from the stress of the situation.

The doctors were still mystified, though they had been in touch with Professor Smythe. He had actually given them his information, in hopes that by some small chance they could artificially synthesize some kind of antidote, but so far nothing solid had been accomplished to that end. Samantha sighed in her hospital chair, realizing that once again, The Professor was probably correct in his judgement that for an antidote to be created, a sample of the plant which had produced the poison would have to be acquired. It looked like her career as a time-traveler was far from over.

The police, too, had been in contact with The Professor. He had given them the same information that he'd given to the hospital, though had understandably withheld any further knowledge that he possessed relating to the situation. There was, Samantha was beginning to realize, a real chance that the government could pierce their bubble of secrecy and infiltrate it, seal off the museum and exploit the site like some alien crash-landing area in a science fiction movie. Would she ever speak to her mother again if this was to happen? She didn't think so.

She had arranged for Jason to bring her to the museum at four, it being Friday now, almost an entire week that her mother had been in a coma. Todd and Aunt Tina had actually expressed interest in coming with her, as her explanation for going had been that she was helping Professor Smythe research the toxin that trickled ever-so-slowly through Cindy's nervous system. Reluctantly, they had agreed to let her go alone after she fabricated a story about The Professor being a very reclusive man who didn't function well around people that he didn't already know. It had finally been agreed that Aunt Tina would pick her up at seven at the museum, and that afterward they would all have dinner together somewhere.

Jason was at the hospital at three and escorted Samantha out to the waiting car service car, kissing Cindy's forehead before they left and making sure that Tina and Todd were okay. Samantha decided that he was a very good man despite his simple, sometimes immature behavior and made a mental note to try really hard to keep him and her mother together. The car ride was mostly silent, though he too expressed an interest in accompanying her to The Professor's labs, hoping to be of help in some way. Samantha looked at him after giving him the same story she had told her family and smiled slightly through her tears, which welled up frequently in the past week. Yes, he was possibly a keeper.

She waved goodbye to Jason from the steps of the museum, having thanked him profusely for having been so concerned about her mom and for being there for her as well. It was a particularly cold night, and she tried to search her memory for a feeling of warmth that she'd had as she'd stood on the same stairs in the altered reality.

The Professor's office was once again a lively center of activity. All her friends were, once again, already there and had apparently been being briefed on the details of their mission by the aging, many-degreed Englishman. They all hugged her as she entered, even the stoic 'Dr. Marvy.' She felt good.

"Everything's ready Samantha," The Professor began. "Suki, Marvin and I have been planning the mission details for days. We've even constructed more wrist-communicators so that everyone will have one now."

"Thank you all so much," Samantha spoke quietly, trying to hold back tears. "It really means a lot to me."

"I need only relate a few things to you, as I have already to the rest of the team. Please listen carefully, for these things are very important, though they may seem trivial." He cleared his throat. " Do not touch anything, speak to anyone or in any way interact with the environment around you unless it is absolutely necessary. This means life or death, or mission failure. We have supplied the team with food and water enough to last for three days. If you cannot complete your mission within this time, you *must* return nonetheless to our present time. No exceptions." Samantha nodded, swallowing gravely. " Do not eat or drink anything from your surroundings; this is truly the distant past, and doing so will most likely result in violent illness for one or all members of your party.

"Be invisible if at all possible. Your mission, though it may seem a simple one of gathering samples, should not in any way affect the existence of other plants, animals or especially human beings you may inadvertently come in contact with. This is of the utmost importance.

"Do not camp where you might be noticed. Do not dally in distractions that may pique your interest; you have but one primary mission and your only other function should be to absolutely minimize any possible effect you could have on the ancient world around you. Remember, even a chance encounter with a harmless-seeming native could result in none of us ever being born."

The friends all looked at each other, feeling almost as if they were some adult team of astronauts about to fly into the sun. Clearly, this was serious stuff.

"Finally," The Professor concluded, "make sure you've got the *right plant.* I've given Marvin and Brianna palm computers detailing the plant's visual, textural and olfactory, that is, scent characteristics. Brianna also has the little chemical testing kit I whipped up. Performing the chemical test should be fairly elementary, nothing beyond what any of you have had in school. And I know you're all very bright," The Professor cracked a smile. "I can't think of any team I'd rather be sending to perform this task. Just *please* be careful." He patted Marvin on the back and then indicated that they should follow him to the time machine room.

*

The time machine was as awesome as ever. Everyone had now experienced its effects, and all had consequently developed a healthy respect for the megalithic construction of some ancient pre-Mayans. The Professor had managed to duplicate the original stick of 'chalk' through painful research and questionable materials requisitions that he had submitted through the museum, giving them each their own hunk of the mysterious compound. He had also seemingly refined his knowledge of the device's controls, and now manned them with a much more reassuring air of confidence. In a short time, the party found themselves clustered together atop the machine's stone platform, fingers crossed for good luck.

It began. Once again, the world turned an electric blue and started to flicker. Incomprehensible symbols flashed through the minds of the would-be adventurers, dancing like fireflies on the insides of their eyelids. Reality seemed to ripple, like the spot on the surface of a pond where someone had just tossed a pebble – it was entirely surreal. Samantha and the others stared at their feet, trying to focus, trying to ground themselves in some awareness that they *did* exist, that they were real things, standing on solid earth. It was difficult.

Again, as before, it was over in an instant. The friends looked around, trying to get their bearings. They were standing in the middle of a desert area, with nothing but wide-open space around them. The edge of some encroaching jungle could be seen in the distance, the only interruption in an otherwise perfectly flat, dusty horizon. They turned to look at each other and almost simultaneously remembered the necessity of the chalk. Fortunately, perhaps, they had appeared on a plateau of rock, so it was easy to trace their footprints on the hard surface. Samantha wondered for a moment what would have happened if they'd appeared directly on the plain of sand, or even (heaven forbid) on the surface of a lake or river. She shivered at the thought of it as she dutifully traced her feet on the floor of thousand-year-old stone.

"Yo, that was, once again, *criz-azy*," M.C. Marvin piped up, always the smiling, willing adventurer.

"I feel like I'm going to puke," Brianna added sincerely.

"Time travel sure is, well, dizzying," Suki put in. "It feels kind of like being on a roller-coaster without actually moving."

"Word," Marvin agreed.

"Well, it looks like we made it to somewhere resembling the right place," Samantha opined, looking around at the arid landscape. There were some small desert plants in evidence, but the information they had suggested that the one they were looking for would most likely be found in a moister, more forested area.

"I guess we should head for that jungle over there," Marvin said, a little unsure of himself. "At least, I think there's more of a chance that we'll find our sample in there." The others agreed and the group began marching toward the ominous-looking horizon of dense trees and undergrowth, shrugging their backpacks higher onto their shoulders.

The company had brought a good amount of supplies with them, three days worth of food and water, a large, four-man tent and plenty of matches with which to build fires. It was, however, quite warm, being (theoretically) Central America, and no one was worried about freezing overnight. Their other supplies included sleeping bags, a few compact pots and pans and the various scientific equipment The Professor had given them: palm computers containing relevant information, the chemical analysis kit that Brianna carried and other small, useful items such as flashlights, fifty feet of strong nylon rope, razor blades and of course, duct tape. One never knew when such things would come in handy. They also each carried a high-voltage stun gun, in case they needed to protect themselves. The legality of anyone their age possessing the latter was questionable, but Marvin had come through again, finding a way to procure some from some street acquaintance or another, with Professor Smythe's money.

It was a pity, Samantha thought, that they had been forbidden to bring any sort of camera or sound-recording device. The ancient landscape was truly wild and very beautiful; even the sparse desert they trudged through now was abuzz with the minute details of life that could hardly be documented earnestly in the twenty-first century. The jungle they marched toward, she imagined, would be even more filled with the sights and sounds of a world forever lost to naturalists of the modern era, and the budding scientist within her lamented the lost opportunity to capture the essence of what they experienced on video or audio.

The sun became hot on their backs as they walked. Even after only twenty minutes, everyone was sweating and trying not to break into their supply of water. The line where desert met jungle had initially seemed not so distant, but it quickly became evident that the trees that defined it were much larger than they had originally presumed, and that their chosen destination was in fact rather some miles away. Within the first hour, though, they were aware of their wrist-communicators crackling.

"Hello?" The Professor's voice came through, weak and staticky but understandable. "Alpha Team, are you there?" He had given their group a catchy code name and seemed determined to use it.

"Yes," Samantha replied, tapping the talk button on her unit. "We're here, Professor. All's well, I suppose. We're sort of in the middle of a desert, but we're heading for a wall of jungle about three or four miles away."

"Oh, so that's," The Professor converted, " six or eight kilometers. Good for you, then, agents! You're on the right track. The plant you're looking for is called, if you'll recall, *Phylathimus Phylathum.* It supposedly grew in small ponds of brackish water, usually in the same area that trees with hanging moss would be found."

"We'll keep that in mind," Samantha spoke back, wiping sweat from her brow and staring at the powerful sun. *No wonder these people worshiped the sun so much,* she thought to herself.

"Very good," The Professor continued, sounding as if he was having trouble receiving them clearly. "We shall try to keep radio contact to a minimum unless something crucial is happening. I'm having trouble tuning you in perfectly; the time distortion to the signal is considerable. Also, if you hear any beeps like this," the wrist-communicator beeped, "*Do Not,* I repeat, *Do Not* contact me until I contact you. This is in case there are any police or federal agents who may enter my office while you're away."

"Roger that," Samantha replied. It seemed that, whether because of her slightly more extensive time-travel experience or her close personal involvement with the mission's outcome, she had become the team's de facto leader. Surprisingly, she decided that this role suited her fine.

"One more thing," the crackly voice intoned.

"Go ahead, Professor."

"Unless you need them to talk to each other, keep all of your wrist-communicators switched off, excepting one. Rotate which one is left on, if you can. This will save battery power."

"Got it," Samantha acknowledged, signaling to the others, who had all heard, to switch off their units.

"Very well, Samantha. Marvin, Brianna, Suki – good luck. Smythe out."

"Alpha Team out," Samantha cringed as she absent-mindedly spoke the cheesy code name.

"Why do we have to be 'Alpha Team'?" Marvin voiced the question everyone had wanted to ask while they snickered quietly.

"Well," Samantha guessed, smiling for the first time in what seemed like a week, "I suppose The Professor thinks it's safer if we don't use any of our names, though," she giggled, "I don't particularly like his group designation, either. Got a better name, Dr. Marvy?"

"You know it," Marvin rose to the challenge as they hoofed along through the ancient desert. "How about 'The Tasty T.T. Posse'? Or 'The Fly Travelin' Crew'?" Everyone laughed good-naturedly.

"That is the stupidest name I've ever heard," Brianna chuckled.

"Well, what then?" Marvin began a gestural dance of mock

agitation. "What you got for us, Buttermilk?"

"*Buttermilk?*" Brianna raised an eyebrow. "*Please.* Talk to the hand." She stretched out her arm to block her view of the clownish friend's act.

"What about 'Kitty Troop?'" Suki asked quietly but hopefully.

"Aw, man!" Marvin slapped his hand to his forehead. "Somebody call the *Dork Police!*" Suki pouted and frowned at him.

"Look, it's certainly not by any means the most important thing for us to worry about right now," Samantha refereed. "Let's just try to focus on getting to that jungle over there."

*

After half a day of walking, the group found themselves coming up against the wall of vegetation that formed the edge of the jungle. They had begun to feel humbled by its vast, dark mass as they approached it; some of the trees that stuck through the top of the rainforest's canopy were at least two hundred feet tall, and everyone's eyes strained to see anything that might serve as some sort of traversable path through the dense undergrowth of the forest's floor. They also wondered if they should just camp where they were for the night; the sun was rapidly sinking and they began to think they might prefer the relatively obvious dangers of desert snakes and scorpions to the unknown and surely more numerous threats of the thick, noise-filled jungle.

Despite their fears, they decided to push onward. They still had at least two or three hours of light left in the day, dim as it was once they entered the forest.

"We forgot to bring a machete," Marvin noted with frustration as they struggled through ferns that came almost up to their necks. The going was a lot slower than they had expected, and bushwhacking was taking its toll on the less than tough members of the party.

"This is absolutely *awful,*" Brianna moaned, pouting and making a fearful expression as she pulled a palm-sized beetle off of her shirt. "I'm sorry, there are just *way* too many bugs in here, it's totally *gross.*

And the humidity, *Gawd*! Look – just look at my hair, Samantha! I look like, like *The Bride of Frankenstein* or something!"

Samantha couldn't help but giggle. Everyone's hair was pretty frizzed-out by the humid weather, except for Suki's. Brianna looked as if she felt pretty miserable, but so was everyone else, and they weren't complaining. It wasn't long before the pampered princess learned that her complaints, also, were already assumed, and therefore vocalizing them was both unnecessary and unwelcome as the party schlepped along. Still, she pouted a lot and made sounds of being grossed-out by bugs, spiders, snakes, mud and the other hundred or so things in the jungle that could make someone squeamish.

Thankfully, about a half-mile into the bush, they came upon a little creek that they could follow and so wouldn't have to bushwhack as much. As much as they had wanted to follow it upstream, probably to rock formations and more solid footing, they were advised via wrist-communicator to head in the opposite direction. *Phylathimus Phylathum* would most likely be found in standing water, Professor Smythe reminded them, and standing water would most likely be found downstream. It was with little enthusiasm that they followed The Professor's instructions, for the path became wetter on their feet and the clouds of gnats, mosquitos and some tropical equivalent of giant blackflies became thicker and more frequent as they went.

Luckily, they were prepared to some degree for these conditions. Having anticipated the type of terrain their target plant would be found in, The Professor had equipped them with heavy rubber boots and some industrial-strength bug repellent that he'd whipped up himself in the lab. The stuff smelled absolutely disgusting, and Brianna refused to put it on – until it was discovered how well it worked. Then she sensibly submitted to the stench in preference to the hundreds of welts the bugs surely would have given her.

To distract herself from various discomforts, Brianna periodically checked her palm computer against the backdrop of flora around her, trying in vain to identify the correct plant. In fact, the picture she had of it on the miniature screen was actually only a very good computer simulation, not a photograph at all. Of course, this was understandable as the plant in question had become extinct some eight hundred years before the invention of the camera. Still, it made the matching game more difficult, and Brianna was frustrated. To make matters worse, it was getting quite dark.

Samantha found a clearing of relatively dry ground, and the group made ready to pitch their tent. They piled handfuls of long grass over the root-infested earth, trying to create a softer bed, and then put their tent up on top of it. They smeared a good bit of The Professor's bug repellent all over the outside, and Marvin began attempting to build something like a fire. It certainly wasn't cold, and the food they'd brought didn't need to be cooked, but the fire was comforting in the strange, wild jungle and the team agreed that it would probably help to keep away any predatory beasts that might be sniffing about for a meal of Samantha steak or filet of Suki.

"You know," Brianna said, chewing on a piece of dried apricot, "this is the most pleasurable thing I've done all day." She looked satisfyingly at the remaining piece of fruit in her hand as she sat on a large, round stone. "Thanks, Suki."

Suki had been in charge of stocking the mission's food supplies, and had tried her hardest to balance out nutrition, taste, non-perishable qualities and space-savers. The resulting selection of rations was mostly dried fruit and nuts, cereals, meat jerky and a wee bit of smoked salmon. Everyone echoed Brianna's thanks as they each nibbled on some snack or another.

The night became thick and felt like it was closing in all around them. It seemed somehow almost hotter than it had during the day, and the multitude of noises that came from outside their tent made their imaginations run wild. The three girls had zipped their sleeping bags together and huddled in one corner of the tent, which for no logical reason they had decided was the safest one. Marvin stayed outside and stoked his fire, which was indeed *his* fire – he was very proud of it, and rightly so. To have gotten anything to burn in this half-jungle, half-swamp was an accomplishment indeed. He tried to build it up enough so that it would burn slowly through the night, though he soon decided that he was hardly even tired, and would probably stay awake for a while anyway. When he informed the girls of his insomnia, they breathed a sigh of relief and fell promptly asleep, reassured that a strong male would be awake and guarding them, as it were. Still, Samantha asked to be woken up when he did get to feeling tired and agreed to take the next watch. Marvin nodded and zipped them into the tent.

For at least half an hour he sat, staring into the deep darkness of the noisy jungle and imagining he saw jet black panthers leaping at him or shiny black cobras slithering into his little ring of firelight. In truth, the only real wildlife that invaded his sphere was an occasional bat, sometimes large ones which made him wonder if they could be vampire bats – they were, after all, carnivorous and would probably be attracted by the heat of the fire. Everything else, however, seemed to have a healthy respect for the flame and stayed well enough away. This made Marvin happy.

He decided after a while to buzz The Professor on his wrist-communicator.

"Dr. Marvy pagin' Professor Smooth-move," Marvin giggled into his wrist.

"I say, what was that, Marvin?" a voice came back.

"Nothin'. What up?"

"Well, no more police yet. How goes the hunt for *Phylathimus Phylathum*?"

"Nothin' new. We're camped for the night. I'm on watch and the girls are all sleeping."

"I see. You haven't had any serious trouble with animals or anything, have you?"

"Not really," Marvin shrugged. "Lots of sounds out there, though. You know, Professor, I think you did the right thing putting Brianna in charge of looking for the plant." He chuckled to himself. "I don't think anyone wants to get out of this swampy fly-trap faster than she does."

"I suspected as much," Smythe replied, probably smiling though Marvin had no way of knowing. "Well, if there's nothing else, I'm going to get back to my work. I need to at least keep up the appearance of being the bumbling old academic, you know. And you, young 'Dr. Marvy,' should turn off your communicator and save batteries."

"Okay, Prof," Marvin sighed. "Alf-alpha team out."

"That's *Alpha* Team, Marvin. Smythe out."

"Whatever," Marvin mumbled, switching off his unit.

*

Morning in the jungle was the noisiest time of day. Everything that could chirp, creep, croak or screech felt the imperative need to do so. Suki was on watch, Marvin having woke her after his attempts to rouse Samantha failed utterly. It was understandable. The poor girl's mother had been in a coma for a week and she had hardly slept a wink in all that time. Suki actually felt oddly at home in the jungle. It was weird because she, like the others, had spent pretty much her entire life in huge, bustling cities. There was something peaceful about it despite its noisiness – it wasn't noisy like the city. She got up and threw some more thick grass on the fire; it made huge billows of thick, white smoke, which was a little annoying though it certainly did a good job of keeping the bugs away.

"Aaaaaaaaaaaaahhhhhhhhh!" A scream that sounded like Brianna woke up every snail that might have still been sleeping. In a flash, everyone was up and out of the tent. Brianna was jumping up and down and pointing at their giant, three-part sleeping bag.

"There's a – a," she stuttered. "There's a s-s-s-,"

"A *what*!?" Samantha yelled.

"A snake!"

"Oh, dear," said Suki.

Marvin shook his head, wishing he could've slept a bit more and went to pick up a somewhat long stick. This he used to poke around in the sleeping bag while Brianna and Suki made sounds of fear. Samantha didn't seem so terrified. Sure enough, a long, shiny black snake appeared.

"Oooohhhh, there he is," Marvin said. "He looks poisonous." This was obviously the wrong thing to say, as it caused the two shrieking girls to dart away from the tent and make even more noise. He poked at the snake, trying to coax it out of the tent. It was very fast. Suddenly, it found the door and slithered out with astonishing quickness, heading straight for the girls. With lightning speed, Marvin brought the stick down on top of it with a mighty *whack,* and it spasmed up into the air and then came down again onto the ground. It appeared to be dead.

"Wow," Samantha stared. "Good work, Marvin." Marvin grinned.

Suki and Brianna breathed a massive sigh of relief. They stood, paralyzed, for a moment, then burst into chatter.

"Oh, my *Gawd!*" Brianna squeaked. "Let's get this stupid plant and get out of here!"

"Yeah," Suki agreed. "I'm with Bree."

"Did you *see* that, Samantha!?"

Samantha nodded. The snake no longer showed any signs of moving.

They cautiously pulled out all their things from the tent, checking for any other critters that might have somehow snuck in during the night but finding none. They detached their sleeping bags and rolled them up, packed up backpacks and pulled on their rubber boots. In fifteen minutes or so, they were ready to go.

"I think we should keep following the creek downstream," Samantha directed, starting to walk that way. "Brianna, stay on that palm computer and let us know if you see anything that looks like a good match. Brianna nodded and pulled out the little hand-held device, fumbling a bit with it. She was still visibly shaken.

The group moved along at a brisk pace, everyone feeling decidedly awake after their harrowing morning experience with the unwelcome reptile. The terrain became more and more swampy as they went, and they all began to appreciate their rubber boots more and more as the creek they had been following dissolved into a puddle-strewn marsh. Brianna became excited when they began to see trees with hanging, "Spanish" moss, which was supposed to be a sign of the preferred environment of *Phylathimus Phylathum,* according to Professor Smythe. After an hour or two of further penetration into the thickest part of the marsh, she spied something next to a tree root that greatly resembled their object of desire.

"Look," Brianna indicated the stubby, bulbous plant. "What do you guys think?" The team gathered around and shifted their gazes back and forth between the plant and the palm computer's digital simulation of what they were looking for. The two seemed promisingly similar in appearance. With the others' approval, Brianna unpacked the little chemical test kit The Professor had entrusted her with. It was a fairly simple apparatus; one only needed to clip a small piece of the plant in question, place it in a jar and add two chemicals to it. Brianna performed the operations dutifully, and after a tense ten minutes they had their answer. The mixture turned a deep purple. If The Professor's notions of chemistry were sound, this was indeed *Phylathimus Phylathum.*

The team commenced harvesting as many samples of the plant as they could, placing them in the plastic containers The Professor had supplied them with for just such a purpose. They all felt a deep sense of relief as they collected the plants; perhaps their mission was not to be so difficult as all that. All that remained between them and home was a day's trek through jungle and desert back to where they had arrived in this time. They gathered together around a last patch of the curious plant and optimistically clipped its leaves, stem and even its roots into a final container, smiling and chatting cheerfully with each other.

"I am *so* taking a bubble bath when I get home," Brianna shared.

"That sounds really good," Samantha thought out loud, her closed eyes and imagination transporting her back to the tub in her Brooklyn home.

"Ya know," Marvin stopped to think for a moment. "I should've brought Flacko along. I think he would've really liked it here."

"I think he would've liked it a little too much," Suki offered.

"Yeah, he probably would've flown off into the jungle looking for other parrots or something," Brianna agreed.

"No way, Jose!" Marvin defended his pet. "Flacko's smarter than that. He'd come back. He's loyal, too – way more loyal than a human friend."

"I'm pretty loyal, I think," Samantha shrugged. They were almost done collecting all the plant's parts. They had to get all of them, including its long, veiny roots that stretched several feet outward under the water, because they weren't sure exactly what part The Professor would need to extract the maximum amount of 'antidote.'

"Yeah," Marvin continued his rant on loyalty, "but how loyal are you, Samantha? I mean, one week you drink Coke, the next you drink Pepsi. One month you only want to listen to Heatwavvve and the next it's all Britney – "

The last word of Marvin's sentence was eerily timed, as at once, they all looked up to find themselves surrounded by several small, brownish men who were pointing long, metal-tipped wooden sticks at them menacingly.

"...Spears," Marvin concluded, swallowing hard.

*

Alpha Team marched along through the swamp, hands bound behind their backs with tough, scratchy vines. The natives had, at least, apparently decided not to kill them immediately, which was a very good thing of course, though not all that comforting. They might indeed still be in for some gruesome deaths, worse even perhaps than spear-point. They seemed to have one thing going for them – the little, light-brown men were fascinated by the girls' appearance. They had, possibly, only seen an Asian person once in one of their families' histories, and had probably never seen Caucasian people at all. The general feeling the girls got was that they might somehow be being regarded as 'witches.' The men kept them at a spear's distance from themselves, except for one, who was much more covered in body and face paint than the others and who kept shaking some sort of powder at them. He seemed to be their witch-doctor or holy nan, someone with spiritual authority among these people. Whatever his function or intentions, the girls did their best to hold their breath and not inhale any of his strange jungle powder.

Marvin they almost totally ignored. He looked enough like one of them that he most likely wasn't a warlock or a god, and it seemed that they probably perceived him to be a servant of the girls. As if it hadn't been bad enough dealing with Brianna's complaints, sleeping alone in a far corner of the tent and saving them all from snakes, he now had to suffer the disgrace of being viewed as 'servant boy,' even though he was at least two years older than any of them. There would have to be major payback for this, he decided, if they lived.

They marched for what seemed like hours, the marsh eventually turning back to jungle and the jungle in turn giving way to a sandy beach. *This,* Samantha recalled her geography lessons, *must be the Gulf Of Mexico.* It was indeed a vast body of water, stretching all the way to the horizon and displaying no farther shore. The group turned right at the shoreline, which was probably south, and continued along for at least another hour. Samantha guessed it was early afternoon when the shore began rising up into rocky cliffs, making their trek a more athletic one, and the team began to sweat as their feet found the difficult uphill trail.

The view, however, became spectacular. The Gulf, if that was what it was, shone with an intense, magical blue in the powerful afternoon sun. Looking out on it from atop the cliffs was truly exhilarating, and a cool sea breeze began to ease their feelings of roasting. Though they were all quite frightened on some level they were also very excited to be in a beautiful, untouched place such as this one. There was nothing like this in New York City.

They had all been smart enough to keep their wrist-communicators switched off, so as not to alarm the natives. At least none of their possessions had been taken from them thus far, though most had been transferred to Marvin's back in accordance with his apparent new role of porter. Samantha felt bad for him, but she couldn't think of anything that she could do about it other than pray they would soon reach whatever destination these strange little men had in mind. On the other hand, she wasn't at all sure if this was a good thing to wish for, as for all she knew they would all be cooked up and served for dinner upon arrival.

At a point where the seaside cliffs had at last leveled off they reached a place where a narrow pathway sloped steeply downward, looking as if it had actually been cut through the cliff with human hands. As they walked down it, straight rock walls rose up on either side of them, and they descended into a hollow which was situated at an elevation halfway between the cliff tops and sea level. In this hollow was built a most amazing little village, bustling with the activities of at least a hundred little people like the men who now marched them along at spear-point.

There were many thatched-roof houses, as well as a larger central building, and a stream of water ran through the village's center as it cascaded down from its cliff-top origin through a sometimes shallow, sometimes deeply-cut channel that eventually poured out into the gulf below. A short strip of beach could be reached only by a path of winding stairs that had been cut into the rock alongside the narrow, multi-leveled waterfall. Samantha thought she could make out something out in the gulf just off the shore – some sort of stone edifice or wall – it was too far away to see in any detail.

Her attention snapped back to front-and-center as they entered the village, their group being met by other warrior-types while old men, women and children gathered to watch them pass. They were truly a curiosity, and the men with spears became very alert, guarding their prisoners as if they were some great treasure. The 'witch doctor' led them, somewhat ceremoniously, to the village's large central building, which they entered. It was a single great room, at the far end of which sat a very important-looking man, bigger than most of his kind and adorned with gold, turquoise and multi-colored feathers. He was engaged in conversation with someone who looked to be a priest, possibly a man of the witch doctor's order, though dressed to indicate a position of greater authority. Both stopped their conversation and looked up as the witch doctor entered, beckoning the party in and gesturing for them to stand before the elevated leader figure.

The 'chief' remained seated in his throne-like chair that was woven intricately from twisted, knotty tree branches, while the 'priest' kept standing, though he now faced the party and stared at them with a fascinated look on his face. The 'chief' spoke something to the 'priest' in a totally incomprehensible language, who in turn questioned the 'witch doctor.' The 'witch doctor' then exploded into what must have been a highly descriptive story, complete with illustrative hand gestures and body movements that recalled the day's events. A long conversation then ensued between the three of them, mostly sounding like questions and answers. The prisoners' eyes wandered about the room, not being able to understand the discussion that would probably determine their fate. There were many decorative items in this hall: Shields, spears, masks and the like. Samantha noted, somewhat uncomfortably, that they all bore a common symbol – a great fish, or – *well*, she thought, *it looks more like a shark than anything else.* Her mental exploration was ended abruptly, however, when an unexpected voice came from the building's main entrance. It was a voice that turned all the blood in their veins to icewater, spoken in modern English but in no way comforting. Samantha's heart practically stopped. It was Jordan Anderson – Jordan Slane.

"Well, well, well," Jordan spoke smugly as he walked in, dressed more or less like the natives with only a sort of animal-skin skirt on. "If it isn't my favorite group of fans, here, a millennium before I'll even think about starting a band. Comfortable?"

Samantha fumed, half in livid anger that the person who had put her mother in a coma was standing in front of her, smirking, and half in disgust at herself for thinking about how good Jordan looked without a shirt on.

"Go choke on some coffee," Marvin said defiantly. The men with spears instantly raised them to his chest, a couple of which poked him with their sharp tips.

"Now, now," Jordan smiled. "I believe they think you're a slave here, Marvin." The party looked shocked for a moment that Jordan knew his name. "Oh, yes," their enemy went on as if sensing their unspoken question, "I know your name, *Marvin*. And yes, I do remember our coffee incident from 1931. Strange," he scratched his chin and momentarily stared at the high ceiling. "Isn't it just *bizarre* that here, in nine hundred and twenty-four A.D., I should *remember* something from 1931?

"Yes, I know all your names," he continued, walking by each of them as he spoke. "Suki – lovely girl, you are, though I fear your father will be underwater once we've worked this all out. Tokyo's one of the first to go, as I recall. Brianna – that was a clever little trick you pulled at the Heatwavvve show, though it won't do you any good, I'm afraid. Samantha – ," his gaze settled on the skinny Brooklynite. "My first and favorite time-traveler. But you've always

162

sort of... admired me, haven't you?"

"Pig," Samantha spat, shocking everyone in the room. "Whatever you're trying to do, it won't work."

"Won't it?" Jordan smiled, raising an eyebrow. He looked around at the prisoners and then broke into a grin. "Would you like to know what you've been fighting against? Hmmm? Oh, come on, I know you're a curious lot." He surveyed their faces but no one responded. "Very well," he said. "Since you are about to die anyway, in the distant past, I'll tell you.

"My father, Vassily Slane, is the last in a long line of... well, beings, shall we say, who've evolved, unknown to mankind, from sharks. I, too, share these incredible genes with my father, but my mother was a human woman. My father planned this, engineered me, actually, so that I might walk amongst men in their world of land and air. As a result, I can assume many shapes." He grinned and stopped his pacing in front of Brianna. Suddenly, his head and shoulders began a grotesque, hardly-believable transformation, his flesh bubbling and changing color, until the entire top half of his body had morphed into that of a shark's. The natives, all but the chief, fell instantly to the ground in worship, the warrior-types shaking in fear. The members of Alpha Team felt equally shaky, though they stood their ground.

"The little natives think I am a manifestation of their god," Jordan laughed, his features snapping suddenly back to normal. "In fact, this is not far from the truth. The shark-god these people worship is one of my oldest ancestors – they call him *Vasche*. It is he whom my father and I are descended from, and it is to him that you will be ritually sacrificed at dawn tomorrow."

Samantha's mind was racing. They had determined that the Slanes could not physically interact with people or things from other time periods, but these natives could obviously see and hear Jordan, even if they couldn't touch him. It had also been proven through their experiences in 1931 that their enemies *could* physically affect other non-natives of a timeline, i.e. Alpha Team, or perhaps anyone from the same time as them – and Marvin had proven that Alpha Team could physically affect Jordan.

The 'Brooklyn Bandit,' as he sometimes called himself, was at this moment already thinking along the same lines. The warriors surrounding him were all still on the ground in some semblance of terrified worship, leaving him free to discreetly struggle at freeing his hands from the coarse vines that bound them. It had taken a little while, but he had managed to work one hand free and was silently unwrapping the other. When at last this, too was free he felt inside one of the many bags still strapped to his back. In under a minute he had located one of the stun-guns and wrapped his fingers firmly around it.

"Unfortunately," Jordan went on, "you have already caused some trouble. Even though you will die here and now, you were sent here from the future, or, I suppose, what to us is the present. Before you were sent here, however, you did disrupt our 1931 operation *already*. Now, we could send someone else back to that time after we kill you here, but you would now still already be there to stop us because you *were* there – or *will be* there, in what is *your* past, though to these natives it would be the distant future. It's all very confusing, isn't it?" Jordan grinned. "Let us just say that you *are* there to stop us, so now we must find another way to achieve our goal."

"And what exactly is that?" Samantha growled her question through clenched teeth.

"Why, I thought that much, at least, was obvious, Samantha. *Warm saltwater.* What more could a shark-man desire in a world? You humans – you're dirty, inefficient and obsessed with manipulating objects in the world around you. You even manipulate each other, every day, all the time. Sharks evolved to perfection millions of years ago; they know exactly what they are, they know that everything around them is either an enemy or food, or both. They do not pretend to work together as humans do for some 'common good,' they never have – that is, until now. Now we have evolved to a final stage, we have become a species that rivals your own in intelligence, but also that retains its incredible decisiveness and instinct to survive. We *shall* re-make the world to suit *our* needs; you are merely obstacles in the way of this achievement."

The team members stole looks at each other. Jordan's speech was exceptionally arrogant, though, sadly, some of the things he had said about humans rang true, and they almost felt pangs of guilt for their own species. There was more.

"For centuries, you have poured poison after poison into our world, the sea, stolen most of our food and in many cases hunted us almost to extinction. You are clearly an enemy. *And... ,*" Jordan smiled an impossibly wide, toothy smile, his mouth morphing again into a shark's, "... a very tasty food as well."

This was all Marvin needed to hear. He suddenly turned sideways and leaped over the bowing warriors that surrounded him, dropping the vines he had wormed his way out of and shedding his burden of packs onto the surprised men. He ran for the main entrance, still clutching the stun-gun he had worked out of one of the bags. Jordan was right behind him, yelling in the natives' strange language, inciting them to rise and pursue him. The others, still bound and surrounded by now vertical warriors, stood stunned. Marvin cut a sharp left just outside the entrance and darted off into the small maze of huts that made up this strange, ancient village.

Now, Dr. Marvy had never been the fastest kid on the block. He was a little on the pudgy side and perhaps spent a bit too much time sitting in front of a computer, though these adventures were beginning to take a few pounds off of him. He did have one advantage, though: He was a city kid, and knew very well how to get around in a city, even if it was made of grass huts. He wove between buildings like a practiced alley-cat, ducking this way and that, jumping over low barriers and scampering under high ones. But these little men were very quick.

He was almost nabbed a couple of times but managed to wriggle away and keep running until he reached the rock wall through which they had first entered the village. He turned right and ran along it until he came to the narrow pathway they had come down through. There were two guards posted there, but he ran right between them, deciding it wouldn't make much of a difference if there were two more warriors after him. They were startled but soon started up the path after him, being met by the other warriors that were already pursuing him at a lightning-quick pace.

Toward the top of the path, Marvin came to a realization and then made a split-second decision. Concluding that he would most likely never be able to outrun these jungle-trained hunters, he turned around and stopped, pointed the stun-gun at the man in the front of the pack and yelled the only word he was sure they would recognize, hopefully to some effect.

"*VASCHE!!!*" he blurted out, at the same time activating the stun-gun. A flash released two arcs of 200,000 volt blue-white electricity through the air and into the warrior in the front of the pursuing posse. He flew back into the others and lost consciousness, drooling and soiling what little clothing he had on. A faint smell of ozone hung in the air and the pursuers looked terrified, perhaps thinking that their leader was dead.

Marvin's gambit paid off. They all hit the ground in 'worship' position, the utterance of their shark god's name in combination with a very visual display of power had been enough to scare and confuse them. He stood, breathing heavily and still holding the weapon out in front of him, then yelled "Vasche," once more and lightly kicked the closest man to him. The native looked up at him, and Marvin gestured to him that they should all leave immediately. They didn't seem to quite get the idea, so he blasted the man and made more obvious gestures for the rest to be on their way. This seemed to work. It was a good thing, too – you couldn't usually get more than two good shots with the stun-gun without needing a recharge. The natives turned tail and ran, leaving Marvin with two messy warriors who would regain consciousness in a moment. He ran. Up and out of the village, into the boulder fields of the cliff tops.

Jordan had returned quickly to the chief's building, having abandoned the chase to the warriors. He fumed and cursed, and the girls feared that their treatment would be somehow worsened in response to Marvin's daring escape. Strangely, however, this was not the case. Jordan gathered all their belongings and stripped them of their wrist-communicators, but then went suddenly away, perhaps to see about Marvin, and left them in the warriors' care. After a very brief discussion between the chief and the priest, they were led away to a small hut, where they were looked after by several small, mostly older women.

The new situation wasn't that much more comfortable. Their clothes were taken from them and they were given ritualistic dresses to wear, leaving little doubt that they were scheduled for sacrifice to the shark-god. They were also brought fruits and fresh meat, which they accepted reluctantly in their hunger. All the while the little women kept muttering prayers and sprinkling water on them, and the girls were beginning to get very nervous as the night wore on. *I sure hope you can figure us out of this one, Marvin,* Samantha thought, batting away a palm leaf that one of the women had been fanning her with.

*

Marvin slid down into a crevice between two massive boulders, out of breath and with his heart racing like that of a hunted animal's. This, he decided, must be as safe a place as he could find. Catching his breath, he repeatedly stuck his head out the side of the crack to gaze back in the direction of the village, though he had probably run at least a mile from it on the cliff tops. At last, feeling that no one had followed him, he switched on his wrist-communicator and pressed the talk button.

"Professor?" Marvin gasped.

"Marvin!" the familiar British voice came back. "How goes it? Any luck with finding the plant yet?"

"Uh – yeah, we got the plant. Sort of. Listen – "

"Sort of? What do you mean you 'sort of' have the plant?"

"*Listen,*" Marvin pleaded. "The girls are being held in a native village by Jordan Slane. I, uh, escaped, used a stun-gun. We need *help,* Professor!"

"Oh, dear," The Professor's tone turned to one of concern.

"Marvin, are the other wrist-communicators in the enemy's possession right now?"

"Um, well, yeah, I mean – the girls still had them on when I busted out an hour or so ago, but – yeah, he's got 'em."

"Very well. This line is no longer secure. I want you to do something for me, Marvin," The Professor's voice said calmly.

"Sure, man. What?" Marvin replied.

"Take the wrist-communicator off. Look on its back, its underside. You will see two small compartments that can be opened. The larger one is for the battery. I want you to open the smaller one."

"Um – okay. Hold on." Marvin fumbled with the thing with no success. "I can't get it open, Professor," he despaired.

"If you had a very small stick or a – a, well, I don't know exactly – but something small and thin..."

"Oh, wait – got it!" Marvin rejoiced, proud of himself. He had used a little lip of metal on the stun-gun, the only other thing he had, to achieve the desired effect. He smiled and opened the compartment.

"You should see a tiny green button," The Professor continued coaching him. "I want you to press it."

"Done," Marvin came back. His voice was not consistent in volume due to the fact that he had to keep flipping the thing over to talk into it while working on its backside. "Okay. Now what?"

"You can put it back on, after you close up the hatch there," Smythe guided him. "Stay where you are if you can; help will be forthcoming, I promise you. Smythe out."

"What? Wait!" Marvin petitioned their fearless leader. "Yo, what does that mean, 'forthcoming'!?" There was no reply.

*

The night was long and sleepless for the girls, though it was quiet and the distant sound of waves lapping against the shore was somehow slightly relaxing. It did not, however, change the fact that morning would come, which it did. A little before sunrise, the attending women came to fetch them, and along with a couple of spear-toting warriors led them out of the hut that had been theirs for a night. They were taken down the winding stairs that were cut into the rock next to the waterfall, down, down, down... until their bare feet suddenly felt soft, fine sand underneath them.

The shore was bathed in a warm, pink light as the sun rose over the gulf, each wave tipped with a taffy-textured crest that made the morning world look like an impossible candy-land. As the girls were marched out to the water's edge they stared at the beautiful picture, half hoping that the Good Ship Lollipop would appear to rescue them and whisk them away to a place that wasn't so tense, so angry and so vengeful as the reality of Jordan Slane. They each thought about their lives, reflecting on happy moments and sad, wondering if the world would go on without them or if the Slanes' fiendish plan would in fact succeed with them out of the way.

Samantha tried to keep her wits about her, tried to pay close attention to what the natives were doing and wondered nervously what ghastly fate lay in store for her and the others. Jordan was directing two crews of canoe paddlers from the shore, waving his hands and speaking in their strange, ancient language. It appeared as if they were to be taken by boat out to the stone platform that sat some hundred yards out from the beach, from which several stone pillars rose up to a height of ten feet or so.

The natives herded them somewhat roughly into their canoes, parting them from their female attendants who threw flower petals on them as they were paddled away from shore. The sun had risen somewhat quickly and the waves now looked bright blue, that brilliant, electric blue that one only sees in travel brochures depicting tropical island vacations. Alas, a vacation this was not, and the girls' hearts and thoughts grew heavy as the boats approached the platform.

As they pulled alongside it, they could see that it was in fact far larger than it had looked to be from land. The pillars were closer to twenty feet high than ten, and the whole structure seemed to have a super-sized, deity-scaled theme that made all the people seem like miniature dolls next to it. They were pulled out of the canoes firmly but gently and each was led to the base of a pillar, two guards to a girl. Some sort of iron manacles had been anchored into the stone in each one at about six or seven feet off the platform, and the girls were shackled in these, their arms high above their heads. The closing of the manacles around their wrists was a frightening, very physical feeling of finality, of the last possibility of escape vanishing, and Suki began to whimper. The natives backed away and let Jordan have the platform to himself as they piled back into their canoes.

"And so it ends," Jordan smiled an evil smile. "The race of sharks, as always, tears the race of humans to pieces. Oh, trust me, ladies, we'll find your friend Marvin – I wouldn't count on his coming to your rescue. But even if we don't find him – well, he may fancy himself something of a survivor, but let me assure you, thousand-year-old Central America is no Brooklyn, New York. I suspect some other of the land-dwelling species will finish him off." Jordan smiled his impossible, morph-toothed smile again, walking back and forth in front of the girls.

"And then what!?" Samantha burst out angrily. "Say you succeed, and the earth *is* covered with saltwater – what then!? Do you think you can build half as beautiful a society as humans have? Will you – will you create wondrous works of art? Will your shark-men write sonnets like Shakespeare's? Will they make music? Or build incredible buildings?"

"Your society holds no beauty for us," Jordan turned serious, stepping closer to Samantha. "Your race is no better than ours. Your 'artists' are inspired by pain, by violence. These qualities we accept as natural; we embrace them. We do not, as you do, deny our own nature." He stood very close to her face now, his head morphing into an angry shark-expression. "The world we build will be, if nothing else, an *honest* world, free of deception, free of duplicity. We will let *nature* be the world's artist, the world's poet and architect, the world's composer. All that will remain for us to do will be what comes naturally to us – the urge to hunt." Jordan's toothy grin hovered inches from Samantha's face, drooling with what appeared to be genuine appetite. Suddenly, however, his face snapped back to normal and he turned away from her.

"But to others, some respect is due. You three we give now to Vasche, my ancestor, for it is in his time that your end is scheduled." He paced back toward the canoes and began laughing maniacally, then got back into one of them. Both boats then pushed off and headed back toward the shore.

Though Jordan's close-up teeth had felt threatening and unnerving, Samantha knew in the back of her mind that he could not actually touch her. Unfortunately, this was probably not the case with Vasche, who was presumably a regular denizen of this time. She racked her brain for some means of escape as she helplessly watched the natives' canoes paddle away. But it was too late.

*

Brianna screamed, pointing out to sea as best she could with her manacled hand. A huge, dark shape was approaching the platform, moving fast. A fin cut through the surface of the water as it came, heading straight for them. Just as it reached the platform, it leapt out of the water and grew legs, or arms, straddling the stone ledge and heaving its massive, primitive form onto the flat surface. It was huge, much bigger than they'd expected, and it paused for a moment on the platform and shook water from its body like a dog. A crowd of natives was cheering from the shore, and everything began to blur into a surreal collage of horror and fear. Vasche, for it must have been Vasche, the Slane ancestor, the shark god, sniffed the air as if deciding which of the girls to devour first. Samantha stared over at her two friends, her heart pounding in her chest. Brianna had fainted and now hung limp from her manacles. But Suki – Suki was staring up at the sky, as if totally entranced by something... else. Samantha craned her neck to follow Suki's gaze, wondering what could possibly be more interesting than their imminent death at the hands (or jaws) of a gigantic, hideous, primitive shark-man. She heard before she saw.

Thuk! Thuk! Thuk! Several Javelin-like objects pierced the thick hide of the Vasche-creature, causing it to writhe in pain and let out a horrible screaming sound. It morphed erratically, trying to regain its pure shark form and slipping, badly wounded, back beneath the gentle waves of the gulf, trailing blood as it went. Then Samantha saw it, the agent of their rescue. It was a small speedboat, dangling from a sort of giant, square parachute, quickly descending and angling itself toward the stone platform. There were spear-guns mounted on the boat's front, and at their triggers – Marvin, and Professor Smythe!

It would almost have been funny to Samantha if she hadn't been purely terrified a few moments earlier. The boat-chute looked like some scene out of *Chitty-Chitty-Bang-Bang* as it touched down on the water, Marvin engaging its engine. The two rescuers zipped quickly over to the platform and Marvin got out, carrying a glass vial with him and leaving The Professor at the controls.

"Hold *very* still," Marvin instructed as he uncorked the vial and poured what must have been some powerful acid onto the chains of Samantha's manacles. The metal hissed and smoked, then gave way almost instantly. Some drops had fallen onto the platform and were fast eating holes through the stone, a sight that made Samantha gulp for a moment, looking down at her wrists, which held the remains of the manacles.

"Help me," Marvin instructed, handing her another vial of the stuff and then running over to the pillar that held the unconscious Brianna. Samantha followed suit, rushing to Suki's column and imitating what she had seen Marvin do with the acid. There was a collective roar coming from the shore and canoes were already paddling out to them, fast.

The girls jumped into the flashy speedboat, helping Marvin to carry onboard the limp Brianna. The Professor, presumably not wanting to leave any evidence of their presence in this time, had pulled the deflated parachute aboard and was packing it away inside the hull of the boat. Marvin slid behind the wheel and gunned its engine. It was very fast. The girls were thrown backward as the vessel sped along the cliff-lined shore, and it seemed for a moment as if they were heading straight for the canoes full of warriors in pursuit.

"Marvin!" The Professor yelled, but Marvin had ideas of his own.

He floored the accelerator and shot right at the pursuing natives. It looked as though they were going to collide. Wide-eyed warriors threw their spears and jumped overboard from their canoes. None of the spears came close to hitting them, though one glanced off the front of the fiberglass boat. At the last moment before impact, Marvin jerked the wheel to the right and tore off north along the rocky coastline.

"That was *stupid,* Marvin!" The Professor chastised the 'Brooklyn Bandit,' honestly angry. "One of us could have taken a spear to the head! Cackling Quetzlcoatls! Don't *ever* do anything like that again!"

He was holding his heart in an 'I'm too old for this sort of thing' way.

"Well," Marvin sighed, smiling a little, "No one will be following us for a while."

"That is true," Samantha chimed in. "But that *was* a stupid stunt, Marvin; someone could really have gotten hurt. I suppose it's hard for me to be angry, though, when I was expecting to die moments ago and you've just saved all our lives – you, too, Professor." She kissed the old, flustered Brit on the cheek, making him blush uncharacteristically.

"Well, uh, yes, well, of course!" Smythe stammered. "Aaaahhh – Marvin?"

"Ya, boss," Dr. Marvy replied, focused on his speedboat driving. He was quite enjoying it and wishing that their real time didn't require silly things like drivers' licenses.

"You know where to head to, correct?"

Marvin looked down at the boat's dashboard, which featured a bright digital display with many numbers and some sort of wavy lines on it.

"Yup, I figure about fifteen to, oh, twenty or twenty-five minutes."

"What's that?" Samantha's scientific curiosity kicked in. She slid closer to Marvin and studied the dashboard's readout, which seemed to be changing as they traveled along.

"Built-in terrain recognition," Marvin explained. "You know, navigation stuff. They use it in fighter jets and things like that. It scans ahead of you with radar and feeds the information back to here," he pointed at the wavy lines with his finger as he drove. "Then the computer compares it to all the radar maps in its database and lets you know exactly where you are."

"Cool," Samantha cooed. "Where'd you get this boat, Professor?"

"I, er, *borrowed* it from the Chelsea Piers on Twenty-third Street. I'm, ah still working on a way to replace it; I fear we can't get it back the way we, ah, got it here." Smythe fretted.

"G.P.S. would've been easier, and easier to find a boat with," Marvin displayed his geekiness. "That is, a global positioning system. It guides you by a very precise satellite signal."

"I'm actually considering building G.P.S. into the next round of wrist-communicators," The Professor took up the topic, equally zealous in his knowledge of popular electronics. "I daresay it'd be quite useful, on any mission. There is a problem, though..."

"What's that?" Samantha asked.

"Well, you see – it won't work on any mission into the past beyond 1995 or so, because – "

"Because there aren't any guidance satellites," Samantha finished his sentence, understanding.

"Precisely. Sort of a disadvantage to traveling in the past, you know. Unless – well, I did manage to perfect a sort of wireless closed-circuit that lets us communicate through time. If I could somehow patch the satellite signal into that frequency, well, I might be able to get it to work."

"So, we'd be able to get global positioning from satellites – in the future?"

"Yes, well, I suppose so. But, I mean, it's just a signal like the one that carries my voice, and you've been getting that from 'the future.'"

"*Anyway,*" Marvin steered the conversation back to the 'present,' "The terrain recognition is working fine. Luckily we're on a coast, which makes it a lot easier, right Professor?"

"Indeed," Smythe replied. "I programmed the map databases for this specific area, though I'm sure the coastline has changed a bit over the last thousand years."

They zoomed along, pulling gradually back towards the shore as they went. The cliffs had blended down into the jungle they had marched through, and it stretched out like a vast, dark cloud of green that covered the land completely. The boat ride reminded Samantha of their stint in the alternate timeline, and suddenly she grew concerned.

"I hope Polly's all right at Aunt Tina's," she spoke, mostly to herself. She remained troubled, staring at the jungle as it flew by on their left. She thought of their uncomfortable bug-infested time in that place and then once again felt a sense of alarm, remembering the original purpose of their mission.

"Professor, what about the plant!!? What about my mother!?"

"It's all right, Samantha," The Professor tried to calm her. He pulled something out from under one of the boat's seats. It was one of their backpacks.

"How – how did you – "

"Get this?" The Professor chuckled. "You can do amazing things with time travel, you know. I simply transported myself to the coordinates of your three confiscated wrist-communicators – to you it would have been last night. I used a stun-gun on the single guard they left with your belongings – rather a tense moment for me, I should say! But I gathered up everything, the backpacks, wrist-communicators and what have you, and transported back to the lab. Actually, I dropped everything off there – this pack is full of sandwiches – delicious turkey and cranberry chutney, from the Carnegie Deli. Would you like one?" He reached into the pack and pulled out a very tasty-looking sandwich, offering it to her.

"Uh – sure," Samantha responded, stunned. The Professor handed out sandwiches to everyone, and the group devoured them hungrily, although Brianna was still out like a light.

"I couldn't risk leaving everything there," Smythe continued, chewing a bite of his own sandwich. "Though I still believe that Jordan can't physically interact with things in other times, the Slanes did somehow manage to synthesize a poison from that very plant that

I sent you after, so they have some sort of... means to achieve such things. I don't know – perhaps they instructed one of the natives to preserve some of the plant somehow and went to collect it from a specific spot a thousand years later. They are a clever lot, too, you know – and no doubt at least as well-equipped as we are.

"In any case, I certainly didn't want them to have the communicators, or the 'chalk.' It may, I believe, have something to do with their inability to time-travel as effectively as we can. And, of course, I needed the plant. I think I've extracted the basic essence of an antidote, Samantha – I shall get back to work on refining it as soon as we get back, I promise."

"I, uh, um – thanks," Samantha said earnestly, overcome with a moment of emotion at the thought of seeing her mom again, awake and well. She was still pretty stunned at The Professor's extreme effectiveness, as well as by the tense and bizarre events of the past day or two.

On their left, (Samantha couldn't remember if this was "port" or "starboard" in nautical terms), the jungle began to thin and gave way to what looked like the beach of a familiar desert area, most likely near to where Alpha Team had arrived in this time. Marvin eased up on the throttle and slowly began guiding the boat to shore. It grazed some rocks as they pulled into a sort of shallow cove and the jostling woke Brianna, who opened her eyes and immediately let out a blood-curdling scream. The others quickly made to comfort her, stroking her hair and quietly reassuring her that they had, in fact, been rescued, and that they were no longer about to die a grisly death. She gradually began to accept this, reluctantly allowing herself to be helped out of the boat and onto the desolate-looking shore.

It was here that The Professor informed them that they must part ways. They would have to walk a mile or two to get back to the bleak slab of rock that held their 'magic' footprints, apparently still their only viable means of return to their own time. The Professor would have to pilot the boat back to his point of entry, the return to which was considerably more complicated. He had transported the boat, parachute and all, to a high cliff top just outside the natives' hidden village and had propelled it over the edge by means of a modified trailer. The motorized trailer, he had related to them, had then plummeted into the gulf below, whereupon a special polymer he had coated it with would have its chemical properties activated by contact with saltwater, causing the entire thing to dissolve within hours. This assured that no evidence of the thing from the future would be left in this primitive time, though the boat itself presented its own problem in this respect.

The Professor had, purportedly, somehow got boat and trailer into the time-machine room, which sounded impossible. He had shrugged off further questions about this feat, saying that there wasn't time to explain it to them. He did have a plan to destroy the vessel as well, in a presumably similar manner, and acknowledged that it would not be making the trip back home with him. It was a mystery that Alpha Team could only ponder, at least for the moment.

The girls, (and even Marvin to some extent) remained concerned about how The Professor would get back to the cliff-top, but at this, too, he smiled and assured them that he would have no problem doing so, patting something in the boat that looked very much like an astronaut's rocket-backpack. Samantha looked at Marvin and they grinned at each other. Suki and Brianna smiled too, and they all waved to their undoubtedly resourceful leader as he spun the boat around and sped out of sight.

The trek back to their footprints was hot and tiring, as expected, though it was earlier in the day than it was on the day that they had arrived, and so at least somewhat cooler. They also were mercifully free of the extra weight of their backpacks, for which they were all very grateful. Brianna in particular was in much higher spirits and hardly complained at all, which everyone was equally appreciative of.

Marvin kept checking a compass that The Professor had given him, eyeing the disturbingly homogenous horizon carefully as they went. It was only an hour or so before they came to an area that looked at least somewhat familiar to everyone in the party, and 'Dr. Marvy' instructed them all to split up and begin looking for the slab of rock upon which they had materialized a couple of days earlier. He passed out the wrist-communicators, which The Professor, in his wisdom, had been thoughtful enough to bring back and leave with them, and instructed each party member to signal if any of them came upon the correct spot.

It wasn't long before the devices squawked with Suki's voice, excited that she had been the one to find the glowing tracks they sought. The others turned around and quickly made for her location, arriving some minutes later.

There they were – four sets of footprints, glowing a bright blue in the sun of late morning, their salvation. The girls huddled around them, then hugged each other in an unspoken acknowledgment of all they had been through in the past forty-eight hours. Marvin, too, smiled and put on a look of relief that no one had seen on his face for a while. They held hands and stepped into their respective tracks, each saying a silent goodbye to the ancient world that had been their home for the past two days, and with a dazzling blue fizzle of light and temporal energy, vanished from where they had stood.

*

The feeling in Cindy Smart's hospital room was one of nervous anticipation. Though nearly a dozen people stood around her bed, everyone maintained a sort of hush, fingers crossed. After two days of conferencing between Professor Smythe and Dr. Amesbury (The physician assigned to Cindy's case), they had administered The Professor's lab-synthesized antidote. At first the doctor had been very skeptical, but after a few trips to The Professor's lab with an accompanying colleague, he had concluded that Smythe's science was sound, that his synthesized antidote could only help and not worsen Cindy's condition, and that it was in fact within the law to administer it with a signature from an immediate family member. Aunt Tina supplied this, reluctantly, after many assurances from Samantha, Professor Smythe and Dr. Amesbury, and so the injection had been given that morning.

It was now close to noon and there were as yet no signs of the antidote working. Around the bed stood all the members of Alpha Team, Jason, Todd, Aunt Tina, The Professor and a few doctors and/or med students. The Professor looked the most nervous – he had literally been awake for days working on perfecting the serum and probably felt largely responsible for the whole of the situation anyway. He had become angry at himself several times during setbacks in the antidote's development, wishing he had been able to figure out how to defeat the Slanes' time-bubble blocking devices – it would have been so much easier to go back and prevent Cindy from ever having been poisoned in the first place. It was a study to which he decided he must devote a lot of time to in the near future.

"There!" Samantha shout-whispered. Cindy's fingers had twitched. "You all saw that, right? I'm not seeing things?" Everyone in the room nodded, and even if Samantha wasn't sure whether or not to believe her own eyes, the issue was rendered moot when Cindy's whole body stirred and she took a deep breath. The crowd of onlookers was completely on edge.

Suddenly, Cindy gasped a deep, panicky breath and sat straight up in her hospital bed, almost ripping the I.V. tube out of her arm.

"Mom!" Samantha yelled, tears in her eyes.

"Mom?" Todd echoed.

"Oh – Samantha? Todd? Jason – " she looked around her, dazed, and tried to piece together where she was and why.

"Where am I? What – why am I ... in a... hospital? What happened? Is everyone all right?" She was obviously quite confused, very disoriented and more than a little scared. They all did their best to calm her, took turns hugging her while Dr. Amesbury checked her pulse and breathing and then tried to explain what exactly had happened to her.

The official explanation, compiled by the N.Y.P.D., had been that Cindy had been 'drugged' by some twisted, drug fiend concert-goer, though no one had ever heard of or seen a drug such as the one they found in her bloodstream. The F.B.I. and D.E.A. had even been called in to speak with all the witnesses, which in itself was frightening. It was indeed a good thing that their adventure into the distant past had only taken up an hour or two of present time, for almost immediately upon returning Samantha was requested for interviews by both Federal agencies. Though she wasn't the best liar, she had managed to mostly plead ignorance, and the government 'experts' were more than happy to try to explain the incident themselves. Presumably they were now out looking for some previously unknown drug and the massive criminal organization that surely must surround it.

To make this Fed-preferred story more believable, The Professor had also supplied the agencies with some of his synthesized antidote and formula for creating it, for study. He had been momentarily concerned that they would somehow be able to concoct their own poison from it, which might be employed questionably in the area of intelligence missions, but then remembered that there wasn't any of the actual plant left and doubted they could completely artificially synthesize the necessary chemicals without it, at least in the next decade or so. Still, it made him nervous about the possibility of adversely affecting the future.

Another result of all this was that there was now also a federal agent in Cindy's hospital room, who had until now sat quietly, almost invisibly in the corner in a chair. It was a woman, in fact, named Agent Stiles, whose purpose here was supposedly to record and judge the efficacy of Professor Smythe's antidote, as well as to continue questioning in the ongoing investigation. As Cindy regained consciousness and began catching up, Agent Stiles commenced typing calmly but with sizzling speed on her portable laptop computer. Stopping occasionally to ask questions of The Professor, the doctors and Jason, she embodied a feeling of confidence and composure that Samantha greatly admired. Every now and then Stiles would catch Samantha looking at her and would smile. Samantha blushed, turning back to her mother.

"Really," Cindy was saying to the doctors examining her, obviously adjusting nicely, "I feel *fine*. I just want a shower and to go back to my own house."

"You're welcome to take a shower here, Ms. Smart," Dr. Amesbury offered, gesturing toward the bathroom that was attached to her hospital bedroom. "But we need to monitor you, I'm afraid, for just one more day. We need to do a few more tests and make sure all your vitals are stable, over a twenty-four hour period. And, if you feel... up to it, Agent Stiles from the F.B.I.'s Manhattan field office would like to ask you some questions." Cindy looked over at Agent Stiles, who smiled and waved her pen in an unobtrusive self-introduction.

"Oh. Um, sure, I guess. Maybe, uh, a little later."

"That's fine, Ms. Smart," Agent Stiles replied. "I'm just going to go get some lunch. I'll be back later this afternoon, if you feel more like chatting. Glad you're feeling better." Her tone was cheery in an honest-sounding way.

"Thanks," Cindy acknowledged, perhaps slightly uncomfortable.

The group of spectators gradually left the hospital after various well-wishings, returning to their respective homes or places of work, all but the immediate family, which now consisted of Samantha, Todd, Aunt Tina and Jason. Agent Stiles returned, mid-afternoon, and gently put to Cindy the many questions that the F.B.I. apparently had to ask her. Though she was very polite and amiable, she asked a bit too much about The Professor for Samantha's liking. Samantha played along, trying to act surprised at some things and casually dismissing others; she hoped her contributions to the federal investigation were significantly misleading, believably ignorant-sounding and not overly dramatic. It was hard to gauge Agent Stiles' reactions, and Samantha decided to inform The Professor of the government's sudden and specific interest in him (assuming he didn't already know) at the earliest opportunity.

"And so, this... Professor friend of yours managed to synthesize an antidote for this unknown poison, or drug, in under a week?"

"Thank God!" Cindy said. "I guess it pays to surround oneself with well-equipped geniuses, even if I never was quite one myself."

"The Professor's really smart," Samantha agreed, playing dumb. "He's shown me how to do Carbon-14 dating, and spec-tral-a-nal-y-sis..." she trailed off, trying to sound as if she were struggling with the words. Cindy gave her daughter a strange look, wondering why she was pretending to not be able to pronounce words that she'd said a hundred times; her daughter was no dummy. Samantha hoped the agent hadn't noticed the look and kicked herself mentally.

"Is that so?" Stiles smiled and raised an eyebrow. "Well, anyone that good we could certainly use in the F.B.I. Where exactly did he get the plant sample that he was able to extract the necessary chemicals from?"

"I have no idea," Cindy mused. Samantha shrugged, hopefully not looking guilty.

"That plant's been extinct for a thousand years," the agent offered provocatively. Samantha exchanged a quizzical look with her mother.

"I don't know," Cindy repeated honestly. "I mean, the museum's got hundreds of fossils – thousands even. Plants, animals, up to, oh, I don't know – three hundred million years old. Maybe he squeezed it out of one of those." Samantha smiled inwardly while outwardly nodding. *Good answer, Mom!* She thought.

Agent Stiles made a bit of a crooked pout and raised her eyebrows, looking downward. It did seem the most plausible explanation.

"All right," she closed her laptop and smiled. "Just one more question, then – and I hope you don't find it too weird – we just have to look at all the angles."

"Okay," Cindy said.

"Do you have any reason at all to believe that Professor Smythe would want to hurt you or your family?"

"No!" Cindy almost laughed. "I've known Ainsley for years! I mean, I know he's a bit odd and all – geniuses usually are, don't you think? He'd never harm a fly, though, really. He – he used to always ask if we had any scones back when I still worked in concessions," she said the word 'scones' in a mock-British accent. "And Samantha's been learning all sorts of interesting science things from him for the last two years or so – sometimes working a bit too hard at it, if you ask me, picking up some of his absent-mindedness and forgetting to call her mother," she eyed her daughter sternly, privately referring to Samantha's 'missing week.' "But no, no. He would never hurt us, never. In fact I'm eternally grateful for what he's done for me today."

"Of course," Stiles smiled again. "I wouldn't think he would. He seems like a very gentle man. It's just that, at present, we know of no one else who's manufactured *anything,* drug poison or antidote, from this extinct plant. You do see the need for us to be curious about him?"

"Mmmm," Cindy nodded. It *was* strange indeed. The whole thing was strange, though. Her whole life seemed very odd lately, and she had to admit to herself that all the strange happenings had either surrounded her daughter or Professor Smythe. It made her head hurt to think about it all now, though, and she sighed and closed her eyes.

After Agent Stiles had departed (everyone having been left with one of her business cards), the family made their plans for the next few days.

It was decided that Todd and Samantha (and Polly) would spend one more night at Aunt Tina's. It was Sunday night, and Tina had to work early Monday morning, so the siblings said an early goodnight to their mother and left her to spend some quality time with Jason, who was, despite his unfortunate averageness, turning out to be a real hero in everyone's book.

Polly was beyond ecstatic to see Samantha. Between her time at the hospital and the museum, the junior adventurer had hardly seen her faithful canine companion at all in the last week. To Samantha it had seemed even longer, having spent an entire two days in a completely different world in the space of an hour – thinking of it like that was weird. She had had something like a seventy-two-hour day in there somewhere – Friday, she guessed it had been. Of course, time away from your favorite person is always very, very long for any self-respecting dog, and Polly smothered Samantha with dozens of sloppy, wet kisses, sproinged all over her like a maniac and wagged her stumpy little terrier tail at amazing speeds.

"Polly, stop!" Samantha began laughing. "Stop! Okay! Okay! I love you, too!" It was clearly a most happy reunion. "Thanks for walking her and stuff," Samantha said, turning to her brother. She wasn't used to thanking him for anything or even being nice to him at all, but having gone through a week of their mother being in a coma had forced them to make a sort of peace pact. Samantha was surprised at how uncomfortable she felt – it was quite different from their normal mode of operation.

"Yeah, no problem," Todd blurted out with equal discomfort. "She's pretty spunky – Polly, I mean."

"Yeah, she is," Samantha giggled, still trying to control the hyperactive little dog.

Aunt Tina had set about fixing some dinner, and Samantha was helping out, cutting onions for a quiche that was to be the main course. Her eyes stung and tears rolled down her face as she gathered up the pieces and put them into a bowl. Next, she began chopping some broccoli and her mind began to wander as she focused on the simple task. She was a little worried about Agent Stiles watching The Professor, or even interviewing him to see if their stories matched. She thought she should contact him and at least let him know to watch out for the F.B.I., to be extra-secretive in his actions, but she decided that his phone might well be tapped (this was what federal agents did in the movies, anyway). She resolved to talk to him later in the evening via wrist-communicator. Surely the F.B.I. hadn't learned about those, and even if they had, the devices used a pretty obscure frequency.

The quiche came out perfectly, and Samantha and Aunt Tina did a high-five in celebration of their cooperative effort. They sat at the table and ate, unhurriedly, and talked about normal family things.

"So, I guess you guys won't be going back to school until Tuesday?" Tina asked, pretty much knowing the answer to her question but wanting to make some light dinner conversation.

"Yeah, well, I guess we're going to bring Mom home tomorrow," Todd replied, adding, "Mmmm, good quiche, guys."

"I've kind of missed school," Samantha spoke up. "I mean, *literally,* I've missed a lot of school lately, but I also mean I'm kind of excited to go back."

"Mmmm," Tina nodded, taking time to swallow a bite. "I heard all about your 'missing person' stint, Samantha. Your mother was worried sick. What exactly were you doing?"

"I, um - aaaahhh," Samantha stammered and then sighed. "I was helping Professor Smythe do some research at the museum. I couldn't leave because, well, we were doing an experiment that required constant monitoring. I know, I know, I should've called home but, well, I just wasn't able to."

"Well, you scared your mother half to death, you know," her Aunt went on in a scolding tone. "God forbid you should have a child as precocious as you are."

'Precocious' was a word Samantha had heard often enough; it was quite frequently used by many adults to describe her behavior, and though she still wasn't sure exactly what it meant she had taken it to mean something along the lines of a person who acted more grown-up than they actually were. Perhaps the adults were right. She did sort of fancy herself more able to function independently than most kids her age. She just shrugged in response to her Aunt's comment, though, and continued to eat quiche.

*

Late that night, curled up on the futon in Aunt Tina's tiny guest room, Samantha attempted to use her wrist-communicator. She pulled the covers up over to try and create a more silent place to talk, then tapped the button that called The Professor. It seemed to take a long time, but The Professor did eventually pick up.

"Who is it?" his voice came back, sounding nervous and hushed.

"It's Samantha. Where are you?"

"Samantha! I – uh – I'm at home. Brought the desktop set here, you know – I don't want to leave it in the office anymore."

"I understand, Professor. I'll be quick. I just wanted to warn you about that Agent Stiles – she was asking a lot of questions about you at the hospital."

"Yes, I know," The Professor continued in his whispery voice. "She's been following me, I think. Shivering Shadows! I wouldn't be surprised if she's eating jelly rolls in a car right outside, you know!"

"Um, it's *doughnuts* here, Professor. At least, if you believe all the cop shows on TV."

"Doughnuts, then! It's very unnerving, Samantha. I don't think they can tap this communications band, however. Hmmmm..." The line went momentarily silent and Samantha could tell that he was thinking hard. "Samantha, as much as I know that the Slanes are out there working against us, I'm afraid we have no choice but to completely halt all operations for at least a few weeks."

"Understood, Professor," Samantha acknowledged after a brief silence. "What do you want me to do?"

"Nothing. Try to live like a... a normal American girl. Go to school, meet with your friends – all the things you'd normally do. I suspect you should check in at the museum once a week as well, seeing as that's normal for you, though we mustn't speak of anything related to time travel or the Slanes in the office until I'm sure it's not being bugged. Please relate this to the others as well, in secret, and all of you should keep your wrist-communicators switched off and in a safe hiding place until further notice. Is that all clear, Agent Smart?"

"Clear," Samantha promised.

"Our next discussion of what needs to be done will take place in person, when I'm sure we are absolutely free of surveillance. Smythe out."

Samantha switched off her communicator and slumped down under the warm covers. *It's going to be a long, cold November,* she thought to herself. She was glad, however, that it was *her* November, the November of her proper timeline. She pulled the covers closer and whispered to Polly, who came up onto the bed from her chosen spot on the floor and snuggled up to her much-absent-of-late owner. It was nice to sleep with Polly again, to have her warm little companion back. Tomorrow night she would have her bed back, too.

*

Everyone was in a cheery mood at the hospital the next day, and

Samantha was no exception. It was great to see her mother up and dressed, ready to go. The family thanked the doctors and nurses on their way out, and Dr. Amesbury informed them that he and Professor Smythe had agreed to correspond about possible collaboration in future research. Jason had taken yet another day off of work and had arrived, in his own car at the front entrance to bring Cindy and the kids back home. Aunt Tina would follow in her own car (which they had all come in) and would join the family in Park Slope for a small celebration. It had been their job to procure food and drinks for the occasion, which would include doughnuts, punch, a cheese and vegetable platter and champagne for the adults. Though she really wanted to be with her mom, Samantha politely elected to ride with Aunt Tina back to the apartment so that she wouldn't have to drive alone.

They followed Jason's car down First Avenue, crossing Twenty-third and then Fourteenth Street, through the East Village. Traffic was fairly heavy, it being Monday, and taxi cabs surrounded them on all sides as they squeezed by the last shades of green cast by the Houston Street traffic light. Samantha, still a little sleepy, looked at the cabs through heavy lids and tried to remember what the taxi-boats had looked like, and the streets all filled with water. It was very much fading from her memory, like a strange and distant dream, and as more time passed it became increasingly less real to her. Artificial trees, shark-men and ancient Central American warriors – all the elements of the last few weeks of her life were totally bizarre, she thought. It had been exciting, though having her mom so affected by her involvement with the time-travel bunch had been stressful and guilt-inducing.

The cars rolled through Soho, passing chic art galleries and hip coffee shops and finally got snagged in gridlock at the southern end of Allen Street, just before they patiently merged into the flow coming from south and west and onto the Manhattan Bridge. The line of cars crawled at a snail's pace across the East River, bottlenecked up from three streets worth of Manhattan traffic as well as runoff from the nearby FDR Drive. Samantha didn't mind, really. It was a clear, sunny day, if a bit on the chilly side, and the views of both Brooklyn and Manhattan were beautiful, sunlight reflecting sharply off the glass towers of the financial district.

The bright panorama seemed somehow strangely wrong. The huge twin towers no longer stood as the city's biggest reflectors. It was more than a decade now since that day in September when terrorists had flown planes into them, killing thousands of innocent people. It always made her sad to think about it. She was too young to remember it – it happened right around the time she was born – and she wasn't that in tune with global politics at all (they usually depressed her), but her personal experiences of the last two months had made her think about one thing in particular: since that day, it seemed like the world had been at war. Every day more innocent people died in foreign lands because of what had happened. And, the fact was, in the Slanes' altered timeline, there was no war. Those towers were still standing; she remembered them vividly, one or two stories shorter like every other building but still dominating the landscape and reflecting sunlight even more because the city's streets were all surfaced with water. In that world, they had been a weird, almost ghostly presence that Samantha had done her best to ignore. But they had been there.

She furrowed her brow while her mind grappled with these difficult truths. She wondered how many people would still be alive today if the Slanes' reality was what had prevailed. Tens, maybe hundreds of thousands, probably, in New York, Washington, Iraq, Afghanistan. *But,* she thought conversely, *How many people died from the global warming?* Flooding, heat stroke, starvation – the elimination of all trees and many plants had wiped out primary food sources for millions of people, perhaps billions. And the future of that timeline was bleak, for humans at least. She decided to put her mind at rest on the issue, concluding that this reality was indeed, despite its troubles, the more preferable of the two to live in.

They spilled out onto Tillary Street and turned onto Flatbush Avenue, where traffic was at least moving at a reasonable pace for once. It was mid-day, so rush hour was a long way off yet, and they cruised along comfortably, turning up Fourth Avenue before Samantha was even aware of it. Aunt Tina was a good, solid city driver and managed to make good time on the road whenever it was possible. The lights flew by now and the car slowed down to make the left turn up Ninth Street, one of the few two-way roads in Park Slope.

Aunt Tina found a parking spot up on Eighth Avenue, a few blocks away from the familiar brownstone that Cindy Smart somehow managed to make the payments on every month. The only reason that they owned it at all was because Cindy had won it in the divorce settlement with Samantha's father, who now lived in Seattle and worked as a computer programmer. It had been a while since Samantha had thought about him – he was so generally absent from her life. She got e-mails from him once a month or so and he would call once in a great while. She used to try to call him a lot, right after her parents' divorce three years ago, but he was almost never home and when he was he explained to her that being a programmer meant you had to work all the time. In some ways, Samantha still resented him for leaving them; on rare occasions she would just well up with anger and feel like it wasn't fair that her family had fallen apart when other families seemed so happy and functional. As she grew older, though, she had gradually begun to see that her mother, for all her goodness, had a hard time staying with one person, and that really, no family was perfect or without its own troubles and complications. Still, she missed her dad.

Polly took advantage of the three-block walk and took care of a little dog business, (thankfully unwitnessed by anyone as she had absent-mindedly forgotten to bring a bag to pick it up), and everyone was happy to be back home. The brownstone had been empty for almost a week and it smelled a little stale and un-lived-in when they opened the door. Still, being surrounded by the comforts of home was a feeling of great relief to all, and Samantha flopped down on the couch with a huge sigh of satisfaction. Aunt Tina started unwrapping the food they'd brought for the celebration brunch, and Cindy was touched by the ribbons, balloons and "welcome home" letters that

Jason had somehow found time to put up in the last twenty-four hours. The adults popped the cork out of a champagne bottle and the family began celebrating with smiles and optimistic conversation.

Samantha relaxed for what seemed like the first time in ages. After a few hours of talking with the family she went into her bedroom, breathed another sigh of relief and began the task of unpacking her backpack. She and Todd had been at Aunt Tina's for nearly a week (when they hadn't been at the hospital), and between that and her excursions to alien timescapes, she had begun to feel less and less like she had a home, anywhere. She was glad to be back now, looking around her familiar room, and was also excited to return to school and something like a normal life. She placed her wrist-communicator in a little jewelry box that locked, turned the key and then took it, attaching it to her house key-chain. She sat down on her bed and wondered at all she and her family had been through, thanked the powers that were for her dog and her friends and then stretched out, thinking that if anyone deserved a nap, it was she. Her eyes closed and she smiled slightly, and she was briefly aware of Polly coming up to lie next to her. It would be almost seventeen hours before she would wake again.

Snow was falling on Prospect Park as Samantha shivered in her winter coat and Polly did likewise in her Gortex dog sweater. The cold of winter had come on somewhat suddenly, or else it just seemed earlier or more extreme than usual. It was only two days until Christmas, and New Yorkers were everywhere scrambling around at an even more frantic rate than they typically did. Samantha's family was Jewish, and had done the Chanukah thing already – she was sporting a fancy new pair of boots and had also received many other clothes, books, CDs, DVDs and a fair assortment of other gifts from her mom, dad, brother, Aunt Tina and scads of other relatives that she hardly ever saw. Overall she had made out like a bandit, some would say; Chanukah wasn't really a big holiday compared to Yom Kippur or Rosh Hashanah, but, this being America, consumerism was pretty much the religion of now, and so everyone got presents at every holiday opportunity. Her absolute favorite of all her presents was a new, top-of-the-line laptop computer that Jason had given her. Samantha wondered briefly if maybe he was trying a little too hard to become part of their family, but then decided she didn't really care. She liked him a lot, anyway, and he seemed like he might stick around for longer than the average boyfriend her mother had historically had.

The computer was totally awesome. It was cutting edge, with a lightning-fast processor, a 500 gigabyte hard drive and a Blue Ray/DVD burner. It had a superfast wireless connection that even had a 4G network option so she could connect to the net through cellular towers if no WiFi was available. She wondered if The Professor could modify it to work through time – it would surely be very handy to be able to access the modern Internet if she was stuck back in the fifteenth century or some other, more primitive place.

Polly was tugging on her leash, suggesting that she was ready to go back to someplace warm and indoors and pulling Samantha out of her daydreams and back into the normal reality she had been living in (again) for the past few weeks. School had been fun, though she was now on vacation, and she had had to work very hard to catch up to her classmates, having missed so many days. She had enjoyed it, though, writing all those papers and even making up dozens of missed homework assignments. Her teachers had been understanding, having heard of the hard times her family had been going through, and Samantha was, after all, always at the top of her class, so the challenge actually kept the catching up interesting.

It was nice to have a break from it again, too, though. She didn't have to be back at school until something like the tenth of January and would have lots of time to read, explore or hang out with her dog. She hoped she would get to spend more time at the museum, both with her mom and with The Professor. Smythe had been tight-lipped as promised; their once-a-week meetings focused exclusively on non-time-travel-related research and experimentation. She was happy to learn more about forensics and chemical analysis, though she wondered if he would ever again mention their still very real, very important mission. Try as she might, it was impossible to tell how much they were or weren't being watched by F.B.I. agent Stiles or others. Both she and The Professor had become paranoid, always glancing over their shoulders, noticing 'suspicious' things and people that hardly would have made them think twice a month ago. Still, "better safe than sorry" was their new philosophy, for heaven only knew what chaos would be unleashed if the government were to get their hands on the time-traveling technology.

Samantha's mother had, in fact, received a call from Agent Stiles which Samantha had eavesdropped on. It sounded as if they had arrested someone in connection with Cindy's 'drugging.' She felt weird about this; whoever it was, they had not committed the crime, which she had fairly clearly witnessed or at least confirmed her suspicions about through her conversations in the past with Jordan Slane. He was obviously the guilty party. So whom had they arrested? She fretted, hoping it was some mob-connected drug kingpin who deserved to be in jail anyway, but how could she be sure? What if it was just some kid who happened to have been at the Heatwavvve show, maybe with some small prior record for stealing a candy bar or a video game? Surely someone like that, though perhaps guilty of other, more minor crimes, didn't deserve to go to jail for attempted murder!

Her uneasiness was amplified when she and Polly returned home and she took off their winter coats. Agent Stiles was there, sitting on their living room couch and enjoying a cup of tea with Cindy.

"Oh, hello Samantha," the pretty, sharply-dressed woman got up and gently shook her hand. Polly growled under her breath.

"Polly!" Cindy yelled, quieting the little terrier.

"Oh – sorry about that," Samantha added. "Hi." She petted Polly calmly.

"That's all right. Polly's just being a good, loyal protector. That's an admirable quality. One we look for in an agent, actually. How are you?"

"Oh, I'm good – I mean *well*," Samantha blushed a little, correcting her own poor grammar. "I've been back at school a lot."

"Your mother and I have been chatting a little, you know. We caught the person we think is responsible for blow-gunning her at the show."

"Really? Uh – um, I mean, wow! Who is it?"

"Sadly, it seems to be – a teenager. We'd actually like you to come downtown and see if you could possibly help us I.D. him."

"Um, sure... I guess," Samantha half-gulped. "I mean – I'm not exactly sure that I can, specifically."

"No?"

"Well, yes - and no. I mean, well – I could probably tell if it definitely *wasn't* the guy."

"Probably, definitely?" Agent Stiles raised an eyebrow and stared at Samantha for a moment. "I see. Well, I'd appreciate it if you could come with me anyway and aid us with whatever knowledge or memory you may have. We've put a lot of work into finding him."

"Yes, please, Samantha," Cindy was nodding, "whatever you remember, I'd feel a lot safer if I knew that whatever freak did this was locked up."

"Yes, all right," Samantha said nervously, unhitching Polly's leash. "I'll do whatever I can."

"It's not necessary for you to come, Cindy. I can get Samantha back home when we're done. It shouldn't take more than a couple of hours," Stiles assured them. Cindy nodded and Samantha tried to put on a 'helpful' smile.

The two departed, saying a quick goodbye to Cindy (and Polly). Todd was gone, off to Seattle to spend a week with their father. Samantha was jealous in a way, but had declined to go in case something came up with The Professor. She knew she'd hardly see their dad anyway, if she went; he was always so busy. She had sent a present for him along with Todd, however, a deluxe shaving kit. She laughed to herself when she thought of it; it was sort of an ongoing joke as their father generally wore a perpetual beard, which she disapproved of.

The car ride got interesting fast. Agent Stiles was as sharp as she looked, and the questioning began immediately.

"So, Samantha," she began, "I'm going to be straight with you. I know you're a very bright kid. In fact, I know a great deal about you that you probably don't think I know. The F.B.I. doesn't mess around, Samantha, especially when people could be in danger. I know that you studied aborigines in school two days ago. I know the exact route that you take through Prospect Park when you walk your dog. I even know that for lunch today you had a cheese and tomato sandwich, embellished with Marmite, a particularly nasty spread which you were no doubt introduced to by your mysterious British friend, Professor Smythe. But, Samantha, do you know what the most unsettling thing I know about you is at this moment?" Samantha shook her head, intimidated. "I know that you're hiding something from me.

"Now, despite watching you and your friends quite closely for the past few weeks, I'm still not sure what it is that you're hiding. What I do know, however, is that it's something big, something dangerous and, chances are, something that's way over your head. If I were you, I'd ask myself how many people could be affected by whatever it is that you know, and whether maybe you should seriously reconsider keeping quiet. You're only *eleven*, Samantha." She sighed, pausing for a moment in her lecture.

"When we get to the station, you're going to look at a sixteen-year-old Hispanic kid who's the only person we've been able to even loosely connect with this Heatwavvve fiasco, and if you I.D. him, he probably goes to jail for a lot of years and this case gets closed. If you don't I.D. the kid, we're all over you until this is solved one way or another. So, what's it going to be, Samantha? Is your memory getting better yet?"

Samantha was cowed by Agent Stiles' directness. This was the F.B.I. This was hardball. But what could she do? She trusted The Professor's judgement, more than anyone's. And he was an adult – he could get into much bigger trouble than she or any of her friends would, legally being minors. And they had agreed over and over again that for the time machine to fall into the government's hands would surely be disastrous. But she couldn't send an innocent person to jail. She couldn't live with that. She wished she could've talked to The Professor about this possibility days ago, but in the absence of his advice she was forced to act on her own.

"Your suspect is innocent," she blurted out, still trying to think of what to say next, if anything. She wished at this moment that there had been a law school for eleven-year-olds.

Stiles pulled over to the side of the road and put the car in 'park.' She looked over at Samantha with a deadly serious look.

"Samantha," she said sternly, "if you know who's responsible for putting your mother in a coma, *why* won't you tell me who it is!? Was it Smythe? Was it some accident, some experiment of his gone wrong? What!?"

"I can't tell you," Samantha said as calmly as she could. "If I told you, many, many more people would be endangered. The future – "

"The future!? I'm talking about the *present*, Samantha! The Bureau is stumped here, and if you don't give us some answers, we'll find them, and you'll wish you had. Now I'm going to ask you one last time: Do you know who is responsible for this?"

"I'm sorry," Samantha swallowed. "Your suspect is innocent."

There was a long silence as the two looked into each other's eyes, Samantha's sad and pleading and Stiles' frustrated and confused.

"All right," the agent turned away, turning the car around and going back up Fourth Avenue. "Tomorrow we'll have a search warrant for Smythe's office and labs, and don't be surprised if we show up at your door with one, either. I'll give you tonight to figure out how you're going to explain this to your mother."

Samantha nodded, almost in tears. Had she done the right thing? She was very worried.

*

Samantha was frantic. Agent Stiles had dropped her back off at home with something of a smirk on her face, one of those looks that said something like 'I'll get you, my pretty, and your little dog, too!' It had been tricky explaining to her mom why she was home so soon after leaving, but it had worked. Cindy was expecting Agent Stiles tomorrow so that they could 'finish their business.'

She went into her bedroom and closed the door, sat down on her bed where Polly was lying patiently. She wagged her tail hopefully; a walk was always a possibility. Samantha took her little key and unlocked the box that held her wrist communicator. She was about to call The Professor when she stopped and thought a moment. Even if the F.B.I. couldn't tap into its frequency, they still could have easily bugged the room, even placed tiny cameras in it. She quickly put the communicator in her pocket and looked around feeling as if she were being watched. She racked her brain for a safe place to try to contact The Professor. She could take Polly for a walk, but she had just done that and her mom might get suspicious, and once outside, agents could be lurking anywhere – hiding in bushes with highly sensitive directional microphones or binoculars powerful enough to read lips through. In a moment of inspiration, she walked out of her bedroom and over to the front door.

Cindy had most accommodatingly fallen asleep reading on the couch, and Samantha slipped noiselessly out into the hallway, silently shooing Polly, who was trying to follow. She walked halfway to the outside door and then made a U-turn following the stairs that led down to the brownstone's basement. It was a dark and somewhat damp place, but she was worried it could still contain bugs or cameras – The F.B.I. had a certain knack for being thorough, if they really wanted something. Samantha walked over to the laundry machines that were fit in under the staircase, opened the door to the dryer and got in. She pulled the door shut behind her and was suddenly enveloped by a most intense darkness. With her heart racing, she tapped the talk button on her communicator, having fished it out of her pocket.

"Professor?" she whispered loudly. There was no response. "Professor!?" she tried again, louder. Again, nothing. She waited, trying repeatedly over the next half hour. It was around six o'clock and her mother would probably wake up soon and start cooking something for dinner. Thankfully, there was no laundry in the dryer or she would have worried that her mother would come down and find her, though perhaps she would just laugh and wonder what in the world she was doing. Just as she was about to give up and go back upstairs, The Professor's voice came over the tiny receiver.

"Alpha Agent Prime? Come in, this is the Clockmaker. Are you there?"

"Yes!" Samantha said with great relief.

"All chatter to be coded," The Professor said, indicating that no names should be used. They would have to be creative in their speech.

"Is the frequency compromised?" Samantha asked, feeling very professional.

"Negative," the reply came back. "But still unsure about the premises. Calling from non-business location." That meant that The Professor's desktop unit was still at his house.

"I have important information," Samantha went on, trying to decide how to convey that Agent Stiles would be showing up at his lab the next day with a search warrant. "The... uh... hawk will be searching tomorrow. She'll have official papers. We must prevent her from looking at the... clock." She figured if Smythe was going to be the "Clockmaker" then the time machine must be the "clock," and Agent Stiles definitely had hawk-like qualities.

"This problem has been solved, Alpha Prime. We were expecting the hawk, so the Brooklyn Bandit and I made a few adjustments. The hawk will find nothing. Now, we must meet. All of Alpha Team. There is work to do regarding the sharks. I have located their base of operations. It is imperative that we infiltrate it and disable their... clock. It will be a complicated mission and may take days, but once we're gone, it won't matter if the hawk notices our absence. If we succeed, the threat to the world is over. We can disappear back into the background." The Professor sounded almost genuinely American in his attempt to disguise his voice.

"How do we meet?" Samantha asked.

"Go to your mailbox. There is a CD in it. Put this CD into your notebook computer. This will destroy any potential bugging or spying programs that may have been installed by the hawk while you were away from it. After that, you will take your computer to a public café with Internet access and check the email account we communicated through previously. There will be instructions on where and when we will meet and what you will need to bring."

"Samantha?" It was Cindy, calling her name down the stairs. Samantha's heart leapt.

"Gotta go," she whispered hurriedly. "All is understood. Will proceed as instructed. Alpha Prime out."

"Excellent. Clockmaker out."

Samantha turned off her communicator and slunk out of the dryer, trying not to make too much noise. She waited until her mother had gone looking somewhere else in the house and began walking up the stairs, as if she had been out in the back yard. When she came back up, Polly was jumping on her and her mother was standing in the kitchen with a puzzled look on her face.

"There you are," she said. "Where were you, Samantha?"

"I was in the yard," she replied.

"With no coat on!? It's freezing out there, Samantha! And why didn't you take Polly with you?"

"She just had a good walk an hour ago," Samantha half-mumbled. "I just wanted a little fresh air."

"Hmmmph." Her mother huffed, obviously suspicious. "Well, help me chop some broccoli. We're having chicken and broccoli tonight, and some rice."

"Okay." Samantha smiled. "Sounds good. Remember, Mom, you're only feeding two people tonight."

"Oh, yeah," Cindy said absent-mindedly. "I keep forgetting Todd is at your father's. The house has been mercifully free of sloppy teenagers and the sounds of video game monsters dying, though."

"Definitely," Samantha chuckled.

*

After dinner Samantha made ready to take Polly out for a walk. As she exited the house, she smoothly checked the mailbox, grabbing a parcel out of it and continuing on her walk. She could feel eyes on her even now and stared at every car on the street, wondering if Agent Stiles was sitting in one, watching her. She also wondered how The Professor had managed to get the package into the box without anyone having noticed, assuming F.B.I. Was watching the place round the clock.

No one jumped out at her, so she continued on up to the edge of the park. It was dark already and cold, and even the shivering Polly seemed to acknowledge that this walk would be a short one. She did her business quickly, and the two returned to the house in short order.

Cindy had asked if Samantha wanted to watch a movie upon their return, some girlish flick that Suki and Brianna would have enjoyed more, but Samantha declined and headed to her bedroom with a book, her excuse for self-isolating. Once inside, she quickly opened the package. Sure enough, it was a CD. She hastily took it out of its jewel case and popped it into her new laptop. Its 'Auto-run' kicked in and looked to be something like an Anti-virus program. It searched every file on her computer, finding and destroying at least five different spying "cookies" and seven other mysterious files. She had never seen anything like it and concluded that The Professor must have wrote the software himself, though it wasn't beyond Marvin's capabilities.

When the cleanser program was done, she took out the CD and put it into her little lockbox, locking it securely. Now she only had to think of an excuse to go out one more time so she could check the vital email that awaited her from a safe, random location. Even if she left, she figured, if there were agents watching her they would follow her to the café she planned to go to on Seventh Avenue.

She did, however, have a plan brewing in her head. She went out to the living room and hung out for a while with her mom, then feigned going to bed around 10:30. Cindy had to work tomorrow, so she would most likely be asleep soon. She would probably encounter Agent Stiles in the morning at the museum, but Samantha couldn't worry about that now.

At midnight, she snuck out of bed, shushing Polly, and down to the basement again, her laptop computer tucked neatly under one arm in its stylish, nylon traveling bag. At the opposite end from the laundry machines there was a grate in the floor; it drained to the city storm sewers and had been put in many years ago by a handyman whom her father had called when their basement had had troubles with flooding. She and Marvin had gone down it one day, as nine-year-olds (well, Marvin had been older), and found that it led into tunnels that ran underneath the entire neighborhood. It had been scary, and Samantha did not relish the thought of going down there again, but necessity demanded it, so she pulled off the grate and descended into the cold, wet underworld of Brooklyn.

She had been smart enough to bring along a flashlight, and turned it on as her feet hit the bottom of the tiny tunnel. The first hundred feet or so was the hardest: she had to crawl on her hands and knees through a tunnel that was barely wider than her, especially now that she was almost twelve and had grown considerably since her last adventure through this maze of brick and old stone. Luckily, she was still very thin, and the journey wasn't as bad as it could have been, though the tunnel's floor was coated in a thin sheet of December ice. She doubted that Marvin could have traversed the passageway at his current size.

She reached the larger tunnel that ran beneath Twelfth Street and extracted herself from the smaller one, finally able to stand. She turned right and began walking, keeping her flashlight pointed down lest some alert agent notice it through a street-gutter grate. The storm sewers were absolutely frigid and ice crunched beneath her feet. Under the ice was, of course, freezing cold water, which promptly soaked her new boots and made her fairly miserable and most unlikely to enjoy the trip back. *At least there are no rats,* she thought to herself, trying to look on the bright side of things, which was difficult in a dark, wet, freezing cold sewer.

She passed under Eighth Avenue and continued on; she could hear cars whizzing by above her and caught the occasional glimpse of the city above through grates. She kept moving, faster now as the sounds died away, and in about five minutes had reached Seventh, she thought. The sounds were busy and she came to a spot where she could see lights through a grate above her. These signs also corresponded with another crossroads in the tunnel, and she chose to turn right, which she was pretty sure was North, or at least toward Flatbush Avenue anyway. The cyber-café was down around Ninth Street, and she hoped that in the three blocks in between she might encounter a manhole with a ladder, or at least stepped grooves cut into the stone below it.

Almost immediately, she found one. An alcove was visible off to the left about a half a block down, and she made for it. The semi-circular well beneath the manhole cover was layered in graffiti;

obviously she wasn't the only one who had been down here. She slung her laptop over her shoulder, put her small, two-battery flashlight between her teeth and set to climbing the worn grooves in the old concrete wall.

When she got to the top, she stuck the flashlight, facing up, in her back pocket, so she still had some light to operate by. The manhole cover was very heavy and she almost despaired when she found that her arms could not lift it. Her small size had been an advantage up until now, but at this moment it betrayed her, and she felt quite helpless. She was not one to give up easily, however, and in an instant had wedged herself between wall and manhole, her feet on the highest notch in the subterranean concrete and her back pressed hard against the iron cover above her.

It was enough. The manhole cover rose slightly from its hole and slid some inches to the side. Worming her body into the crescent-shaped space she had made, Samantha flexed outward and edged the cover away from the hole as much as she could. It took her breath and she relaxed after her effort, though suddenly realized she was staring straight into an oncoming army of cars and quickly dropped back down below street level, holding onto the hole's rim with only her fingers. She sort of dangled there, wincing as the horn-blaring cars zoomed over her; she was certain at least one would crush her fingers as they sped by.

It seemed, however, that luck was on her side. The wave of evening traffic passed over her without her sustaining a single injury. When the cars were all gone, she hoisted herself up, finding in alarm that she had surfaced smack in the middle of Seventh Avenue, which was almost as busy a thoroughfare as Flatbush at this hour. She scurried quickly to the sidewalk, clutching her laptop to her chest and breathing heavily.

To the credit of her sense of direction (something that Marvin claimed females "simply didn't have"), she was more or less where she thought she would be. She brushed herself off and continued in the same direction, looking around as if she were still afraid agents were watching her. She walked quickly, (which she figured wasn't suspicious as most New Yorkers tended to move along at a brisk pace), hoping that the F.B.I. hadn't staked out the entire neighborhood.

Two blocks further she reached the café, looked quickly both ways and turned into the tiny storefront, her heart still beating fast with nervous energy. She smiled innocently as she purchased a hot cider from the attendant, who looked at her with some suspicion; it must have seemed a bit odd, a girl her age coming in alone after midnight. She sat down at an empty table and unpacked her computer, turned it on and let it locate the WiFi signal. There was only one other person in the café, a thirty-something man who looked bleary-eyed and over-coffeed, perhaps some kind of writer or web designer who was up late struggling to meet a morning deadline.

She accessed the Hotmail website and hurriedly typed in her 'secret agent' email address, *Timetraveler11*, which quickly yielded two new messages, one from The Professor and one from what had to be one of Marvin's web alter-egos, *'Dr.M@brooklyn.com*. She opened The Professor's first:

To: <u>Samantha Smart</u>
Re: <u>Further Operations</u>

<u>S.</u> - Communication is difficult. Surveillance is high. Our mission must, however, proceed. Alpha Team will meet in two days' time, at 2:00 p.m. in the women's bathroom in the 14th Street subway station, on the middle level. Bring your wrist-communicator. Plans will be discussed at this time. Try to avoid being followed.

Yours,
A.E.S.

Samantha noticed The Professor had shortened his signature to just initials, an extra precaution, no doubt. She mentally filed away the new information and opened Marvin's email:

204

To: <u>Samantha Smart</u>
Re: <u>Observation</u>

   <u>S.</u> - What up, girl? You'll probably get a visit from 'the hawk' tomorrow, and you can bet she'll be rooting around in uptown basements as well. Not to worry! We've got it all figured out. Pressure should ease off a little by the time Alpha Team comes together. Hope you had a good Hanukkah. See ya soon, lady.

Peace
Dr. Mashizzle

   She snickered at Marvin's signature. *Always the clown,* she thought. Both messages contained post-scripts instructing her to delete them immediately after reading them. This she did quickly, after sending brief replies of acknowledgment to each. She packed up and headed back outside, flashing a smile at the young man behind the counter. He gave her a subtle nod, unhappily eyeing the slight trail of water that her soaking wet boots had left on the floor.

   Samantha shivered as she walked back to her manhole. New York was a bleak sort of place sometimes in the winter, and she clearly hadn't dressed warmly enough. The lid was still ajar when she reached it, and traffic on Seventh Avenue seemed to be conveniently stalled at a light a block down, so she took the opportunity to wiggle back in, pulling the cover behind her as best she could. The route back was familiar enough, and in short order she was crawling back through the hole in her basement.

   She left her wet boots by the dryer and snuck quietly back up the stairs. It was a small miracle that Polly didn't bark as she re-entered the apartment; it seemed the little dog was content to just greet her quietly at the door, thankfully with a minimum of sproinging.

   Another five minutes saw her wet socks off and her computer stashed under the bed. She put on her flannel pajamas and crawled under her covers, inviting Polly and wondering fretfully what the morning would bring. Marvin had always taught her not to worry, though, that whatever was going to happen was going to happen, and so with only a little difficulty she slipped off into a warm, peaceful slumber.

*

As Samantha had expected, morning came violently. At what seemed like the crack of dawn, F.B.I. agents were banging on the front door. Cindy was not happy, throwing her robe on and eyeing the perfectly-put-together Agent Stiles with daggers as she walked through the door.

"Ms. Smart," the intimidating woman addressed Samantha's mom, "We have a warrant to search these premises, in connection with our investigation into the attempt on your life." She held up an official-looking piece of paper and nodded to her two male subordinates, who began searching the apartment.

"What!?" Cindy shrieked. "What in the hell do you think you're doing!? What, do you think I made this all up or something, now!?"

"I'm sorry, Ms. Smart," Stiles said calmly, almost appearing to smile. "It is actually my belief that you are indeed innocent of any crime. Unfortunately, I'm afraid that I can't say the same for your daughter."

"Samantha!? What are you, nuts? She stayed at the hospital with me every day! She rode in the ambulance with me! I've been a good mother to her for almost *twelve years*! No," Cindy waved her hand, walking to the telephone. "You're crazy. I'm calling the police."

"Suit yourself," Stiles shrugged. She walked over and handed Cindy the search warrant. "Just tell the desk Sergeant the number in the upper left-hand corner. He'll be able to confirm the warrant's validity." Cindy scowled and dialed the number for the police.

At this point, Samantha was out of bed and dressed, and she loosed Polly, who was barking furiously, from the bedroom. The terrier ran out into the living room and growled fiercely at one of the agents, who was kneeling behind a low chair looking at something or another. Slowly, he looked up with a thin, slight smile on his face. Suddenly, Polly let out a little whine, laid down on the carpet and was silent. Samantha was shocked. So was Cindy. They stared in disbelief at the dog and then at the agent, who broke into a large grin and shrugged.

"Hello, Samantha," Stiles greeted her icily. "Perhaps you'd like to end this little charade of yours right now and save yourself the trouble of putting your home back together."

"I don't know what you're talking about," Samantha lied. "I thought you were helping us."

You don't have to talk to her, Samantha," Cindy snapped, on hold to speak with the local police.

"No, and you obviously don't want to, either," Stiles frowned. "All right, be difficult. Gentlemen, let me know what you find; I'm going to meet the other team over at the museum. Perhaps I'll see you ladies there later?" She raised her eyebrow and turned to leave. This was obviously a rhetorical question, one that she didn't really expect an answer to.

After she left, Cindy finally got a desk Sergeant on the phone and grudgingly acknowledged the legitimacy of the piece of paper she was holding in her hand. She sighed and looked at the remaining two agents, black-suited and sunglassed just like the familiar stereotype.

"Well, go on, then!" she barked, clearly unhappy. "But if you leave this place a wreck I'll sue you from here to Jersey City." Cindy could be intimidating, too, if she wanted to be.

The agents were thorough. They confiscated Samantha's laptop, which made her very nervous. She had, of course, deleted all the possibly incriminating emails, but she knew that the 'professionals' had ways of extracting information from computers that you thought had been safely erased. She was actually surprised that The Professor hadn't told her to re-boot the whole system to insure that anything on the hard drive would be wiped. It was unlike him to not have calculated in details like that; she was also a little angry at herself for not having thought of it on her own. In any case, it was too late now. At least they had promised to return it "as soon as possible."

They had also found her lockbox and taken it. The 'cleansing' CD was still in it and Samantha kicked herself mentally for leaving it there. She hoped they wouldn't be able to somehow trace it back to The Professor. Her one consolation was that the wrist-communicator was still in her pants pocket when she woke up, and this she transferred to her shoe in case the agents would be searching their persons as well.

She needn't have worried, though, as they did not. They were most pleased with their finds of computer and CD, and had made her open the box with the little key on her keychain. Likely they, too were serious computer geeks, and couldn't wait to get the stuff back to their lab to try to pry loose any electronic secrets they might find. After they left, Polly got a brief walk and then it was time to go. Even though it was Christmas Eve day, the twenty-fourth, Cindy needed to go to work and demanded that Samantha accompany her. Her own brand of interrogation began on the walk to the subway station.

"Do you know what's going on here, Samantha? Why is this Agent Stiles suddenly all over our lives? Is there something you're not telling me?"

"I don't know why she's doing this all of a sudden," Samantha tried hard not to lie outright. "She thinks I know who blow-gunned you and that I'm not telling her."

"Well, do you?" Cindy asked, peeved.

"Mom, I *told* you," Samantha did her best tweener whine. "I didn't see exactly where the dart came from." This was essentially true, though she had dodged the more direct question. They reached the Ninth Street station and descended the stairs.

"Well, what happened with the guy that they caught?"

"It wasn't him, Mom. He was just some teenager with a little bit of a record. I *know* it wasn't him, and I didn't want him to get in trouble for something that he didn't do."

"Did you even go and look at him? You were home so fast yesterday – how could you know?"

"Agent Stiles described him to me. Just a poor Hispanic kid. It wasn't him, Mom – I remember the guy she described – he was at the show, but he was way too close to us to have used a blowgun. If you think hard enough, you'll remember him yourself."

"Well... all right," Cindy grumbled as they boarded an inbound F train. "I'll believe you. My own memory is pretty, well, fuzzy, as you might expect. But I would hope that you would want whomever is responsible for this to answer for it! This was no prank, Samantha; I was in a coma for five days! And let me tell you, I can always think of things I'd rather be doing than eating my dinner through a tube!" She grabbed a pole as the train started moving, taking Samantha's hand with her free arm. It was crowded – more last minute Christmas shoppers, no doubt.

"Of course I want them to answer for it, Mom. And they will, if I can do anything about it. It just wasn't that kid, I swear!"

They rode along in silence until they reached the Fourteenth Street station, where they had to switch to the C train to get uptown. They walked up the stairs through hundreds of rush-hour commuters and more frenzied shoppers and Samantha scoped out the women's room on the way. She asked her mom to wait so she could stop and check it out, feigning an urgent need. Cindy decided she might as well come in, too, so Samantha had to fake that she was using one of the toilet stalls. There didn't seem to be anything particularly special about the place, but this was to be Alpha Team's rendevous tomorrow afternoon. She marked the bathroom's location in her memory, flushed the toilet and came out to wash her hands.

"Come on, Samantha, we don't want to miss our connection," Cindy tried to get her moving.

They hurried to the uptown platform and just squeezed onto a C train before the doors closed and it left the station. It didn't really matter that much - there were lots of different lines that ran this route and they had taken a B, a 3 or a 4 at times when they'd had to. The C was probably the fastest, though, and they got off at Seventy-second Street no more than ten minutes later.

"I wish they'd fix that other damn stop," Cindy complained as they emerged from underground into the frigid air. Samantha silently agreed. She actually enjoyed the walk in the warmer months, but all travel was a pain in the winter, especially walking. It did perk the both of them up, however, and Samantha felt more awake and aware as they climbed the museum's steps. This was a good thing. From what Samantha could tell, they would want their wits about them to contend with Stiles.

The museum seemed normal at first glance. People were milling about as usual and the gift shop was especially busy due to the holidays. Cindy greeted Luann as they walked into the office behind the ticket counters, who immediately went into an excited account of the Federal agents' arrival that morning. Apparently, they were still there somewhere downstairs, likely tearing apart Professor Smythe's labs and office. Cindy grabbed Samantha's hand and headed for the stairway, assuring her somewhat dim-witted co-worker that she would be back shortly to commence her ticketing duties.

After walking down the stairs and traversing some length of hallways, they arrived at The Professor's office. Samantha gasped. It was in a shambles: Books and papers were strewn everywhere, CDs and floppy disks lined the floors and The Professor's main desktop computer was packed up in a pile of cords and wires. They could hear Smythe's voice coming from his back room, his closet-library, emphatically trying to protect his books, notes and databases.

"Lingering looters!" The familiar English accent almost shrieked. "This is my work! And – and my library! These books are priceless! If you harm a page of any of them, I'll have the mayor on you!"

"Relax," Stiles' silky voice replied. "We'll return everything exactly as we found it."

"When!?" The Professor blurted out in exasperation.

"When we're finished," Stiles said calmly.

"Wonderful," Smythe quieted down. "When you're finished. Well, I suppose I'll just have to start some new research in the meantime," he went on, almost just babbling to himself at this point. "Perhaps something useful this time, like how to breed the curiosity out of Federal agents or how to dissolve Federal agents in a red wine vinegar solution..."

Agent Stiles frowned at him, but her face quickly changed into a slight smile when she saw Cindy and Samantha coming toward her, picking their way through the debris.

"Ah, our other favorite suspect," she said, looking at Samantha.

"Cindy! Samantha!" Smythe ran up to them. "What's going on? Why is this woman destroying my office, my – my labs!?"

"I don't know, Ainsley," Cindy replied.

"They're tearing our house apart, too!" Samantha tried to play her best little girl.

"What are you people looking for!?" Smythe barked at Agent Stiles, who was just then whispering with a fellow agent.

"Actually," Stiles smiled a tight, thin-lipped smile, "we may have just found it. Professor, Samantha, would you follow us please? Ms. Smart," she turned to Cindy, "you're welcome to come as well, or you can return to your ticketing station, whichever you prefer." The way she said "ticketing station" made Cindy's blood boil. It was a snobbish, looking-down-the-nose tone the agent had used. Cindy decided to follow.

They walked out of The Professor's office and past his two main laboratory rooms, both of which contained agents hauling away some of the smaller machines and photographing those that were too big to easily move. Gallons and gallons of chemicals had also been impounded, and one agent was busy stuffing plant samples into large, plastic zip-lock baggies.

"I don't know what it is you think you're going to find," The Professor sighed deeply. "I've already given you all the information about the plant, my antidote formula and my process for getting it, Agent Stiles. What have I not made completely transparent to you?"

"Our scientists have studied your antidote – and your story, Professor," Stiles walked on, her words punctuated by the clack of her heels on the basement's tile floors. They were now heading straight for the time machine room. They reached the door and Stiles looked up at Smythe. "They've concluded that your explanation is implausible, and that they were unable to reproduce your experiments in their lab. Live DNA could not be extracted from the fossil samples you provided. This leads them to believe that your antidote could only have been synthesized from a recently harvested plant, that plant being *Phylathimus Phylathum,* which accepted knowledge holds has been extinct for at least nine hundred years." They reached the door with the keypad lock on it. "Combination, please."

The Professor looked up at Agent Stiles, then at Cindy and Samantha. Samantha tried not to gulp obviously but began to break out in a nervous sweat. Stiles smiled as The Professor started punching in the correct numbers and resumed putting forth the conclusions of her investigation.

"Therefore, it follows that you either a) know of some secret supply of this plant that's growing somewhere that no one else, except perhaps the perpetrator of this crime, is aware of, or b) – " The Professor finished dialing the combination and the lock clicked open. The little LED indicator light went from red to green. " - you've found a way to retrieve things – living things, even, by manipulating... *time*." She barely smiled and turned the doorknob, pushing the door open. Samantha held her breath. One of the lesser agents reached in and flicked the light switch on... and found nothing.

Well, it wasn't exactly nothing. Samantha let out her breath, closing her eyes for a split second in relief. Agent Stiles looked puzzled, her usually perfect composure somewhat shaken and uncertain. She looked all around, her hawk-like eyes seeking out the slightest sign of a cover-up. She bit her lip.

"Check it out," she said quietly to her subordinates, who began to move around the room. It was nothing like it had been. The time machine had somehow miraculously vanished, and in its place were dozens of artificial trees. The agents explored the entire room, examining the virtually identical devices and shrugging at each other until at last Stiles spoke up.

"What are these devices, Professor Smythe?" she snapped.

"Well," The Professor said slowly, "they're, ah, they're what I've been working on lately. Ah – look," he bent down to the controls of the nearest one. "You see the readout? Here we have numbers indicating the intake of carbon dioxide. And the other set of numbers is oxygen output. They're, ah, essentially artificial trees."

Stiles stared at Smythe, who smiled hopefully. She was not happy.

"It's, well, I've been sort of trying to keep it a secret, you see.

They take in carbon dioxide, process it just like plants, and release oxygen into the atmosphere. The extra, er, carbon and such is stored here, in the base." The Professor knocked on the hollow metal bottom of a 'tree.' "I planned to patent it, actually. Maybe retire somewhere nice, like the Caribbean, you know? In any case, as you can see, there's nothing here related to *Phylathimus Phylathum* or, eh, any other sort of *real* plant."

Stiles stood, listening, and fumed. It was plain to see that the perfectionist investigator had not found the necessary evidence to prove whatever theories had been cooking in her head, and it sounded to Samantha as if those theories had been dangerously close to the truth. However The Professor had pulled this off, it was sheer genius. The artificial trees were so 'out of left field' that they had even surprised Samantha, and defending himself about the plant, *Phylathimus Phylathum,* was another brilliant distraction. Neither of these things really had much to do directly with time or time machines, but they were believable eccentric pursuits for Smythe to convincingly feign a passion for.

"Grab a few of these for our lab," Stiles bitterly chewed her words. "Professor," she spun around quickly, trying to penetrate his soft old British eyes with her razor-edged glare, "I'm afraid I owe you an apology." She sighed and relaxed a little. "We'll return these as soon as possible, within the week, I promise. We'll also have all your notes, books, computers, files and lab samples back within that time. I'm sorry if this has been an inconvenience to you. We're just trying to follow every lead or theory we can come up with to try to apprehend Ms. Smart's assailant. I'm sure you understand."

"Certainly," Smythe said calmly. "Of course, as always, I offer whatever I can to help you. I just don't see what you're looking for here, agent, and I think perhaps your methods of obtaining assistance might be a little, er, extreme, if you know what I mean." Stiles momentarily looked at the floor, then back up at The Professor.

"Yes, well, as I said... I do apologize." She turned to her subordinates. "Have any and all evidence brought immediately to the Canal Street labs," she said curtly. The men nodded and two of them began carrying an artificial tree out of the room and toward the lobby stairway (it was definitely a two-man job). Stiles nodded and began to walk out the door. "Anytime you want to talk, Samantha," she said as an aside. Samantha nodded silently.

"Agent Stiles?" The Professor called after her. She turned in the doorway to acknowledge him. "Does this mean I can have tea and biscuits somewhere without being on film?" Smythe grinned a hopeful grin.

"Pretty hard in this town," Stiles replied. "Just ask Jordan Anderson." She smiled slightly and then was gone.

Christmas morning came with something of a whimper, though of course ever-commercial New York City did its best to put the 'bang' into it. Even in Brooklyn there were Santas roaming the streets, advertising holiday sales for electronics stores or hawking candy canes to bored neighborhood children. Samantha and her mother had gone to meet Jason for a holiday brunch down at Katina's on Seventh Avenue, and had enjoyed some eggs and toast in relative peace.

Jason and Cindy had made plans to go to a party, which suited Samantha just fine. By noon she had the house to herself and was formulating a plan to get to the Fourteenth Street station by two, and she hoped that her friends would be able to escape any holiday duties that might inhibit them from meeting to commence the next step in whatever plan Professor Smythe had cooking.

She decided to slip out secretly, through the sewers again, which was probably a good idea, all things considered. Agent Stiles had given no indication that surveillance would ease up, despite the fact that her investigation had hit a major wall thanks to The Professor's ingenuity. Samantha remained just as wary of the F.B.I., however; Stiles' mention of Jordan Anderson had been disturbing, another hint that she knew a lot more than she was letting on.

Polly would not sit still this time. She followed Samantha's every step, and eventually Agent Alpha Prime gave in to her dog's loyalty and let her get into her familiar backpack.

"Polly," Samantha whispered, "Not a peep out of you until we're somewhere safe, okay?" The little terrier hunkered down and quieted her excited panting – it was almost as if she understood.

The sewer trip was easier this time – there was, at least, some light down there in the middle of the day. It was also wetter, though, for the air was warmer today and the ice on the sewer floor had thawed. Nonetheless, Samantha made a quick trip of it and was soon emerging from a different manhole she had found that opened up in a nice, safe curbside location on less-trafficked Sixth Avenue.

Deciding it was best to travel as 'low profile' as she could, she walked down along Twelfth Street, avoiding her local subway stop and opting to hoof it down to Fourth Avenue, where there was also a station at Ninth Street. She had worn some uncharacteristic clothes: sweat pants (her mom's) and an old, lined leather jacket that had been Todd's favorite until he had outgrown it. Her hair was all tucked up inside her warm winter hat with the Yankees' logo on it and she had on a dark pair of glasses. She looked very much like any New Yorker, she hoped.

The F train was waiting as she reached the platform and she just made it through the doors before they closed and the train started rolling. She thought she had glimpsed a few men in black staking out the station about thirty feet down from her, but who knew? There were plenty of sharp dressers in this city and for all she knew they could just as easily have been Mafia as Federal agents, or even just expensive car salesmen.

The train ride was quick, as there were surprisingly few people traveling at this hour. Samantha guessed that most people were probably already at whatever place they had been going, and she was grateful for the unusually spacious subway car. In contrast, though, she was nervous after disembarking at Fourteenth Street, which was normally crawling with people and would have been a much more anonymous place had it been so today.

Even so, her walk up to the bathroom proceeded uneventfully, and she didn't notice any suspicious-looking people on the way. She reached the bathroom quickly, without incident, and looked both ways before entering the unlikely meeting place.

It looked completely normal – no one was there that she could observe. It had to be about two o'clock by now, and she looked around for any sign that might indicate the presence of The Professor or Alpha Team. There was a slightly larger, handicapped stall at the back of the bathroom and she entered this, half-expecting to find all of her friends huddled quietly on top of the toilet seat. But there was nothing.

She looked the stall up and down, her eyes catching various bits of graffiti that ranged from phone numbers to obscene comments to pictures of kittens and band logos, rendered in fairly well-done 3-D text. She sighed and sat down on the only seat available, nervously playing with her thumbs. After a few minutes of sitting in silence, she thought she heard something; it was a voice, for sure, but where was it?

There, she thought. It was coming from the pocket of her – of Todd's jacket. She had brought the wrist-communicator but had opted not to put it on in an effort to draw less attention to herself from any knowledgeable party. She took it out and pressed the talk button, shushing Polly who was starting to whine from inside her backpack.

"Um... Clockmaker?" She whispered hopefully into the thing's tiny microphone.

"Alpha Prime," the familiar British voice responded. "Stand by." Samantha sat, waiting.

In an instant, reality warped. The stall was enveloped in the now-familiar flashing blue lights, and a second or two later The Professor was standing in front of her, glowing chalk in hand.

"Trace your feet," he said hurriedly, handing her the chalk. She did so as quickly as possible, looking up at him and smiling slightly.

"Merry Christmas," she said.

"Thanks," Smythe replied. He pressed the talk button on the wrist-communicator that he was wearing. "Now, Marvin," he spoke into it.

Once again the light show commenced, though Samantha felt she was almost getting used to it at this point. The Mayan symbols were all now somehow familiar, almost like things she knew the meanings of, though she still couldn't have translated them literally if anyone had asked her to. In a moment, they were somewhere else.

And what a 'somewhere else' it was. Samantha's jaw dropped immediately upon arrival. It was a place unlike any she had ever been in. She stood, with The Professor, on the time machine's central stone platform. Around them was, of course, the Stonehenge-like configuration that made up the rest of the amazing Mayan apparatus – but even this was visually dwarfed by the incredible structure that surrounded it, and them.

They were on a vast, flat plane of floor that was encased in a gigantic dome, a sphere almost, made up of thousands of triangles. The whole of the thing must have stretched the length of a football field in diameter, and the structure's ceiling was almost as far above their heads. Sunshine poured in through the translucent, triangular windows, illuminating everything with a glassy, reflective glow. Samantha's eyes wandered the breadth of the place, then came at last to settle on what was closest to her: Marvin's devious smile.

"What up, girl?" he grinned. "Merry Christmas."

"Felice Navidad," she answered in Spanish, smiling back at him. She turned to The Professor. "Is this the future?" she asked.

"Montreal. 1967," he replied matter-of-factly. "If you knew your history, you'd recognize it." He stepped down from the platform and walked over to a table with books and maps on it. "We're in a geodesic dome – that is, a partial sphere composed of triangular supports, designed by R. Buckminster Fuller. Theoretically, there's no limit to the size of such a thing that could be built; it's one of the near-perfect applications of this model for structural integrity. Affectionately, they're known as 'Bucky Balls.'"

"Bucky Balls..." Samantha repeated, dazed and still staring at the amazing building around her.

"Bucky Balls," Marvin echoed, capturing her gaze and grinning again.

Polly poked her head out of the backpack at the mention of the word "ball." She knew this word very well from playing fetch in the park, and wondered now if some game of fetch was afoot. Marvin greeted her loudly and with a friendly head-scratch; she was happy to see him. Samantha, sensing her dog's excitement, let her out of the backpack and allowed her to run around on the spacious floor of the dome.

"It's a few months after the World's Fair," Smythe went on, already deeply involved in some text on the table of what was obviously their new makeshift headquarters. "I found most of a day when no one was here and figured out how to transport the entire time machine. Marvin helped out..."

"Yeah, *whatever!*" Marvin cut in. "I had to do almost everything!"

"Well," Smythe shot Marvin a look, "in any case, I've got the thing on a sort of loop. There is a window of some five hours when no one was in this place, and I've set the time machine to keep transporting itself – and everything within its perimeter, of course – back to the beginning of the five hour period, every four and a half hours. I've had to adjust it so as to erase what was there before, so we don't keep piling up multiple Smythes and Marvins and Samanthas, all doing different things in different time-streams, but I think I've calculated everything quite properly. Do you follow?"

"Yeah..." Samantha scratched her head, trying to understand. "So, I guess you've gotten pretty good at programming this thing, huh Professor?"

"You've no idea," Smythe looked up, appearing exhausted.

"Professor." A voice rang out halfway across the vast chamber. It was Suki. She and Brianna were standing over a table whose surface appeared to be a computer screen of some sort. "I think we've got a lock. I'm feeding the coordinates into your main computer." Suki looked up and smiled at Samantha, as did Brianna.

"Excellent," Smythe beamed with genuine excitement. The girls walked over to The Professor's station. They both exchanged greetings and hugs with Samantha and Brianna bent down to scratch Polly behind the ears, as the team's unofficial mascot had come back around to sniff everyone and make sure everything was in order. The four kids then gathered around The Professor to stare with him into the makeshift headquarters' central computer. Onscreen was a map of what looked like a chain of islands, following a slight curve that described some deep undersea chasm. A flashing point indicated the sought-after coordinates, whatever it was that they represented. The Professor held a key on the computer keyboard and outlined the area with the mouse so that the picture zoomed in on the selected area.

"The Mariana Trench," he said, leaning back from the screen and assuming one of his looks that meant he would probably start talking to himself. "I suppose that makes perfect sense for super-evolved sharks. Though it seems like it would be too cold for them. Can we get a depth on those coordinates, Suki?"

"Sure, Professor," Suki responded, going back over to the other computer and punching some keys. "It looks like... wow. It says it's approximately five thousand meters below sea level – I think that's like, what, three miles down?"

"Indeed," Smythe scratched his beard thoughtfully. "Very deep. And probably very cold. Too cold for sharks – unless..." He trailed off.

"Unless?" Samantha looked up at him.

"That's it. There must be a vein of very warm water down there somewhere, probably next to an open fissure. The area is, after all, composed of active volcanoes."

"What exactly are we looking at, Professor?" Samantha finally submitted, very much confused at this point.

"Hmm? Oh – sorry, Samantha, I suppose we should bring you up to speed here," he said, stepping back and looking at Alpha Team once again. "We have determined that the Slanes are operating out of some sort of base in the Pacific – apparently an undersea base and not, as I originally suspected, a boat of some sort. The flashing point on the screen is a signal from a homing device that Jordan was just foolish enough to bring there with him – albeit through a little, humph, shall we say, brilliant trickery." Smythe looked quite pleased with himself.

"How did you do it?" Samantha took the bait.

"Well, it was nothing really. Just a bit of, oh, psychological warfare, you know. Back in Central America, when I rescued your carelessly misplaced wrist-communicators from Jordan's hut, I replaced them with duplicates, exact copies of yours. Of course, they were somewhat altered: None could actually broadcast or receive on the unique band we use and each contained a powerful homing device that I was able to track from this computer. We gave them some frequencies, of course, useless ones really – I think all they could tap into was... what was it, Marvin?"

"Nepalese radio, I think. Short wave," the Brooklyn Bandit grinned.

"Right," Smythe chuckled. "Nepalese radio. Anyway, I had hoped that the lad would be curious enough to bring at least one back to his base of operations, to try to figure it out or attempt to crack our 'Nepalese code' or some such, and evidently that's just what he did. Save those coordinates, Suki."

"Done," Suki piped from the other computer.

"Wow," Samantha marveled, giving Marvin and The Professor an impressed look. "Clever boys," she smiled and patted them on their backs.

"So what's next, then?" Brianna spoke up.

"Some sort of... probe, I imagine," Smythe replied. "We need a more concrete set of coordinates if we're going to transport ourselves in there." This got a shudder from Suki. "I believe I can, er, borrow such a probe from a colleague of mine. We need to get a good visual on the place as well. Marvin, if you can operate the controls, I can fetch it and be back in a minute. Are you confident enough in your abilities yet?"

"Yeah." Marvin suddenly dropped his cockiness, as if a bit unsure. "Yeah, I can do it, Professor. Just set the initial settings for me and I can get you back."

"Are you *sure?*"

"Yeah, I'm sure. I got you, man." His tone was very serious.

In a moment Professor Smythe was on the stone platform and Marvin was at the time machine's ancient controls. The Professor winked at Alpha Team and gave the 'thumbs up' sign, and Marvin moved the loose pieces of obsidian around that somehow controlled the time machine's functions. In an instant, the old Brit was gone. Polly gave a quick, yelpy bark as he disappeared from sight, and for a second everyone tried to place themselves inside her canine mind. She must, they all concluded, be very confused indeed about the whole time travel concept.

Now they were faced with their own confusion: Time travel presented many mental conundrums; it was hard to wrap one's mind around all the possibilities of it. The Professor had been transported back to the nominal 'present,' presumably to spend 'time' conjuring up some deep-sea probe from a scientific colleague of his that worked in that field. Though this process would take him several hours or even days, he could be transported back to a mere minute after he had left, thanks to his looped time machine setting that constantly erased occurrences and so prevented more than one of each of them from existing in the same place at the same time.

The problem was, at least initially, Alpha Team had to wait for The Professor's call in 'real time,' in other words, they had to wait, through approximately thirty-five hours of looping, for his call, with not much to do.

They talked about their holidays, their families and what they'd all been doing for the last month or so. Suki had apparently traveled to Tokyo for a week to spend time with her father, and had, in the process, encountered Samantha's brother Todd. It seemed like an amazing coincidence but wasn't really, if you thought about it. Both had left on the day after school got out, and both had been booked on a flight to Seattle, though Suki's had left earlier than Todd's. They had run into each other in the SEA-TAC airport, Todd being picked up by their father and Suki waiting for a connecting flight to Japan.

"Did you, um – did you see my dad?" Samantha asked in a hopeful tone. Suki had met her father on one occasion when he had visited New York a couple of years ago.

"Yeah – he said to say 'Hi' to you, and that he misses you. He said he'd call soon."

Samantha nodded. That was her father's way; maybe he would actually call. "Thanks, Suki." She smiled slightly.

Brianna was, of course, covered from head to toe in new clothes and jewelry, sporting the latest smart phone and a faux-snake-skin handbag that was simply to-die-for. She seemed to be in a wonderful mood, and insisted she be allowed to photograph the team with her new toy. It was a fairly nice phone-camera, and so even allowed Brianna to be in the picture thanks to its automatic timer function. It was funny how it came out, and they all had a good laugh looking at Marvin's mischievous devil-horn-thumbs that he had ungraciously (and unbeknownst to her), embellished Suki's head with, and the caught-in-action Polly who had just squirmed free of Samantha's grip. They decided to keep it, and Suki downloaded it onto all the computers as background wallpaper, adding some neat 3-D text in a photo-editing program that said "Alpha Team," like something from a comic book or cartoon that made them look like super-heroes.

Marvin had had the hardest time getting away on this, Christmas morning. He came from a very large, very Catholic family, and so after going to church and then back home to prepare for a day of extreme feasting, he had slipped out his bedroom window after changing his clothes. He had evidently been the most active team member, however, and killed some time by relating to the girls how he had helped The Professor move their base of operations to this wondrous dome.

They feasted on apples and granola bars that Suki had had the aforethought to stock the place with, and she had even remembered dog food and a water bowl in the event that Polly would be joining them. The hours ticked by, everything around them and even they themselves occasionally flickering as the time machine projected itself and them backward in time, recording over, as it were, their previous existence in that spot in space and time. At some point they all grew tired and fell asleep on mats that Marvin and The Professor had brought along with the equipment.

After a day and a half had passed, the desk unit communicator crackled.

"Marvin?" The Professor's voice came through.

"Right here," the Brooklyn Bandit answered after scrambling to his feet to answer the thing. "Any time now..."

"Okay. Hang on a minute, Professor," Marvin concentrated, remembering the sequence of obsidian placement, hoping he wouldn't screw up and transport their leader into the Spanish Civil War or something. Alpha Team all looked at each other knowingly, as the machine was set to bring The Professor back to a minute after he had left, effectively rendering their last thirty-five hours non-existent, an alternate timeline with a dead end. Marvin sighed and finished the operation, still a bit apprehensive.

There was no need to worry. In a crackle of blue energy, The Professor appeared, holding a very heavy-looking piece of technology. No one was aware that he'd been gone for more than a minute.

"Help me out here, would you, mate?" Smythe's voice was strained, though he was smiling. Marvin ran over and helped The Professor with his burden. Together they managed to place the thing on a large, flat table. It was about five feet long and perhaps two feet wide, made of shiny yellow metal with black rubber seals all over it. It was outfitted with wires as well, which were all covered with black, waterproof-looking insulation, and had two cameras like eyes that stuck out from its main body on firm steel stems, giving it the overall appearance of a giant metal bug or frog. At its rear end were four sturdy-looking propellers, mounted independently so as to enable their individual movement for turning, diving and such.

"The mighty UD476," The Professor grinned, obviously eager to educate them as to the machine's capabilities. "Compliments of Dr. Thor Stevenson, marine archeologist. Functional to a depth of ten thousand meters – er – theoretically, anyway. Stereoscopic camera imaging with ten watt light amplification. Shielded, multi-layered stereo microphone and a transmitter I modified myself using the wrist-communicator technology." He beamed, looking proud of himself. "That's what took me so long."

Everyone stared at him, a bit confused. Finally, Brianna spoke.

"You were only gone for a minute, Professor." Smythe stared at her for a moment.

"Puttering Paradoxes!" he exclaimed. "I'm sorry. I forgot – you all must have no memory of the last day or two. My mistake." Alpha Team looked at each other and shrugged.

"Anyway," Smythe continued, "we should be able to transport this unit to the proper coordinates, underwater, and have it transmit sound and images back to here – er, now. It also has a temperature sensor and something of a primitive capability for water analysis – er – salt and mineral density and those sort of things."

"Well," Samantha said after assessing the faces around her, "let's get crackin'."

*

The images on the computer screen were faint at first, but The Professor cranked up the power on the light-amplification module to "high," and a crisp, deep-green-tinted world began to materialize before their eyes. The probe was clearly zipping through some beautiful undersea canyon, the bottom of which could only be guessed at; the Mariana Trench was the deepest, most remote part of the Pacific Ocean's floor. The temperature sensors were reading very cold, only thirty-five degrees Fahrenheit, a few degrees above freezing.

As it progressed through the rift, however, the graphed bars on the computer screen began to rise. There was also a noticeable increase in the sulfur content of the water, which The Professor had predicted.

"The Slanes' base must be located close to an underwater volcano," he observed. "Sulfur is leaking out of some fissures somewhere – cracks in the volcano's cone. The water will become much warmer as well. We'll likely see bubbles of sulfurous smoke escaping from a steep slope around here somewhere."

As usual, Smythe was correct. As he guided the probe from its remote control unit, it rounded a bend in the chasm and encountered a massive, steep-sloped undersea mountain, belching steady streams of smoky bubbles from several cracks in its sides.

"Cool." Suki stared, mesmerized.

"Bear left," Marvin chimed in; he had been put in charge of watching the GPS map on the other computer screen which showed the probe's proximity to the proper coordinates.

The Professor edged the probe around, appearing a bit nervous as it passed through one of the columns of smoke bubbles.

"Hot stuff, volcanic gas," he grinned uneasily. "Not too hot, I hope."

The probe seemed to withstand the temperature change with little effort. The bar graphs on the screen went haywire, at one point reaching some two hundred fifty degrees, but the little drone held, emerging on the gas plume's opposite side into a sea of other, smaller ones. The Professor tried his best to maneuver the thing in-between the pillars of undersea fire, taking navigational cues from Marvin as necessary.

"You're almost there, Professor," Marvin said excitedly. "Just edge upward and a little bit to the, uh, west."

The next few moments were spectacular. The probe skimmed up the slope of the volcano and through another, almost sheet-like wall of escaping gas, rounded a ridge and – there it was.

"Amazing," The Professor whispered.

There, built five thousand meters below sea level, into the side of an active underwater volcano, was the Slanes' base of operations. It was pearly white and donut-shaped, perhaps two hundred feet in diameter, though half of it was enveloped by the volcano's rocky slope. It had several long, oval-shaped windows in its bulging upper section, and its lower half was smaller and more of a flat-walled cylinder, with what looked like bay doors in two or three places. The temperature of the surrounding water read at eighty-nine degrees, and dozens of sharks were in evidence, swimming around the place as if it were some sort of nest to them. Alpha Team looked at each other with fear in their eyes – this was where they would have to go to stop the Slanes.

"All right," The Professor said. "I'm going to plant the markers."

"What? What does that mean?" Samantha questioned, getting a little antsy.

"The markers," Marvin explained, letting The Professor concentrate on piloting the probe. "We need to place three markers on the shell of the base so we can triangulate a position to transport to."

"It's got to be a little more precise than the Mexican desert, you know," Smythe volunteered, inching the probe next to a window and releasing a magnetic marker that stuck to the base's outer surface. "You wouldn't want to wind up outside here, would you?" He steered the probe a ways around the donut-shaped upper half of the building and released another marker, at the same depth as the last. "The water's warm enough here, I suppose– you'd be very comfortable, in fact, if you had some scuba gear, if it wasn't for the immense pressure."

"Pressure?" Brianna asked innocently.

"Why, yes, my dear," Smythe chuckled. "Some fifteen thousand pounds per square inch or so. There's an awful lot of water above this place, enough to crush any of your bones to jelly, or..." he looked up with a somewhat devious smile, "perhaps more of a tapioca pudding. Mmm, quite likely." He nodded, returning to his piloting.

Two sharks had, unfortunately, taken an interest in their probe and were occasionally smashing their heads into it, causing the images to shake violently and short out for split-seconds here and there. The Professor tried to dodge the animals, swerving, looping and changing course, and eventually managed to get them into a fight with one another and slip the probe away, back on track to place the last magnetic marker. This was executed with relative ease.

"Marvin, test the markers," Smythe barked orders to the most mediocre rapper in Brooklyn, who shot him something of a sour, 'yo, don't order me around' look, but did as his mentor had asked. On his computer screen, which showed the GPS imaging, he could see the three points that represented the markers. He tapped a few keys and coordinates appeared onscreen above each point. He then moved his mouse and clicked an onscreen button that triangulated them, that is, by doing some fancy math at speeds that only a computer can, gave Marvin the exact point in the center between the three dots, along with its coordinates. This point stood for, hopefully, a spot inside the base on a nice floor somewhere that they could transport Alpha Team to.

"Got it," said Marvin, hitting the print button. The printer spit out a sheet of paper with all the necessary information, and Marvin leaned back in his chair and sighed. The Professor piloted the probe around again, collecting all the markers it had just placed so as not to leave any evidence that someone had been poking around the base. He then guided the remote-controlled drone away from the structure, down, deeper into the almost bottomless trench, until he found something of a cave that he could park it in. He edged the little machine in far enough so that it was not likely to be discovered, but not so far that it would be impossible to get out. It was not within their power to transport it back the way it had come – just like the hang-glider and speedboat in the Yucatan, there had been no way to trace its entrance point with the special Mayan chalk, still the only method they knew of to return things, or people, to their point of origin. They would have to retrieve it with a boat, later.

"Well," Samantha said as Professor Smythe turned off the probe's 'eyes' and 'ears,' "I guess we've got some planning to do."

*

Alpha team stood, together, staring over the odd printouts before them. They were patterns that represented the strange, ancient controls of the time machine, black ovals standing for the pieces of obsidian glass that had to be arranged exactly for the machine to function properly. Marvin paid special attention, as he was to be in charge of programming the Slanes' version of the machine for self-destruction.

"This must be done in the proper sequence," Professor Smythe was insisting. "According to my calculations, these patterns, arranged in this exact order, should set up a *time-hole* effect, sucking the entire apparatus into its own dead-end timeline where no one should be able to access it again, even from our machine." He looked up with a deadly serious expression on his face. "Needless to say, you should all keep well clear of their machine after the reaction has begun, if you don't want to be sucked into limbo with it."

Samantha swallowed hard and the team members all looked at each other and nodded, preparing themselves mentally for the tasks ahead.

"Brianna and Suki," Smythe continued his instructions, "You two are in charge of accessing the base's central computer and transmitting its vital information back to me through these modified wrist-communicators." He handed them the devices and explained how to use them. "These firewire attachments should hook into compatible ports on their computer. Find the ports, attach the communicators and hit the talk buttons. I've installed certain software in them that should automatically access their information and start transmitting it to my computer here, with the most recent files being transmitted first. If the Slanes are up to any new mischief, hopefully we can derail their plans. Understood?"

The girls nodded.

"Samantha," The Professor smiled a grim smile. "I'm afraid that leaves you with the toughest job. I'm counting on your absolute level-headedness and general bravery for this, Alpha Prime. I'm putting you in charge of security."

Samantha did her best to look calm and soldierly, though she became inwardly uneasy when The Professor opened up the mysterious, tall metal cabinet that had occupied a spot near the perimeter of their headquarters and retrieved what looked to be a fearsome weapon of some sort.

"This, Samantha, is a NEPTUNE-60 explosive-tipped spear-gun. It has twenty spears, each tipped with an explosive head that will make mincemeat out of any creature smaller than a large orca – er, killer whale, that is. The spears travel almost as fast through water as they do through air, though hopefully you won't have to worry about that." He showed her how to hold the thing, which was extremely heavy, though a shoulder strap took most of the weight off her arms. "There's a safety switch here," Smythe indicated a slider on the weapon's side. "Red means 'safety on;' it won't fire like this." He slid the switch. "Green means 'safety off' – this will allow you to pull the trigger." The trigger was fairly self-evident, and she nodded that she understood the rest of the process, though he helped her with aiming as well.

"*Never* point this thing anywhere near your friends. It would also be extremely prudent not to fire it toward any essential structural components of the base, windows or critical computer systems. Only use it at all in the most dire circumstances. Do you understand?"

"Yes, Professor," she replied responsibly.

"Good. I would have assigned this duty to Marvin, but I trust your judgement and I need him to handle the self-destruct on the Slanes' time machine, as he is the only one with some experience in programming the controls." He stood up very straight and surveyed his team like an army colonel about to send them into battle. "Any questions, Alpha Team?"

Brianna meekly raised her hand. "Um, how do we get out of there, Professor?" she asked.

"The same way you always do," Smythe responded. "You will use the chalk to trace your feet upon arrival. When you've got their time machine programmed, return to your footsteps and cue me with a communicator. Make sure all of you are ready and in place – we may only have a few seconds."

They stood solemnly. There were no more questions. It was time for action.

*

They stood on the time machine's stone platform once again, feeling dwarfed by the vast dome that surrounded them. Marvin clutched the printouts that would show him the correct sequence for programming the self-destruct, and Samantha shouldered the weighty NEPTUNE-60, prepared to defend their mission's success to the end. The Professor stood at the controls, Polly sitting nervously at his side.

"Ready?" he asked simply.

"Ready," they all responded, taking deep breaths.

Smythe began the process, aligning the black glass beads in the necessary arrangements to alter the flow of space-time. Crackles of blue energy appeared, Mayan symbols flashing in the minds of the four young New Yorkers. They looked frightened this time, more than they ever had before; this was not some mystery to be solved or some scientific reconnaissance mission. They were transporting into the heart of enemy territory, into the enemy's element, onto the enemy's turf.

It was too much for Polly, who must have sensed their fear or uneasiness. In a heartbeat she launched herself at the platform, jumping up into Samantha's arms and inexpertly straddling the NEPTUNE-60. Samantha staggered under the extra weight and opened her eyes just as The Professor was screaming Polly's name, but it was too late.

They stood on the floor of a large, half-domed chamber, not nearly as large as the one they had just left, but sizable nonetheless. At one end of the room was a large control panel flanked by banks of electronic equipment, computers and a huge central video screen. At the other was the Slanes' time machine, a near-perfect replica of their own. There were three doorways, evenly spaced around the room's perimeter, which curved to follow the upward contour of the half-domed walls and ceiling. There was no one in sight.

Seeing Samantha's plight with Polly, Suki immediately traced her teammate's feet with the chalk before she toppled under the weight of terrier and spear-gun, then reached back to trace her own. The other team members did likewise before taking a step.

"Polly!" Samantha yelled as her dog scrambled off of her, then clapped her hand to her mouth. Silence would, of course, be advisable in the enemy's citadel. "Bad dog!" she shout-whispered, looking around nervously.

Marvin was already at the time machine's controls, moving obsidian pieces and referring to his notes on several sheets of paper that he'd brought to aid him in his task. Suki and Brianna, too, were quickly effective at locating the central computer and attaching their specially-fitted communicators to the appropriate ports after a brief discussion as to which ones were the correct ones. It looked like Polly was staying, for better or worse; there was no time to discuss a change in plans. Someone would have to scoop her up and hold her while they prepared to transport back. *If* they transported back...

"Okay, Professor," Brianna spoke to no one, as her communicator was now in use, "here it comes." She pushed the talk button.

Instantly, there was a huge *BOOM,* and they were all knocked off their feet as the entire building shook. Marvin swore as his arrangement of obsidian pieces was scattered onto the floor, leaping off of their pedestal, and he scrambled to his feet, trying to pick them all up and start over.

"Professor!" Samantha piped into her wrist-communicator, "what was that!?"

"Working on it," his voice came back. Suki and Brianna's communicators were still hooked into the central computer and presumably transmitting information to their leader.

Things got worse quickly, however. The temperature in the room was rising dramatically, and it looked as though cracks were forming in one area of the domed roof.

"All right," Smythe's voice came back through all the communicators (evidently Suki's and Brianna's could still receive). "Listen. You seem to have triggered something bad."

"No Duh!" Brianna yelled.

"I'm afraid it's a bit of a self-destruct mechanism for the entire base. I didn't anticipate this, I – I'm sorry. According to some of these files, you can try to stop it by replacing a... wait a minute... a... crystal relay. That must be what we fried by tapping into their computer."

"What's happening!?" Samantha asked hurriedly.

"It's – it's opened a channel into the volcano. We can try to close it again with a new crystal relay. There's – there should be one in a compartment – on the floor, ah, um, under the main control panel. Suki, I'm sending back a schematic of the circuit you'll need to put it in – it should pop up on a screen there. Marvin, as soon as you could finish that, ah, well, that would be jolly good."

"Yo, I'm goin' as fast as I can! You want me to screw it up!?"

"*No!* I mean – take your time, then."

"I've got the crystal – uh – relay-thingy! I found it!" Brianna beamed.

"Good. Suki - do you see the schematic?"

"Got it," Suki replied. A diagram of the circuit board and its location appeared on the huge main video screen.

Another *BOOM* occurred, and everyone again went flying. Marvin managed to fling himself over the control panel so that most of his work was preserved, but the crystal relay flew out of Brianna's hand and over toward the time machine's central stone platform. The most ominous result of this latest blast, however, was that a chunk of ceiling had fallen in where the cracks had begun forming, and glowing, molten lava was now oozing into the chamber.

"Professor, there's lava dripping through the ceiling!" Samantha spoke into her communicator, "and it's getting really, really hot in here!" Marvin was dripping sweat at the time machine's controls and Brianna looked as if she might pass out.

"Hmmm. Not good. How are you doing, Marvin?"

"I – I think I'm about halfway there, as long as there are no more quakes or explosions."

"Cover your work, NOW," Samantha said decisively, wiping sweat from her forehead, "there's going to be one more." She shouldered the NEPTUNE-60 and aimed it at one of the high windows in the domed ceiling. She gritted her teeth, released the safety as The Professor had showed her and squeezed the trigger.

The building shook again, and this time a major spurt of saltwater became a powerful, steady stream through a large crack in the window that Samantha had fired at. It was amazing to her that the entire window hadn't shattered, the explosion had been so loud. She could see now, though, that it was made from glass or plastic that was at least eight inches thick, and only a chunk of about a foot square had been totally blown out by her explosive-tipped spear. The rest was still holding, for now.

"Samantha, what are you *doing!!?*" Suki screamed, almost fainting from the heat.

"She's being resourceful," Smythe's voice came over the communicators, sounding pleased. Indeed, her idea had been a good one; the jet of water that was spraying across the room was cooling the lava – and the air – to a more tolerable level. The flow of lava was slowed and a large puddle began forming on the floor. Also, the room was filling with steam from where the water actually came in contact with the lava and evaporated, instantaneously. In a way this was good – it meant the base would take that much longer to fill with liquid water, which would eventually drown them, though the excess of steam did coat them all in condensation and was beginning to cause visibility problems.

There was, in addition, the fact that there is only so long that a team of adventurers will go unnoticed after breaking into an enemy's central computer and triggering a self-destruct sequence for their entire evil undersea base. This amount of time had, sadly, run out.

"Uh-oh..." Brianna shrank as all the sliding doors in the room slid down, sealing them in to either be encased in burning lava, drown in very warm water or scald their insides by breathing if the atmosphere in the chamber became too highly saturated with steam. And – they were no longer alone.

The circuit schematic disappeared from the main video screen and was replaced by the image of a shadowed figure, shark-like in profile but seated in what looked like a high-backed, Victorian armchair. It appeared to be smoking through a long, plastic cigarette filter, and wheezing or chuckling or something – it was a most unsettling sound, in any case.

"Welcome, humans," a voice half-choked, half-hissed. "Rather inconsiderate of you to arrive in such a fashion, toting guns and making such a mess." Its accent sounded British, but not like The Professor's. Possibly it was Australian – though in fact it could hardly be called human at all. "I suppose I'll have to leave you to your fates here – though I'm afraid I'm going to need that time machine, and any of that fabulous *chalk* I'm sure at least one of you is carrying. We've really had to 'rough it' without our own, as I'm sure you know." Samantha shivered as she watched the gruesome silhouette through the steamy haze. She looked over at Marvin and gestured to him with the 'let's get it rolling' hand motion, as he had become somewhat (understandably) distracted by the sinister onscreen presence.

"You're not getting any chalk, and your time machine is minutes from being history," Samantha said boldly. Somehow it was easier to be brave with an explosive-tipped spear-gun slung over one's shoulder.

"Of course I am, tadpole," the figure chuckled or gurgled. "Jordan will be by momentarily with some friends. They can be very persuasive, Jordan's friends. I'd suggest you give them what they want, or else they might decide they want your legs instead."

"Bring 'em on, Slane," Samantha barked back at who must be Jordan's mysterious father, Vassily, hardly believing it was she who was speaking the words. "The world is a place that evolves naturally – maybe the fact that your kind exists is even proof of this. But you can't *force* it. You can't make the world into something that only supports your kind. I know you think that's what we humans do but, well, there are a lot *more* of us. You're a freak, Slane, an evolutionary accident, one that knew it was it was a mistake and so cut off its own development."

"You know nothing, child," Vassily Slane's voice grew angrier. "My kind is genetic perfection. There are only more of you because you are persistent little bacteria that must – and *will* be eradicated." The screen went blank, to everyone's shock. Samantha looked at her teammates and then back at the blank screen, indignant.

"He hung up on me," Samantha said in disbelief. She nodded for a second and bit her lip a little, then slung her NEPTUNE-60 down and fired another projectile straight into the massive video monitor. It blew into tiny fragments and cracked the wall behind it slightly, and another chunk of thick glass broke through on the already damaged window, increasing the flow of high-pressure water into the now sealed room.

"Watch it with that thing!" Brianna yelled, getting up from a crouching position that she and Suki had assumed when their 'cool, level-headed team leader' suddenly decided to fire a rocket right over their heads.

"Yeah, jeez, Samantha!" Suki registered her astonishment, brushing debris off of her jacket.

"I *knew* I shouldn't have given you a NEPTUNE-60. I *knew* it!" Professor Smythe's voice piped in over the communicators.

"Sorry," Samantha smiled a slightly crazed smile. "I'm better now."

"Yo, da girl smells somethin' fishy, her trigger-finger gets itchy on the NEPTUNE-60, the walls get crispy 'cause Sam Smart's no sissy..." Marvin broke into a nervous rap.

"Okay, Marvin, thanks," Samantha said curtly.

"Almost there, girl," Marvin said, feverishly shuffling through his reference sheets and comparing them with his own arrangement.

There were now at least a few inches of water covering the floor, and Polly, having an aversion to deep water, was starting to 'bug out' a little. The steady influx of ocean had mostly stopped the lava from flowing, though small cracks were opening in new spots in the domed roof that glowed with the orange intensity of molten rock. Suki was sliding out circuit-board panels, trying to locate the one they needed, from memory, since The Professor's transmitted diagram had been cut off by Vassily Slane; there was also the fact that there was no video screen left to view it on now, thanks to Samantha's unexpected cowboy assault. Brianna was over by the time machine trying to find the crystal relay, which now lay somewhere under four inches of water. Samantha held the NEPTUNE-60 at the ready, looking back and forth between the three doors in the chamber. They would have company soon, she wagered.

It was even sooner than she anticipated. They did have a few seconds of warning from The Professor, who was apparently still wired into the central computer and could presumably monitor the movements of anyone or anything within the base.

"Samantha, I'm reading several things in motion, just outside the chamber and closing in on you. They're opening all the doors. Forget the crystal relay. Suki, Brianna, find your footprints and *stand in them.* Samantha, cover Marvin for as long as you can and then get to the footprints yourself."

Smythe's orders were firm and deliberate. Suki and Brianna did as they were told, abandoning their respective tasks and searching for the footprints through the haze. Samantha fidgeted nervously with her trigger finger. Then the doors opened.

An immense wall of water poured in from three directions, almost knocking them all off their feet. Samantha planted hers wide and braced herself for the impact of thousands of gallons of extra liquid, standing her ground with much difficulty. She only weighed around a hundred pounds, if that, though the NEPTUNE-60 probably added another forty, which helped her to stay put.

The other girls, equally small, were knocked over, and began swimming to get back to the footprints. Marvin, who was fairly heavy for his age and was out of the direct flow of the impact, had little trouble maintaining his position. Polly, of course, took the worst of it. She was practically washed out one of the chamber's doors, but fortunately was washed back toward the center of the room by an opposing wave. She swam with all her might toward the stone platform in the center of the time machine's ring of stones.

The water level now stood at just under two feet deep, thanks to the recent addition of thousands more gallons from outside the chamber. Samantha figured that some other windows or walls somewhere in the base must have cracked in the quakes – *They must be bigger holes,* she thought, on the edge of panic. She did not relish the idea of drowning with her dog and all her friends, faces pressed against the ceiling as they gasped for the last two inches of air. There would be no escape. They were miles beneath the surface of the ocean. *Hurry up, Marvin,* she prayed silently.

Her attention was diverted quickly, though, albeit not by anything happy or reassuring. Through the haze of steam she could see dorsal fins moving through the shallow but rising water. She wiped the sweat from her brow and hefted the NEPTUNE-60. *Steady... aim... fire.* BOOM! Water and shark flesh flew into the air. *Aim... fire.* BOOM! Another one went to meet its maker, or at least the wall.

Samantha kept going.

It was like one of the video games that her brother played. One was going for Suki and Brianna and – BOOM! Two went after Marvin, perhaps sensing the importance of his actions or somehow alerted to them by their more evolved masters. BOOM! BOOM! Two more splatters on the wall. Another went straight for Polly, sticking its nose and open jaws up out of the water and about to snap her up like a bite-sized morsel of chocolate and cheese. BOOM! *Don't mess with my dog,* Samantha's voice sounded in her head. The shark exploded all over the time machine's stone platform as well as Polly, who calmly licked some of its fishy remains from her own face and gave a little dog smile, panting. This caused Suki and Brianna to make disgusted faces and sounds of great distaste.

This went on for several minutes, sharks almost reaching Alpha Team members and Samantha picking them off with the NEPTUNE-60 until what looked like a special, much larger shark appeared in the doorway closest to the time machine. She fired at it but missed – it moved like lightning – and the spear exploded part of an internal wall, further weakening the structure. She jerked her head up for a split-second as another chunk of window broke away, and then the entire window. There was now a huge, high-pressured stream of ocean water pouring into one side of the room, which no doubt would have filled the chamber in minutes if its three doors had still been shut. As it was, the water level was now rising by an inch a minute. The huge super-shark morphed, changing into the handsome young image of Jordan Anderson/Slane, and stood, clothing-free, in two and a half feet of water. He was... beautiful.

"Hello, Samantha," he smiled, his flexing muscles in an unfair assault on her hormonal response mechanisms. "It doesn't have to be this way," he said gently, raising a hand and glancing nervously over at Marvin. "We can figure out a way to share the world, if we must."

"Sharing doesn't seem to be in your nature, Jordan," she sneered at him, keeping the NEPTUNE-60 leveled at him. There were only two spears left.

"It's my father," he said almost pleadingly. "It's not me,

Samantha! I don't – I don't really care if we share the planet with humans – all I ever wanted to do was sing, and live, well, as normally as someone like me could live. I know I'm different," he continued emotionally, "I've – I've always been *different,* but I wanted to – to *fit in,* to be *human,* to be *loved* and to *love*... to love... somebody like *you*..." His hands fell to his sides in a gesture of symbolic surrender, a perfect specimen of humanity who wasn't even human. Samantha's heart was torn.

A few months ago, she would've been in heaven to have heard Jordan Anderson of Heatwavvve say those words to her. Every fiber of her being ached, wanted to believe him. Was he just another pawn in this game, dominated by a powerful, abusive father who was more likely the real villain here? He had a genuine air about him, the air of someone who was lost and was just looking, indeed searching desperately for meaning, for a home or a purpose. Samantha looked at Suki and Brianna, who stood in a similar state of confusion. They had all been Heatwavvve fans, and looked equally uncertain as to what the best course of action would be at this point.

She looked back at Jordan. Beautiful, naked, helpless-looking Jordan, hardly an adult himself and begging for forgiveness, direction and any sense of belonging that someone could give him. She stared, closely, at the iris of his eye – it was as black as the obsidian beads that Marvin was moving around on the time machine's control panel. He stared back. A minute passed, another inch of water filled the room. She bit her lip. He shot a quick glance toward Marvin, who had almost completed his task. Something gleamed through the haze, a reflection of a tooth – a very sharp, pointy tooth.

"Jordan," Samantha smiled at him calmly. "Your band sucks." With this she squeezed the trigger of the NEPTUNE-60, firing a spear straight into his incredibly toned, tan abdominal muscles. He tried to avoid it, half-morphing back into a shark and making an awful, loud, inhuman sound of anguish and evil, but it caught him right in the gut before he could react and exploded, blowing a massive hole in his half-man, half-shark torso and throwing what was left of him back against the wall behind the time machine. He floated there, not moving. Everyone stared with mouths open at what had just happened. Samantha wiped a tear from her face and sniffled, turning abruptly toward the stone platform.

"Polly!" she yelled, "come here girl!" Polly ran in circles on the stone platform, whose surface was now only an inch or two above the waterline. She looked around, disoriented in the haze, and whined.

"I've just about got it," Marvin snapped back to the present, then screamed a blood-curdling scream. The creature that had been Jordan Slane was still alive, though barely. It's still half-morphed body had swum, bleeding, over to Marvin and bit his leg with whatever strength it had left, letting out some gurgling sounds of evil satisfaction.

"Marvin!" Samantha yelled, almost in concert with Brianna and Suki.

"Stay!" Marvin winced. "Samantha – get in your footprints! It's done!" He struggled to release the dying shark-man's jaws from his leg. In the next few seconds, several things occurred:

Polly, sensing her friend and favorite dog-walker in pain and in need of help, dove from the platform, landing on Jordan's mortally wounded man-shark body and sunk her teeth into his flesh. He hissed-howled-gurgled in pain and released his jaws from Marvin's leg. Marvin ran for the footprints (as well as an injured boy can run in almost three feet of water), grabbing Samantha on the way. The time machine began to glow blue and crackle. Their footprints glowed quite clearly despite being under a good bit of water, and they planted their feet in them, next to Brianna's and Suki's.

"Polly!" Samantha screamed, her eyes searching the hazy middle distance for signs of her dog. "Polly, hurry!" There was no time. The time machine was producing an expanding bubble of blue energy, the likes of which they had never witnessed before. It would reach them in seconds. "Damn it!" Samantha cried, wiping tears from her face as she pressed the talk button on her wrist-communicator, weeping into it "now, Professor." It was a split-second decision - no one else would have done it – they probably would have waited for Polly, and probably would have all died or been sucked into a timeless oblivion.

She was the team leader, Alpha Prime. She had had to make the call. And she did. It crushed her with guilt as they dematerialized, appearing soaked, injured and exhausted back at the Montreal dome. They had, miraculously, accomplished their mission and made it back alive. Polly had not. Samantha dropped the NEPTUNE-60 onto the stone platform of their familiar time machine and collapsed to her knees. It must have been hours that she cried.

Samantha stared at the gift-wrapped package in front of her, her face devoid of emotion. It was January 19, her twelfth birthday and probably the worst birthday she had ever had. Todd had given her a gift from their dad which he had brought back with him from the west coast, a deluxe "Bratz" doll which was her favorite toy – three years ago. Now it seemed childish and irrelevant. *How little my father knows me now,* she thought sadly. *How much of my growing he has missed.* It made her even sadder than she already was.

She opened the package in front of her at Suki's insistence.

"It's from Professor Smythe," Marvin indicated. Samantha nodded.

Inside the package was, wrapped in a piece of paper, a beautiful silver pocket watch, probably a hundred years old and still ticking. She made a weak smile at the irony of the gift, then unrolled the piece of paper around it. It was a poem, or a statement of some sort, written in The Professor's handwriting:

Time is like a river
Flowing
Sometimes fast
Sometimes slow
Diverging
And Converging
But all of its being
Including we who make it
And are made by it

Come together
At the sea.

It was signed "A.E. Smythe." Samantha choked on a sob. She missed her dog so much, her best friend, her constant companion. It had been almost a month since Alpha Team had returned that same Christmas day that they had left, and they could not go back. Double-occurrences were still one of the biggest no-no's in time travel, creating paradoxes the complications of which might not be evident for centuries. And they couldn't chance screwing up the mission that they had, barely, achieved successfully. It didn't make her feel any better; she had betrayed the trust of the most loyal creature she had ever known, to save herself and her other human friends. She still wondered sometimes if the Slanes had been right, if the world would be better off without humankind. Perhaps Boston terriers should run the world – she didn't know.

She had been forced to lie to her mother once again, something which she was growing tired of. Polly had "run off into the park" and not returned, frightened by some "stray rottweiler" who had attacked her down in the athletic fields. They had also used this imaginary incident to explain Marvin's badly injured leg. Cindy had been very compassionate and had even offered to get her another dog for her birthday, but Samantha had declined. She wasn't ready. Polly was not easily replaced – she died a hero in Samantha's mind, and Marvin's and everyone else's as well. She deserved to live on in memory, unchallenged, for quite some time as the sole object of Samantha's love, respect and admiration.

"Hey, Samantha," Suki said in a hopeful, cheery voice, "is your laptop plugged in?"

"Yeah," Samantha responded, wiping a sniffle away. "It's in my bedroom. Why?"

"C'mere, we should check something out." Suki took Samantha's hand and led her into the bedroom; the rest of her friends followed. "I got this weird email the other day – from *myself.* I don't remember writing it at all. But the weirdest thing was, it was dated November

23, 1967. That's almost thirty-five years before I was born! Anyway, it was just a quick note, to myself I guess, that said to tell you to check your email from me on your birthday – that is, your, uh, *special* email." Suki was referring to the 'agent' account that The Professor had set up for her (and all of Alpha Team). She hadn't checked hers since Christmas day.

She did so now, her friends gathered round, and indeed found one message waiting, with a picture attachment, from Suki, aka *timetraveler13@hotmail.com*. The message was brief. "This never happened," it said. She looked at Suki, who only shrugged. She double-clicked on the attachment and opened the picture file. Indeed, it was a picture that was very mysterious.

It showed them all together, the inside of the massive "Bucky Ball" headquarters apparent in the background. They were grinning, and the picture made them giggle, with its added text that spelled out "Alpha Team" in dramatic, comic book cover letters and Marvin giving some rabbit ears to Suki behind her head. Not one of them remembered the moment ever having happened. It was bizarre.

Samantha decided to print out copies for everyone – Jason had got her a nice new color printer for her birthday to go with her laptop. She tried to smile as she handed them out to her friends.

It was about three in the afternoon, the party-goers having been in attendance for a few hours now and having begun to grow depressed by their hostess's steady air of mourning. There was great anticipation of something better to come when the doorbell of the Brooklyn brownstone rang unexpectedly.

Who could that be? Samantha wondered. Everyone she had invited to the party was here – Jason was out with their mother for another hour, and seemed to have his own key now anyway (an intriguing recent development). She decided as she walked to the door that it must be one of Todd's friends, come to meet him and facilitate his escape from his little sister's boring party. She undid the chains and deadbolts and opened the door – and promptly fainted.

*

The next thing she remembered was a wet tongue licking her face – it was the best birthday present she could have asked for. Impossibly, when she opened her eyes, she saw Polly, furiously licking her and whining with excitement.

"POLLY!" everyone screamed with joy (and bewilderment). Samantha got up onto her elbows and blinked, wondering if she was dreaming. Behind the hero dog stood Professor Smythe – with Agent Stiles. They were both grinning, and all of the party guests looked very confused. Todd was especially perplexed, still totally unaware of what was going on but glad that Polly was back and that the mood of the party had just taken a dramatic upswing.

"Where – where did you find her!?" Samantha whimpered happily, hugging Polly tightly and smiling through her tears.

"Oh, eh – Agent Stiles here has some connections in the, er, Brooklyn Animal Control department," Smythe fabricated, casting glances at Todd, who was still not in on their schemes. "They picked her up from a spot near where you lost her."

"It's all right, Samantha," Stiles smiled, sensing the birthday girl's nervousness. "We're all friends here, now. The Professor here has explained everything, and my... people are in your debt. We've actually been watching the Slanes for quite a while now, and we believe that you and your friends have done a brave, important service to all of us. We'll, ah, talk about it more later, at your convenience, of course." She smiled and looked up at the party-goers. "Good work, Alpha Team!" She gave the 'thumbs-up' sign.

They were, of course, invited in for cake and ice cream, even Polly, though they didn't allow her any of the chocolate cake, because everyone knows that chocolate is especially bad for dogs. Todd's questions about who Alpha Team was and who the Slanes were were brushed off, and though Samantha's mind was now brimming with questions about the fate of their enemies and the rescue of Polly, she decided to leave them for later and try to truly enjoy her birthday party, which was, at least in her mind, a thousand times better than it had been an hour before. In the midst of the celebration, the phone rang.

"Hello?" Samantha said, picking up and giggling through her answer.

"Samantha?" It was her father. Now she was even happier. "You sound like you're having a good time," his voice said good-naturedly.

"Hi, Dad!" she beamed. "Yeah, I'm having the best birthday ever! Thanks for the present, and thanks so much for calling..."

"Wouldn't miss it," her dad acknowledged. "What have you been up to?" he asked.

Samantha looked around her, at her fellow time-travelers, her dog who had somehow been miraculously rescued from a "time-hole," a Professor of forensic anthropology who owned a time machine, an agent who allegedly worked for the F.B.I. and her own oblivious older brother who was stuffing cake into his mouth and watching Marvin attempt to break-dance on his leg that had been wounded by a boy-band singer-turned-man-eating-shark.

"Oh, you know, nothing much." She laughed.

THE END

Glossary

Adrenalin: Pharmacological trademark name for the hormone epinephrine.

A.k.a.: Alias; also known as.

Albeit: Although; even if.

Algae: Any of numerous groups of chlorophyll-containing, mainly aquatic eukaryotic organisms ranging from microscopic single-celled forms to multicellular forms 100 ft. (30 m) or more long.

Analysis: The separating of any material or abstract entity into its constituent elements (opposed to synthesis).

Anonymous: Of unknown name; whose name is withheld.

Anticlimactic: Something trivial or commonplace that concludes a series of significant events.

Apparatus: Any complex instrument or mechanism for a particular purpose.

Arrogant: Making claims or pretensions to superior importance or rights; overbearingly assuming; insolently proud.

Atrophied: Exhibiting or affected with atrophy; wasted; withered; shriveled.

Aztecs: Members of a Nahuatl-speaking state in central Mexico that was conquered by Cortés in 1521.

Behest: A command or directive; an earnest or strongly worded request.

Biological: Of, relating to, caused by, or affecting life or living organisms.

Captivating: Attractive and holding the attention or interest of, as by beauty or excellence; enchanting.

Cephalopods: Any of various marine mollusks of the class Cephalopoda, such as the octopus, squid, cuttlefish, or nautilus, having a large head, large eyes, prehensile tentacles, and, in most species, an ink sac containing a dark fluid used for protection or defense.

***Chitty-Chitty-Bang-Bang*:** A children's story by Ian Fleming; also a movie written by Roald Dahl and starring Dick Van Dyke.

Climate: The composite or generally prevailing weather

conditions of a region, as temperature, air pressure, humidity, precipitation, sunshine, cloudiness, and winds, throughout the year, averaged over a series of years.

CO2: Carbon Dioxide.

Coherent: Logically connected; consistent.

Confounding: Perplexing or amazing, especially by a sudden disturbance or surprise; bewildering; confusing.

Conspiracy: An evil, unlawful, treacherous, or surreptitious plan formulated in secret by two or more persons; plot.

Consequently: As a result, effect, or outcome; therefore.

Conundrums: Riddles or puzzles.

Conversely: In a way that is in an opposite or contrary direction; in a way that is turned around.

Cowed: Frightened with threats, violence, etc.; intimidated; overawed.

Deciduous: Shedding the leaves annually, as certain trees and shrubs.

Debutante: A young woman making a debut into society.

Deity: A god or goddess.

Dematerialized: Deprive of or losing material character; vanished.

Denizen: An inhabitant; resident.

Discretion: The quality of being discreet, esp. with reference to one's own actions or speech; prudence or decorum.

Divergent: Diverging; differing; deviating.

DNA: Deoxyribonucleic acid: an extremely long macromolecule that is the main component of chromosomes and is the material that transfers genetic characteristics in all life forms, constructed of two nucleotide strands coiled around each other in a ladder-like arrangement called a double-helix.

¿Dónde piensa usted que usted va!?: *"Where do you think you're going?"* (Sp.)

Duplicity: Deceitfulness in speech or conduct; speaking or acting in two different ways concerning the same matter with intent to deceive; double-dealing.

Ecology: The branch of biology dealing with the relations and interactions between organisms and their environment, including other organisms.

Edifice: A building, esp. one of large size or imposing appearance.

Embellished: 1. Beautified by or as if by ornamentation; ornamented; adorned.

2. Enhanced (as a statement or narrative) with fictitious additions.

Encroaching: Trespassing upon the property, domain, or rights of another, esp. stealthily or by gradual advances.

Erstwhile: Former; of times past.

Feigned: Pretended; sham; counterfeit.

Felice Navidad: Merry Christmas (Sp.)

Forensic: Pertaining to, connected with, or used in courts of law or public discussion and debate.

Fortuitous: Happening or produced by chance; accidental.

Fungoid: Resembling a fungus; of the nature of a fungus.

Galoshes: A pair of waterproof overshoes

Geodesic Dome: A light, domelike structure developed by R. Buckminster Fuller to combine the properties of the tetrahedron and the sphere and consisting essentially of a grid of compression or tension members lying upon or parallel to great circles running in three directions in any given area, the typical form being the projection upon a sphere of an icosahedron, the triangular faces of which are filled with a symmetrical triangular, hexagonal, or quadrangular grid.

Geological: Of, pertaining to, or based on geology.

Gypsum: A very common soft mineral, hydrated calcium sulfate, used to make plaster of Paris, as a fertilizer, and for other purposes.

Hormonal: Relating to hormones (internally secreted compounds formed in endocrine glands).

Illustrative: Serving to illustrate; explanatory.

Impenetrable: Not penetrable; that cannot be penetrated, pierced, entered, etc.

Infiltrator: One who moves into (an organization, country, territory, or the like) surreptitiously and gradually, especially with hostile intent: The troops infiltrated the enemy lines.

Inquisitively: Questioningly, with an intellectual curiosity.

Insignificant: Unimportant, trifling, or petty; of no consequence, influence, or distinction.

Integrity: 1. Adherence to moral and ethical principles; soundness of moral character; honesty.
2. The state of being whole, entire, or undiminished. 3. A sound, unimpaired, or perfect condition.

Invigorating: Filling with life and energy; energizing.

Iota: 1. A very small quantity. 2. The ninth letter of the Greek alphabet.

Irrevocably: Unalterably; permanently.

Jackelope: An imaginary creature that is part jackrabbit and part antelope.

Los espíritus del muerto: *Spanish.* Ghosts; spirits of the dead.

Lozenges: Small flavored tablets made of sugar or syrup; often cough drops.

Machete: A large heavy knife used especially in Latin-American countries in cutting sugarcane and clearing underbrush and as a weapon.

Megalithic: Very large and made of stone.

¡Mire la cabeza!: "Look at my head!" (Sp.)

Monolithic: Made of one piece of stone, often large.

Mutated: Changed or altered, often in a biological process such as mutating genes or viruses.

Neutralizing: Having the effect of making neutral or ineffective.

Obscene: Offensive to morality or decency; indecent; depraved: *obscene language.*

Obsidian: Volcanic glass, usually black or very dark brown.

Olfactory: Of or pertaining to the sense of smell.

Ominous: 1. Portending evil or harm; foreboding; threatening; inauspicious. 2. Having the significance of an omen.

Paradoxes: 1. Statements or propositions that seem self-contradictory or absurd but in reality express possible truths.

Paranoid: 1. Of, characterized by, or resembling paranoia. 2. Exhibiting undue suspicion, fear of persecution, etc.: "They're all out to get me!"

Perpetrator: One who commits, as a crime. 2. One who presents, executes, or does something in a poor or tasteless manner.

Perpetual: Continuing or enduring forever; everlasting; without interruption.

Phosphorus: Any of three forms of an element that can be both luminous (glow in the dark) or highly flammable.

Pictographs: Pictorial signs or symbols, often forming a "written" language of sorts.

Pique: To excite with interest or curiosity.

Plateau: A high, flat place in a landscape. 2. A metaphorical high point in one's achievement.

Posthumous: Arising, occurring, or continuing after one's death.

Precocious: Unusually advanced or mature in development, especially mental development: *a precocious child.* 2. Premature.

Pre-Columbian: Of or relating to the Americas before they were discovered by Columbus.

Preoccupied: Completely engrossed in thought; absorbed.

Profusely: Plentifully, copiously, or abundantly. *He thanked her profusely for dancing with him.*

Propaganda: Information, ideas, or rumors deliberately spread widely to help or harm a person, group, movement, institution, nation, etc.

Provocatively: In a way that provokes, stimulates or incites.

Prudent: Wise or judicious in practical affairs; sagacious; discreet or circumspect; sober.

Quetzlcoatl: The feathered serpent god of the Aztec and Toltec cultures.

Refereed: Judged, decided, arbitrated or settled, as in disputes or arguments.

Relevant: Having to do with the matter in hand; pertinent.

Requisitions: Demands or requests, usually in writing.

Reverie: Fanciful musing; Daydream.

Rhetorical: Used for, belonging to, or concerned with mere style or effect.

Ritualistic: Adhering to rites or practices, either religious or habitual.

Simultaneously: At the same exact time.

Solemnly: With great seriousness.

Sonnets: Poems expressive of single, complete thoughts, ideas, or sentiments, of 14 lines and using one of two rhyming schemes developed by either the English or the Italians. *William Shakespeare (1564–1616) is famous for writing sonnets.*

Spectral Analysis: An analysis based on a spectrum, as of a range of light, radio waves or chemical composition.

Stereotypical: 1. Simplified or standardized conceptually; invested with special meaning and held in common by members of a group. 2. Obvious or unimaginative.

Subsequent: Occurring or coming later or after.

Sumptuous: 1. Entailing great expense; costly. 2. Luxurious or lavish.

Surreal: 1. Of, pertaining to, or characteristic of surrealism; surrealistic. 2. Having the disorienting, hallucinatory quality of a dream; unreal, fantastic.

Synthesized: Formed by combining parts or elements.

Tangible: 1. Capable of being touched; material or substantial. 2. Real or actual, rather than imaginary or visionary.

Technician: A person who is trained or skilled in the technicalities of a subject.

Temporal: Of or pertaining to time.

Thoroughfare: 1. A road or street that leads at each end into another street. 2. A major road or highway.

Toxicology: The science dealing with the effects, antidotes, detection, etc., of poisons.

Translucent: Permitting light to pass through but diffusing it so that persons, objects, etc., on the opposite side are not clearly visible; Partially but not entirely transparent.

Trapezoidal: Having the shape of a trapezoid, or a not square or rectangular four-sided figure.

Traumatized: Injured by a physical, mental or emotional force.

Ubiquitous: Existing or being everywhere at once; omnipresent.

Unenthusiastic: Without enthusiasm, excitement or zeal.

Vigorously: Robustly, energetically or even forcefully; with strength and life.

Wagered: Bet on.

Writhe: To twist the body about, or squirm, as in pain, violent effort, etc.

Yucatan Peninsula: A section of what is now Central America where the Mayan civilization flourished.

***